Ransomed Jewels

ALSO BY LAURA LANDON

From Montlake Romance

Silent Revenge
Intimate Deception
Intimate Surrender
The Most to Lose
A Risk Worth Taking
Betrayed by Your Kiss

From Prairie Muse Publishing

Shattered Dreams
When Love Is Enough
Broken Promise
A Matter of Choice
More Than Willing
Not Mine to Give
Keeper of My Heart
Love Unbidden
The Dark Duke
Cast in Shadows
Cast in Ruin
Cast in Ice
Cast in Scandal
Where the Lady Belongs (novella)

Ransomed Jewels

LAURA LANDON

Montlake
Romance

Text copyright © 2016 Laura Landon

Published by Montlake Romance, Seattle

www.apub.com

Amazon, the Amazon logo, and Montlake Romance are trademarks of Amazon.com, Inc., or its affiliates.

ISBN-13: 9781503935266
ISBN-10: 1503935264

Cover design by Michael Rehder

Printed in the United States of America

To my readers! I can't thank you enough!

Ransomed Jewels

Prologue

England - February, 1855

Major Samuel Bennett lifted the freshly filled tankard to his mouth and took a long swallow of the ale they served in the Armor's Inn. It was barely passable, but he'd tasted worse. A damn sight worse. Except that hardly mattered now. Even the finest brandy couldn't dull his senses enough to make what he had to do easier.

Sam set his tankard back onto the scarred wooden table and when the door opened, he slowly lifted his gaze. He watched as his friend and fellow agent, the Marquess of Huntingdon, stepped into the smoke-filled room.

Sam lifted his tankard again and took another swallow. His gaze scanned the patrons sitting at tables around the room. None of them cast the marquess a second glance. But that was not unusual. Hunt was still alive because of his uncanny ability to blend in with any crowd.

Tonight Hunt was dressed like the tenant farmers who frequented the inn, in homespun tweed breeches and a worn flannel jacket. Even the sweat-stained hat on his graying head gave him the appearance of a man used to laboring long and hard both winter and summer, the same as each and every one of the workers that filled the taproom. The slight hunch to his shoulders and the hitch in his gait didn't alert them to the fact that Hunt was really a peer of the realm. The heir apparent to the Duke of Bridgemont.

As well as one of England's best spies.

Hunt stopped at the counter. The burly barkeep paused from wiping the worn wooden bar and silently listened, then reached beneath the counter and set a full bottle between them. Hunt leaned closer, and Sam saw the marquess slip a coin beneath the towel. A second later, a key appeared on the counter, which Hunt slipped into his pocket. With a slight nod, he slowly climbed the stairs and disappeared from sight.

Sam smiled behind the rim of his tankard. It was as if he were watching Hunt's incomparable finesse for the first time. The extent of his talent still amazed him. But Sam's smile faded when he thought of the task ahead of him.

After watching to make sure no one followed Hunt, Sam rose and trailed his mentor, his partner—his best friend.

When Sam reached the top of the stairs, he walked cautiously down the hall. The doors to all the rooms stood open, but none of them held a hint of welcoming. Each portal yawned like a dark empty pit, the entryways as foreboding as the narrow hallway.

A faint rustle echoed from inside one of the doorways, and Sam placed his hand over the hilt of the knife he always wore at his side. He took another step, then raised his knife. He spun around just as an arm closed around his shoulder.

Without hesitation, he pressed the blade against the base of the attacker's throat. He pushed it hard enough to let the man feel the threat, yet not hard enough to do injury.

He lowered the knife when Hunt laughed.

"That was a damn foolish thing to do," Sam said, his heart thundering in his chest.

"I was just testing to make sure you hadn't gotten lax while idling these last few months in England." Hunt dropped his arm from around Sam's shoulder and stepped back into the gaping doorway.

Sam followed, then closed the door behind them and bolted it.

"I thought perhaps you had grown lazy. Basking in the success of our completed mission in Paris." Hunt lit a lantern and set it on a small table in the center of the room next to the bottle Hunt had gotten from the innkeeper. "I wouldn't want to see you let down your guard."

"The Foreign Office has hardly given me time to let down my guard. I just returned from another visit to France."

Hunt's eyebrows arched upward. He held Sam's gaze several seconds before he looked at the bottle on the table. "Can I interest you in a glass of the inn's finest port? We'll imagine it's equal to the fine wines in my town house cellar."

Sam smiled. "That will take a great deal of imagining, I think."

"No doubt," Hunt said on a laugh. Then his expression turned serious. "Perhaps someday we can share a bottle together in public."

"You know that's not possible. Not if we want to continue being of use to the government."

Sam pulled out a chair and sat facing the door. Never exposing your back to the entrance of a room was one of the first rules Hunt had taught him. It had saved his life more than once.

Hunt gave him a knowing smile, then moved a second chair so neither man had his back to the door. Before he sat, he took two glasses from the pockets of his jacket. Sam shook his head, amazed at the marquess's ability. Even he hadn't seen him take the glasses. And he'd been watching.

Hunt poured them each a healthy amount and sat down. "I must compliment you, Sam. Your choice of a meeting place is perfect. Quite out of the way. And such an isolated setting."

Sam noticed the grin on Hunt's face. "I'm glad you approve."

"Oh, I do. But I can't help but wonder what was so important that you risked us meeting like this."

Sam took a long swallow of the liquor Hunt had poured and struggled to speak. Hunt's reputation as a loyal agent had never been in question before. His patriotism and love of country had never been in doubt. Until now.

Hunt leaned forward in his chair. "This must be terribly serious, Sam. I've never known you to be so hesitant to speak your mind before."

Sam shoved back his chair and stood, then walked to the cold, lifeless fireplace. He turned his back to Hunt and stretched out his arms, grasping the brick mantel with both hands.

Tension mounted, their silence an uncomfortable barrier between them. Sam knew he couldn't put it off any longer. He turned to face Hunt. "Since we left Paris, have you heard anything concerning our friend Roseneau?"

François Roseneau was a Frenchman who was suspected of being a Russian sympathizer and the reason Sam and Hunt had been sent to France nearly six months before to attend a ball he'd hosted at his Paris home. While they were there, they'd broken into Roseneau's safe and stolen jewels he intended to sell to help Russia finance the Crimean War.

Hunt sat back, his body relaxed, the expression on his face obtuse. "Nothing, other than he departed Paris within days of his ball and is residing at one of his villas in the French countryside. No one knows exactly where."

Sam walked to the window and leaned against the wall. He watched Hunt for any sign he might know more than he was saying. "Do you think the Russians know their jewels are missing?"

Hunt shrugged, then took another swallow of the liquor in his glass. "It's possible. By now they've got to be suspicious, considering they haven't received payment from the sale."

"Then it's also possible Roseneau's informed them the jewels are missing and asked for their aid in searching for them."

"That's a possibility," Hunt said, shifting in his chair. "But not likely. If I were Roseneau, I'd want to recover the jewels on my own."

"But," Sam said, taking a step closer to Hunt, "we can't forget, Roseneau and the Russians aren't the only ones who have an interest in the jewels."

There was a slight pause before Hunt spoke. "Of course. The intended buyer will also be expecting word concerning the jewels."

Sam watched Hunt even more closely. "Any idea who that might be, Hunt?"

"You have just as good an idea as I do, Sam. Unless you know something that I don't."

"No. Except, I wonder how Roseneau is going to explain the missing jewels to the Russians, and to what lengths he'll go to get them back."

Hunt sat forward in his chair, his demeanor unusually bland. The first niggling of unease stirred deep inside Sam.

Hunt took a breath before he spoke. "If I were Roseneau, I'd begin with everyone who attended the ball that night. I imagine the Russians have already put pressure on Roseneau to complete the transaction."

"Yes, I imagine he'll do what he must. And just what do you think that will be?"

Hunt slid back his chair and bolted to his feet. The two men faced off. "Is there a point to all these questions, Sam?"

"Yes, Hunt. There is."

Sam slammed his fist against his thigh in an unusual show of temper. "Foreign agents have been swarming into England in droves since we stole the jewels. More than half a dozen by last count. Some are known Russian agents, while others have fluctuating allegiances that migrate to the highest bidder. I can explain a strange agent or two to the Foreign Office. But not the flood that's crossing to our shores every day. What does it mean, Hunt?"

"How the hell should I know?!"

At Hunt's outburst, a cold chill raced down Sam's spine. In the dozens of times they'd worked together, Sam had never seen Hunt like this. Had never seen him lose his temper. As if, whatever this was, it was a heavier burden than he could bear.

Sam tried to ignore the fear that assaulted him but couldn't. "I think you'd better tell me what the hell is going on."

"Nothing is going on."

"Yes, there is! And I want to know what it is. Now!"

Hunt paced the small space between the table and the door, then stopped and locked his gaze with Sam's. Several long seconds passed before Hunt spoke. "You're not going to give up, are you, Sam?"

"Would you?"

Hunt raked his fingers through his hair, then took a breath so agonizingly deep, Sam could feel the pain across the room.

"I took something else from Roseneau's safe that night."

Sam fisted his hands at his sides and held them tight. "I'm waiting."

Hunt took another swallow of liquor, then looked at Sam. "It's possible we have within our grasp something so significant it might bring about a quicker end to the war in the Crimea." Hunt uttered a bittersweet laugh. "*If* it doesn't get us killed first."

Sam stared at Hunt, seeing clearly the worry and desperation on his friend's face. "What did you take?"

Hunt dropped into a chair and leaned against the rough wooden back. "A red velvet bag containing a diamond-and-ruby necklace. I've since discovered it's called the Queen's Blood, and it's been an important part of Russia's history since the eleventh century."

Sam pounded his fist against the wobbly table. "That necklace wasn't one of the pieces we were supposed to take."

"I know."

"Then why did you take it?"

"That's not important!" Hunt bellowed, then quickly lowered his voice. "The necklace wasn't supposed to be there. I wasn't sure the Russian government realized Roseneau had it until you mentioned the flood of foreign agents. And Russia can hardly raise the alarm, or their people will realize that they lost one of their prized historical possessions for a war that's becoming increasingly unpopular."

Sam raked his fingers through his hair and paced the floor. "Where is the necklace now?"

"It's safe. She—" Hunt brushed his hand across his face. "It's safe."

"But you're not, dammit! Roseneau's not going to give up until he has that necklace back." He swiped his hand through the air as the full impact of Hunt's revelation hit him. "Bloody hell, Hunt. He's already got agents over here searching for it. It's only a matter of time until they find you."

His friend's hand trembled slightly when he raised his glass to his mouth.

"I'm being followed. I have been for weeks now."

"Are they Russian?"

Hunt shook his head. "All I know is they're good."

"How good? Did they follow you here?"

"I don't think so. I'm quite sure I lost them."

"All right," Sam said. "We'll have to figure out how to get you out of this mess."

Sam sat back down, keeping his gaze locked on Hunt's serious expression. He needed to find an answer to get Hunt out of this.

"How did you do it? I was with you the whole time."

"Not the whole time." Hunt leaned his elbows on the table and slowly turned the glass in his fingers. "Remember when you went to the door to make sure the hallway was clear?"

"Yes, but we'd already removed the jewels by then."

"But I hadn't closed the safe yet. When you went to the door, I took a red velvet bag that was tucked at the back of the safe."

"Bloody hell, Hunt. Why? We had specific orders. The Foreign Office wanted the theft to signal to the Russians that we knew what they were doing so Roseneau wouldn't mistake it for a random robbery."

Hunt shrugged his shoulders. "Who knows? Perhaps I wanted it."

"For her?"

Hunt looked surprised. "Claire? No. For . . ." Hunt hesitated. "Perhaps for no other reason than to take Roseneau down a peg. I didn't know the necklace was so valuable. Not until I had time to examine it." Hunt stood, then turned his back. "There's more."

Sam braced his hands on the top of the table and closed his eyes. "What?"

"Hidden inside the bag were some papers."

Sam's eyes shot open. "What kind of papers?"

"Coded messages."

"Where are they?"

"Safe."

Hunt locked his gaze with Sam's. "We were wrong, Sam. All along we assumed someone was buying the Russian jewels and the money was going to fund the war. That isn't what Roseneau was doing. He was trading the jewels for military secrets."

Sam's breath caught. "Do you know what you're saying?"

Hunt nodded. "Oh, yes. I know. Roseneau may be a Frenchman, and is therefore a citizen of one of our allies, but he's greedy. And I think he's made a hefty profit acting as courier between the Russians and someone here in England."

"Stop right there, Hunt." Sam paced the small room like a tiger on a short leash. "If you're right, it means that either a very influential member of British Society who has connections to the military, or someone in the Foreign Office, is a traitor."

The look on Hunt's face told Sam they'd both come to the same conclusion.

"Why is that so difficult to believe, Sam? For months, you and I have both suspected that someone was leaking military secrets to the Russians."

"We need that necklace, Hunt. When the Russian ambassador meets with Her Majesty at the end of June, that necklace could be the advantage we need to save thousands of lives."

Sam slapped his fist against his thigh and spun to where Hunt stood. "And we need those papers. They can lead us to the traitor. Why didn't you give them to someone before?"

"To whom?" Hunt said, slashing his hand through the air. "I wouldn't even trust the Queen with this. Anyone could be our traitor."

Sam sucked in a breath. "Even me? Is that why you didn't come to me with this? Is that why I had to come to you?"

Hunt shook his head. "I didn't want to involve you."

Sam paused. "Roseneau isn't a fool, Hunt. He knows someone who attended the ball that night stole the necklace and the papers, and if he's sent agents over, that means he suspects you. You're not safe."

"And now, neither are you."

"Then we'll have to watch each other's back until we can discover the traitor's identity. Maybe there's a clue in the message that will reveal who he is." Sam paced the small room. "As long as we have the papers and the necklace, we may be able to draw our traitor into the open."

He stopped in front of the curtained window and lifted the worn drapes. The night was black outside, with only a sliver of the moon lighting the gravel courtyard below. "Do you think it possible your wife knew your true purpose for being in Paris?"

"Claire?" Huntingdon shook his head. "No. Absolutely not. I doubt Claire even realizes I'm assisting our government. She'd be appalled to know she's married to a spy."

"But she may have—"

Hunt slammed his fist down on the table. "No! Leave Claire out of this, Sam. To her, the trip to Paris was nothing more than a gay holiday to see a few sights and come home with a new gown or two."

"And what is her connection to Roseneau?"

Hunt looked shocked. "She has no connection to Roseneau. In fact, I'm not sure she even likes the man. She only tolerates him because I told her an association to him is important to me."

Sam watched the struggle on his friend's face, the wretched turmoil that darkened his eyes. Slowly, the corners of Hunt's mouth lifted to form a bittersweet smile. His face held a look of defeat. "Just leave Claire out of this. She isn't involved in anything, Sam."

Sam lifted his gaze and nodded. "How soon can you get the papers to me?"

"Tomorrow night. I'll leave my downstairs study window open. Don't come before midnight. Claire doesn't always retire early."

Sam nodded, then buttoned his jacket. "I want the traitor caught before he causes the death of one more innocent young man."

"Until tomorrow night, then," Hunt said, his gaze locking with Sam's long enough to share a silent vow. Then Hunt turned his back on Sam and walked to the window. Hunt's usual tall and dignified posture was marred by a slight a bend to his shoulders. As if the weight of the lives for which he was responsible was more than he wanted to bear.

Hunt sucked in a deep breath and straightened his shoulders.

"I left a command dinner engagement with my father to meet you," Hunt said, slipping his hands into his gloves.

"How is His Grace?" Sam asked.

"Bridgemont's health is failing. He made it to the Biltmore ball last night, but in a month he plans to retire to the country. I doubt he'll see another Season."

"I'm sorry, Hunt."

"So am I."

Hunt hesitated a fraction, as if he intended to add something pertinent, then appeared to change his mind. "I ran into your uncle last night at the Biltmore ball. He said he hasn't seen you in ages and is most anxious to talk to you."

Sam's smile was hollow. "The Marquess of Rainforth must be on the outs with his son again. Every time he and Ross argue, he seeks me out. My cousin can be quite exasperating. I'll have to drop by when this is over."

"Yes, do that."

Hunt fit the sweat-stained hat back on his head. "I'll be waiting for you tomorrow night after midnight."

Sam nodded.

"Watch your back, Sam."

"You, too."

The Marquess of Huntingdon walked across the room and waited until Sam extinguished the lantern before he opened the door. "You go first. I'll wait to make sure no one follows you."

Sam nodded and checked the dark hallway before going to the stairs. No one was there. He made his way down the worn steps and through the kitchen. He listened, opened the door, then looked around before he stepped out into the narrow alley. He made his way to the side of the Armor's Inn to where his horse was tethered, keeping to the shadows as much as he could. The bay pawed the ground in welcoming. Or in warning. The hairs on the back of his neck stood, and, before Sam could reach for the pistol in his pocket, Hunt's voice bellowed into the darkness.

Sam turned, but not in time. A searing pain stung his shoulder, knocking him off balance. He pulled out his gun, but his fingers lacked the strength to hold it steady.

Sam heard the muffled pop of gunfire as another bullet slammed into the muscled flesh of his arm. He spun around to face his attackers.

"Sam! Get down!"

Hunt's voice came from the side of the inn as a shot rang out, then another. Two of the gunmen fell to the ground, but a third stepped out, his gun pointed at Sam's chest.

"No!" Hunt yelled.

Sam spun to the side, praying he could step out of the gunman's line of fire, but realized it was unlikely. Before he could move, Hunt pummeled into him, using his own body to shield Sam. The gunman fired two more shots.

"Hunt! Hunt!" Sam pushed Hunt's body off him and twisted to the side as a dozen or more men streamed from the Armor's Inn. Sam found his gun and fired, but the attacker was already gone, having run into the thick woods surrounding the building.

Sam lifted Hunt's head to his lap and felt the warm wetness of his friend's blood against his hand. "Lie still, Hunt. Someone will send for a doctor."

"Too . . . late."

"No! Don't you dare die."

"Listen . . ." Hunt gripped Sam's jacket and pulled him closer. "The necklace . . . she has it. My marchioness has it."

The effort to speak took its toll. A fierce, wracking cough sucked the air from Hunt's body, and he struggled to take in air. "I didn't mean for it to . . . turn out this way."

"I know."

Sam ignored his own wounds and held his friend while he gasped for breath. Blood ran from Sam's shoulder and arm, and his head spun in dizzying circles. But that didn't matter. The best friend he'd ever had was dying, and there was nothing he could do to save him.

"The papers . . . and necklace. Get them, Sam. Claire's not safe until you do."

Sam waited while another coughing spasm consumed Hunt's body.

"I'll get them. Don't worry, Hunt."

Hunt lifted a trembling hand to the front of Sam's jacket and Sam leaned down to hear him.

"Tell Claire . . . I'm sorry . . . In my own way . . . I loved her."

"I will, Hunt. I'll"—Hunt's body went limp in his arms—"I'll tell her."

Sam held his friend's body long after his last breath. There was a rush of activity around him, but he ignored it. Just as he ignored the suggestion that he let someone help him up. That he let the men carry Hunt's body back into the inn. That he let someone look at his wounds. He only wanted to be left alone.

When he was able, he helped carry Hunt back into the inn and penned a note to Lieutenant Joshua Honeywell, requesting his help. Honeywell was the only person Sam could trust now.

Sam sat in a room in the Armor's Inn, ignoring the all-consuming pain that enveloped him, and guarded Hunt's lifeless body. He kept his gun drawn in case the assassins returned. But they didn't. Only Honeywell came. When he walked into the room, Sam closed his eyes and let the blessed darkness consume him.

Chapter 1

London - June, 1855

Claire wasn't sure the exact moment she realized someone was in her bedroom. Wasn't sure if she'd heard him move across the floorboards, or if she'd imagined him sifting through the shadows. Or simply felt him intrude on her sleep. But he was here, and she knew why. She'd received enough threats in the four months since her husband's death to know what he'd come for.

A sense of panic washed over her, but she reminded herself she wasn't alone in the house. There were the footmen, and Watkins, the butler. Unfortunately, they were too far away to hear her. She'd positioned them at the downstairs entrances, never dreaming the intruder would climb the roof and enter from an upstairs window.

Claire fought the fear that threatened to engulf her as she slowly inched her hand upward, sliding it beneath her pillow, stopping only when her fingers came in contact with hard metal.

The intruder made his way across the room, his rapid, shallow breaths knifing through the silence. She clasped her hand around the gun and waited, forcing herself to lie still until he was close. So close she couldn't miss.

The drapes were pulled back, allowing moonlight to stream into the room. The bright beams illuminated the large man enough to outline his broad shoulders and massive bulk.

Her heart thundered so loudly against her ribs she feared he could hear it. If he did, it didn't stop him. He slowly inched his way toward her, keeping in the shadows until he was beside her.

With movement as swift and lethal as a practiced marksman, Claire twisted beneath her covers and lifted the weapon. She aimed the barrel at the middle of his chest and—

Before she could fire, his hand slashed through the air. His fist struck painfully against her arm.

The gun flew from her fingers and skittered across the floor, out of reach. Claire opened her mouth to scream, but before she could utter a sound, his big, beefy hand clamped down across her mouth, stopping any cry for help.

Panic surged through her and stole her breath. Fear consumed her. She swung her fists, praying she was strong enough to fight him off. But rough, bruising fingers pulled at her, making it impossible to move.

"Not one sound," he hissed, his Russian accent thick. "Do you understand?"

His breath reeked of day-old whiskey, and his body smelled of sweat and unwashed flesh. Her stomach knotted, and she fought harder to push him away. But her efforts were useless.

With an angry growl, he grabbed her wrists and pinned her arms above her head. His elbow dug into her chest when he lunged over her, and she couldn't breathe. Couldn't do anything but struggle to bring little gasps of air into her lungs.

Every instinct she possessed compelled her to fight him, but she knew she was no match for someone with his brute strength. Instead, her mind searched for another way to save herself. She relaxed her muscles, giving him the impression of surrender.

Slowly, he pulled his body away from her and lifted his hand from her mouth. "Not a sound, my lady, or I'll put a bullet through the first person who comes through the door."

Claire's breath caught and she held still. He eased off her and her heart raced with the hope he'd put some space between them, enough to give her some leverage. But before she could realize any freedom, an even greater terror gripped her as his hand tightened around her throat and squeezed.

"Are you frightened, marchioness?" he whispered, his voice a menacing hiss that sent shivers down her spine. "Or are you really as brave as you want me to believe?"

Claire kept her hateful gaze riveted on him. The evil look in his eyes was cold, and threatening. He laughed.

"I think you are," he said, leaning closer, his mouth opening to a sinister smile. "Very brave. And that is a big mistake. You should be frightened."

As if she weighed no more than a rag doll, he pulled her from the bed and lifted her in the air. His hands clamped around the flesh at her upper arms, his fingers pinching painfully into her skin.

She fought the pain, fought to free herself from his grasp. But her efforts were useless. He was too strong. With a loud grunt, he took a step forward and slammed her against the wall.

Her head snapped back, hitting the wood with a thud. She closed her eyes as the room spun around her.

It took several seconds before everything came back into focus. She had to stay alert. Had to keep her wits about her to have any chance to escape. But before she could catch her breath, he anchored his arm across her chest at the base of her throat and pinned her to the wall.

For a minute everything went black. The pain was excruciating. When her eyes finally focused again, moonlight from the open window illuminated her enemy's face with horrifying clarity. His black-as-midnight eyes gleamed in the semidarkness, and the scar that ran down the side of his face was as vivid as if it were day.

She'd never been so frightened in her life. Never felt so helpless. Claire suppressed a shiver, then bit back a scream when the cold blade of his knife pricked the skin at her neck. She froze, not daring to move lest his knife slice her skin even further.

"You know why I've come, don't you?"

He dug his elbow deeper into her chest, and Claire gave a soft, muffled cry. She swallowed, but her throat was so dry she couldn't have answered even had she any intention of doing so. She took a shuddering breath and shook her head.

She wasn't prepared for his sudden outburst of anger. His hand swung through the air. His fist connected with her cheek.

Her head slammed backward, bouncing as it hit the wall behind her. The whimper she heard was her own. She prayed the end would come quickly and painlessly.

But she knew it wasn't her death the intruder wanted.

"Tell me, marchioness." The tip of his knife again pressed the flesh at her neck. "Where is it?"

Her skin burned where he held the blade, and Claire felt a warm trickle of blood run down her throat.

"Where?" he growled, crushing her against the wall.

She gasped for air. "I . . . don't . . . know."

"But I think you do. In fact, I am sure of it."

He lifted the knife and held it in front of her face. The moonlight reflected off its silvery blade, the tip dark with her blood. With slow deliberation, he touched the knife against the tender flesh at the inside of her arm just above her wrist. Claire fought the fear that raged through her.

"Where?" He pressed the tip harder against her flesh.

Claire tried to keep silent, but her scream echoed in the darkness as the knife punctured her skin. Blood roared in her head, her frantic thoughts spinning to find an answer that would save her. She couldn't give him what he wanted, no matter what he did to her. But if she could get him to let her loose, she might have a chance to escape.

"You will tell me where the necklace is hidden, my lady," the Russian said, moving the knife to her throat, "or this night will become very unpleasant for you."

Claire squeezed her eyes shut. She had to get free for a few seconds. Had to convince him it wasn't here, but in another part of the house.

"Listen carefully," he said, clamping his thumb and forefinger on either side of her jaw. "Monsieur Roseneau is scheduled to arrive in England in less than a month. He expects me to give him the necklace the moment he steps ashore."

Roseneau. It was a name she'd hoped never to hear again. A name as vile as the man himself.

"And to make sure you cooperate, Monsieur Roseneau has provided an added incentive. He is holding your brother, the Marquess of Halverston. His life will be exchanged for the necklace."

"No! My brother doesn't know anything about the necklace!"

"If you want to see your brother alive again, you will give it to me. Now, where is it?"

Claire gasped for air as her heart thundered in her chest. They had Alex! "Downstairs. It's downstairs."

"Then we will go downstairs to get it."

The Russian dropped his hold from across her chest and clasped his fingers around her arm. With brutal force, he shoved her against the bedside table.

"Light the lamp."

Claire lit the lamp with trembling hands, then turned her face away from the bright glare until her eyes adjusted. When she turned back, her eyes rested on the Russian. Her breath caught. He was more frightening in the light than in the dark. The evil she'd only imagined in his eyes was now plain to see. She shivered when he again clamped his fingers around her arm.

"We will go the back way. I have no desire to meet the guards you have posted at the front entrance."

Claire raised the lamp and walked toward the door. The Russian kept a bruising grip on her arm with one hand while pressing the tip of the knife against her ribs with the other. They slowly made their way down the back stairs and into the study from a side door.

"Not a sound, my lady, or you're dead. And your brother will die next."

Claire tightened her hold on the lamp and led the way into Hunt's study. Hopefully, one of the guards would hear them. Even though the room was at the back of the house, surely someone would hear something and come to her aid.

The Russian closed the door behind them and locked it, then quickly went to the windows to shut the drapes. Next, he went to the other door and locked it, too, enclosing them in a tomb from which she couldn't escape. "Now, where is it?"

Claire set the lamp on the edge of Hunt's desk and moved to the side. Hunt always kept a pistol in the top drawer near the back. After the first threat arrived, Claire made sure it was loaded. If she could just get to it . . .

"It's in here." She stepped around the corner of the desk. "In a secret compartment."

The Russian watched her as she sat down behind Hunt's desk and slowly opened the drawer. She reached in and closed her fingers around the gun. She'd only have one shot—she had to make it good.

The Russian watched her closely. She could see by the wary look in his eyes he didn't trust her. Just as she pulled the gun from the drawer, he dodged to the side. Claire fired but the bullet went wide and struck him in the arm instead of his chest.

"Bitch!" he bellowed, darting around the desk.

Before Claire could move away, the Russian lifted his arm and brought the knife in a downward arc. Claire protected her face but felt a hot, stinging pain across her shoulder and down her left arm. In a backward swing, he slammed his fist against the side of her face. Blood poured from her nose and mouth, and Claire clung to the side of the desk as her knees gave out beneath her.

From somewhere in the murky darkness, she could hear the sounds of footsteps racing down the hallway. Help was almost here. They only needed to break through the locked door. And she was not completely helpless. The gun was still somewhere on the top of the desk. If she could only find it, she could . . .

She pushed herself to her hands and knees while the floor shifted beneath her. Her heart thundered in her head as blood streamed down her arm, pooling in a dark puddle on the floor where her limp left hand hung beneath her.

Wave after wave of agonizing pain knifed through her, and she wanted to give in to it. She wanted to close her eyes and let blessed darkness consume her, but she couldn't. Roseneau had Alex. If she gave in to the pain, who would save him? The man rifling through the desk was her only link to where he was being held.

She crawled to the nearest chair and somehow managed to get to her feet. Her left arm was of no use. She had to hold on to the arm of the chair with her right hand to steady herself, but she refused to let the pain control her. She turned her head and watched the Russian frantically rummage through the desk drawers. She knew he didn't have any better chance of finding the necklace than she. And she'd had four months since Hunt's death to search for it.

As if realizing the necklace wasn't there, he threw an empty drawer against the wall. Claire saw the wild look of fury in his eyes as the first thud pounded against the door. The Russian reached for the knife at his waist as if debating whether or not to take the time to kill her, then dropped his hand and darted toward the doors that led out onto the terrace.

Claire stumbled to the desk and searched frantically beneath the strewn papers for the pistol. She couldn't let him escape. The intruder was her only link to Alex.

She found the pistol before he reached the door. Using every ounce of energy she had left, she lifted the gun and turned to face him. Then stopped short. The Russian glared at her with a malevolent gleam in his eyes and a raised pistol in his own hand.

Before either of them could pull their triggers, the door behind her crashed open. A loud, booming explosion rent the air.

The Russian stopped, his eyes wide with surprise, then she heard his last gasp of air before he fell to the floor.

Claire sank to her knees as her legs gave out beneath her. Blood streamed down her arm, dripping from her fingers onto the gray-and-rose Turkish carpet. Hot, fiery waves of pain assaulted her, and she closed her eyes against the burning agony. When she could no longer stand the pain, she crumpled to the floor.

Hunt's handsome face appeared in her mind's eye, his noble features, the sparking humor in his eyes, his ever-ready smile. Suddenly Claire was angrier than she'd been since the day they'd brought his lifeless body home. He'd left her to face this alone. To face his deception and the risks that came with a mission she still didn't understand.

He didn't think she knew what he was. But she wasn't a fool. She'd known for years that he was a spy. She'd lived with his deep devotion to his country and fellow Englishmen since they'd married. His commitment to everyone but her.

Claire listened to the strangely distant sounds around her. With each passing second, she felt further and further removed from what was happening. Until a deep, demanding voice pulled her back from the quiet place where she'd been going.

"Lady Huntingdon?" he said, his hand covering hers reassuringly. "It's over. You're safe now."

Claire thought she should react with some emotion. Wasn't that normal for people when a horror was at an end? But she couldn't. She couldn't feel relief or make an effort to open her swollen eyes. And she wasn't sure this horror would ever end. Roseneau had Alex and the only person who knew where they'd taken him was dead.

"Honeywell!" the man yelled, and a second man appeared. "Hold this light. I need to see how badly she's hurt."

The man called Honeywell lifted the lantern and the other man pulled at her bloody gown.

"Ah, hell, Major," the man called Honeywell whispered. "Look what the bastard did to her."

Claire wanted to turn her face from them but didn't have the strength. Instead she kept her gaze focused on the man hovering over her. The man who gently brushed her hair back from her face. The man who softly pressed a wet cloth someone handed him to her cheek and made the pain seem bearable.

She'd never seen him before. She was certain she'd remember if she had. His hair was dark and his eyes the color of worn silver. He wore the look of intelligence and command. Claire wondered how he'd gotten there.

"I've got to move you. It's going to hurt."

His words registered in bits and pieces, but not fast enough to prepare her for the pain. She sucked in a deep breath when he gently picked her up. She tried to be brave, but the pain was too great. A loud moan echoed inside her head and she knew he'd heard it, too.

"Get me some cloths," he said to the servants who'd gathered in the doorway. "And some water and salve and bandages. And get her room ready upstairs. Now!"

The servants scattered to do his bidding.

"Honeywell," he said, issuing orders as he carried her out of the room and up the stairs, "see if he has any papers on him. Anything to identify him."

The man, Honeywell, left them and came back before they'd reached the upstairs landing. "He's Russian, Major."

Claire saw the muscles at the major's jaw clench. "Get rid of him."

"Yes, sir. Where do you want me to take him?"

"I don't care. Someplace where no one is likely to find him."

"Right, Major."

"Then find Bronnely and tell him to get over here. Fast."

The man nodded and disappeared. The major carried her down the hallway and into her room, where a servant stood outside the door.

"Who . . . are . . . you?"

"Major Samuel Bennett," he replied, his face grim. "Your husband and I were . . . friends."

"You're . . . a spy," she whispered, ignoring the arch of his brows and the dark look in his eyes.

"How did he get in?" the man asked.

"The . . . roof."

Claire thought she spied a flash of guilt before he masked it.

The major laid her on the bed and rinsed out a cloth, then placed it on her face. The cool wetness against her burning flesh was a jolt and she sucked in a quick breath.

"Lie still. You're still bleeding."

Claire shivered; he reached for an extra blanket and put it over her. She felt its warmth almost immediately but still couldn't seem to stop trembling. She closed her eyes and shuddered. When she opened them again, Tilly, one of the upstairs maids, was there with a fresh basin of water.

"Maude's on her way up," the trembling maid announced.

"Who's Maude?" he asked the maid before she left the room.

"The mistress's old nurse. She sleeps in a room off the kitchen," the maid said, then left the room.

The major brushed back a strand of hair from Claire's forehead and pressed a cloth against the cut on her shoulder.

"Your face is bruising already. I'm afraid you're going to be sore for a long time." He lifted the cloth from her shoulder and placed another one on the cut. "The Russian came for the necklace," he said, as if to inform her he knew about the necklace, too.

He kept his gaze on her, the hostile look in his eyes as rigid and unyielding as his military stance. His words were soft and gentle, but what they implied was anything but.

He leaned down over her. His movement brought the sharp, chiseled planes of his face closer to her. The steel gray of his eyes was frigid, his look harsh and removed. An unmistakable warning pelted her with a fresh wave of pain and she sucked in a breath.

"They won't give up until they have it back."

Claire closed her eyes to block out the pain, and the truth of the major's words.

This wouldn't end . . . until they'd killed her, too.

Chapter 2

Sam brushed back a strand of golden hair that had fallen over her forehead and placed another cool cloth against her cheek. He thought maybe she'd lost consciousness, and secretly hoped she had. The less she remembered of this night, the better.

She was paler than when he'd first found her, and the grimace on her face indicated she was in pain. The sticky wetness seeping through the makeshift bandage on her shoulder told him she was still bleeding, although not as badly.

A twinge of guilt touched him when he saw what the Russian had done to her, but it didn't stay long. Only long enough for him to admit that some of what she'd suffered was his fault. He should have anticipated the Russian would climb in from the roof. But he hadn't. He'd expected to catch the bastard before any harm came to her. Unfortunately, he hadn't realized his mistake until he'd heard the gunshot.

The shuffling of aged feet tore his attention to the door. A plump, gray-haired woman in a thick, quilted wrapper rushed into the room. It was impossible to determine her age, but her eyes were sharp and her movements spry.

"My lady," she said as she moved from the door, fussing with the practice of a woman who'd taken care of Lady Huntingdon in her youth. "What has happened—?"

The woman's wrinkled hands covered her mouth the minute she saw her mistress's blood-soaked gown and bruised face. "Ah, sweetling," she whispered, wringing out a fresh cloth and placing it on Lady Huntingdon's face.

"Maude?" Claire whispered.

"Yes, my lady. I'm right here. Maudie will take care of you now. There's naught to fear."

Sam glanced over his shoulder to where the butler stood. "What's your name?"

"Watkins, Major."

"Watkins, get a bottle of brandy and bring it up. Then go back down and wait for the doctor to come."

The butler darted from the room and came back with a bottle. After he handed it to Sam, he left to wait for the doctor.

Sam poured a small amount of the brandy into a glass, then lifted Lady Huntingdon's head and held the glass to her lips. She hesitated a moment, and he knew she wanted to refuse. He also saw she was desperate for anything that might ease the pain. She took a small sip.

"Drink some more of it," he urged, but she shook her head and turned away from him.

Sam wanted to argue with her, but the sound of heavy footsteps coming down the hall stopped him.

"The doctor's here, Major," Watkins announced, ushering the surgeon into the room.

Sam cast a glance over his shoulder as his longtime friend and fellow agent entered.

Silas Bronnely's hair was still slightly disheveled and the buttons of his waistcoat not all fastened, indicating Honeywell had roused him from his bed and not given him much time to dress.

"What trouble have you gotten yourself into, Sam?" he said as he crossed the bedroom floor, his long, gangly legs covering the distance in few steps. "Honeywell said you have someone that needs my—"

Bronnely stopped short, his gaze darting from the bed to Sam's face, then back to the bed. "Well, well," he said to Lady Huntingdon. "Well, my lady. You look as if you've gotten yourself in a bit of a fix."

"A . . . bit," she answered on a gasp, her eyes wary.

"Don't worry about talking just yet, my lady. You have nothing so important that has to be said this minute."

Sam watched her face as her gaze lifted to his, and he felt a stab of something close to anger. Bronnely didn't realize the lady had something very important to say.

Bronnely turned her head to the side to check the knife cuts on her neck, then pushed aside her bloody gown to look at her shoulder and arm. "Whoever got a hold of you was quite handy with his knife. I'm going to have to put in a few stitches. But if I do my best needlework, I can almost guarantee, in time, no one will ever notice."

Sam took in the serious frown on Bronnely's face as he studied the long ragged gash across her flesh and knew it would take more than a few stitches. A hell of a lot more.

Bronnely straightened, then reached into his bag and handed Sam a small brown bottle of laudanum. "Put a few drops in a glass and fill it half full with wine."

Watkins rushed from the room again and came back with a decanter of wine. Sam filled the glass as Bronnely had instructed, then handed it to him.

"Major," Bronnely said without looking at Sam. He was busy cleaning the wounds as he prepared to sew her flesh together. "Why don't you leave us for a while? We can take care of this, can't we?" He looked at the servant.

"Maude. My name's Maude. And of course, doctor," Maude said, rinsing more cloths in the fresh water one of the maids had brought up. "I've taken good care of the mistress from the day she was born."

"Just leave that glass," Bronnely said, holding out his hand to Sam. Sam handed it over. "We'll call you when we're finished."

Sam watched Bronnely lift Lady Huntingdon's head and put the glass to her lips; then he turned his back and walked to the door. "Here," he heard his friend tell her. "Drink some of this. It will help with the pain."

Sam waited to make sure she followed Silas's order, then froze with his hand on the knob when he heard her weak answer.

"No."

He spun to face her. Their gazes locked, and he saw the pain in her eyes. Her face was void of all color except the deep purple bruises growing darker by the second, and a thin film of perspiration that dotted her forehead. Her defiance was unmistakable.

"Drink it," Sam ordered, as if he had the power to make her obey his command.

"I don't . . . need . . . it."

"The hell you don't. I said, drink it."

Her eyes brimmed with pain and still she issued him a challenge she should not have been strong enough to muster.

"I'll not make it . . . that easy for you . . . Major. I know why you're . . . here. I know what you . . . want."

He glared at her with all the anger he'd felt since he'd held Hunt's lifeless body in his arms, and realized that one of the reasons his friend had taken the necklace was because of his infatuation for this woman.

What kind of woman was she that she could bewitch a man as honorable as the Marquess of Huntingdon into betraying his principles and stealing a fortune in jewels to buy her love? What kind of woman could contemplate keeping the necklace that had cost her husband his life?

Only one without a conscience or a shred of decency.

"As you wish, my lady. Far be it from me to force an unfair advantage."

Bronnely gave him a warning look over his shoulder. "Major, why don't you leave now so I can attend Lady . . . ?"

"I'm sorry, Bronnely," Sam said, casting a glance to the doctor. "How remiss of me. Allow me to present Lady Huntingdon. The Marquess of Huntingdon's widow. Please do your best to help her so she'll be healthy enough to face the hangman's noose."

Without another glance at her, he opened the door and left the room.

Chapter 3

Sam stood in the large, masculine study that once belonged to the Marquess of Huntingdon, keeping his gaze focused on the deserted street from the window. For more than a week, he and Honeywell had taken turns watching Hunt's town house.

Sam had secretly hoped Roseneau would come to get the necklace himself, and Sam could catch him. But that hadn't happened. In fact, no one had heard from Roseneau in the four months since Hunt had been killed, which meant Roseneau was still in hiding. But time was running out, and he had to make his move soon.

So did the Russians.

They only had weeks left. Sevastopol was in jeopardy of falling, and representatives from Britain and France were to meet informally to discuss the terms for the conclusion of a war that had gone on far too long. The necklace was a key negotiating tool. It was possible that the British negotiators could use it to convince the Russians to bring about a quicker end to the war. Tsar Nicholas was dead, and his son, Alexander I, was less inclined to continue a war that was increasingly unpopular. The offer to return the necklace might be the one advantage that would tip the balance in favor of declaring peace.

But Sam knew Roseneau would do everything in his power to get the necklace first. The only chance he had of getting out of this alive was to bargain for his life in exchange for the necklace.

And there were, of course, the papers that were hidden inside the pouch.

Sam swiped his hand across his jaw. He wouldn't let Hunt's sacrifice be for naught. He wouldn't let one hint of dishonor tarnish his name.

Sam rolled his shoulder, still stiff from the bullets he'd taken the night Hunt had died. He'd nearly died, too. He should have. Even Bronnely thought he wouldn't live, but Sam knew he had no choice. He'd vowed over Hunt's lifeless body to avenge his friend's death. Even the raging fever that had set in just days after Bronnely had dug the bullets out of his flesh couldn't stop him from his promise to get the necklace from Hunt's widow.

He thought of the woman upstairs. The woman Hunt had loved so much he'd betrayed every principle by which he'd lived. And a small part of him wanted to make her suffer for the price her husband had paid to keep her love.

He braced his hands on either side of the paned window and listened.

Although it hadn't been that long, it seemed like hours since Bronnely had started to work on her. Only in the last fifteen minutes or so had it been deathly quiet. Sam prayed Bronnely was finally finished.

He threw the remaining liquor down his throat and braced his hands again, then hung his head between his outstretched arms. A feeling of dread caused the minutes to stretch by in agonizing slowness. Bronnely should have been down long ago. How much time did it take to put in stitches?

Sam refilled his glass, then stared back out through the window into the darkness. He'd give him another five minutes and then he'd . . .

Sam released a steady breath. He knew the instant Bronnely entered the room. A surprising surge of relief washed through him, but he tamped it down. "Are you finished?" he asked, looking over his shoulder.

"Yes."

Bronnely walked to the sideboard and filled a glass with brandy. "It could have gone easier." He took a long swallow, then sank down on the burgundy settee against the wall. "She refused to take the laudanum."

"That was her choice."

"Because you forced it. She doesn't trust you, Sam."

"Then I'll give her credit for not being a fool."

Bronnely rubbed his temples, then closed his eyes and dropped his head against the back of the settee. "She was in an immense amount of pain."

"If you're trying to make me feel guilty, it isn't working."

"I thought for a moment we might lose her. She was weak enough before this happened."

"Weak from what?"

"Eating poorly. Lack of sleep. Worry." Bronnely took another sip. "The nurse, Maude, told me her mistress hasn't been herself since Huntingdon died. Tonight almost pushed her over the edge. It still might."

Sam stared at Bronnely in disbelief. "You're serious," Sam said, unable to mask his shock. "You really think she might die?"

"It's possible. We have to get some nourishment down her. And pray a fever doesn't set in."

Sam felt an unfamiliar niggling of fear and swiped his hand across his jaw. He needed her to get well. At least well enough to tell him where she'd hidden the necklace. Which would also give him the papers.

"You almost look concerned, Sam."

"Of course I'm concerned."

"How touching. But I have to wonder. Is it the lady you're the most worried about or something else?"

Sam ignored Bronnely's intense look and splashed more brandy into his glass. "It's complicated, Bron."

"That's obvious, Sam. This wasn't some random thievery. Whoever attacked Lady Huntingdon meant business."

Sam took another swallow and dropped down into an oversized wing chair. He couldn't mention the necklace or the papers. He couldn't trust anyone. Not even Bronnely.

"Surely you don't think this is connected to Hunt's death, do you?" the doctor asked, his hand halting midway to his mouth.

"I'm not sure what I think."

"But if it is," Bronnely said, sitting forward, "that means the lady upstairs knows something someone is willing to harm her to find out."

"There is that possibility," Sam said, stretching his long legs out in front of him.

"And your guess would be . . ."

Bronnely waited for Sam to finish his sentence, but Sam shook his head and took another swallow of the brandy in his glass. "I don't know, but I'm not going to rest until I find out."

"Then I don't envy the lady."

Sam arched his brows.

"Face it, Sam. I know seasoned soldiers who shy away from your scrutiny. You don't have the gentlest reputation."

"Then I'll have to take special care with Hunt's widow. If she's as injured as you say, I wouldn't want to do her more harm."

"She is, Sam."

Sam pondered Bronnely's warning as the two finished their brandy in silence.

"I'll be back later," Bronnely said, rising to his feet. "Try to get as much liquid down her as you can. I've told the nurse to fix a broth. See if she won't take some of that." He lifted his bag from the floor, then walked to the door. Sam followed him.

The minute he closed the door behind Bronnely, Sam turned toward the stairs. He didn't care how much the rest of the world sympathized with her. He'd be damned if he'd let Hunt's death be for naught. Damned if he'd let her keep the necklace, or let Roseneau have it.

He took the steps two at a time and threw open the door to her room as if he expected to see the enemy he'd mentally pictured breathing fire and wielding a sword. What he saw sucked the air from his chest.

There was nothing formidable about her. She looked as lifeless as if she'd already taken her last breath. Her coloring was as white as the sheets she lay on, all except the massive black and purple bruises marring her features.

The white bandages Bronnely had wrapped around her shoulder and arm were already stained with blood. She looked as helpless as a child, and yet . . . there was nothing childlike about her. She was all woman. A woman so desirable Hunt had given his life to keep her love.

Sam shot his angry gaze away from her and met Maude's worried expression. "Why don't you get some rest?" he said to the older woman. "I'll stay with her for a while."

Sam almost smiled at Maude's hesitation. He picked up a chair and moved it closer to the bed. "Don't worry. I'll call if she needs you."

Maude finally agreed with a nod. "There's cool water on the table here. That might help keep the fever away. Doctor Bronnely said to give her plenty to drink." She slid a glass closer. "I'll bring up some broth before I retire."

Sam nodded and watched Lady Huntingdon's shallow breathing. When Maude reached the door, she stopped. "If you need anything, just call. I'll hear you."

"Get some sleep. It's been a long night for you."

"Not nearly as long as it's been for her. The doctor tried to be gentle, but . . . she stayed awake through nearly all of it." The older woman swiped her fingers across her damp cheeks, then closed the door behind her, leaving him alone with Lady Huntingdon.

Sam placed a fresh cloth on her forehead. She showed no indication that she felt it. No sign she knew he was here. He sat down on the chair and watched her.

Her hair was more gold than brown, the color of ripened wheat. It fanned out around her face and glowed a deep bronze in the firelight from the brushing Maude must have given it. Even though no one would know it by looking at her now, he knew her complexion was clear and creamy, and that she had exquisitely striking features.

He remembered how she'd looked the night he'd played the part of Hunt's coachman and had driven her to Roseneau's ball; her high cheekbones, the slight uplift to her small nose, the enchanting smile that lit her face.

She'd been the picture of elegance and grace. A most amazing vision. The way her gown clung to her body when she'd walked up the stairs on Hunt's arm was enough to cause any healthy male to take more than a second look. Her sheer perfection made the Marquess of Huntingdon one of the most envied men in Society.

But Sam knew the perfection everyone saw on the outside didn't dwell inside the Marchioness of Huntingdon. Why else would Hunt have felt the need to buy her love? Why would he have stolen a necklace to give to her?

Hunt had paid for his devotion with his life.

Sam looked at her fragile outline beneath the sheet covering her. Bronnely was right. She was overly thin. As if she hadn't eaten well since Hunt's death. The question was, why?

He leaned back in his chair and compared the facts he knew with what he surmised. Surely grief wasn't the reason. It had been four months since Hunt's death. Could she have loved him so desperately that she found it impossible to live without him?

Sam rose to his feet and paced the floor at the end of the bed. No. He knew too much about her to believe that. No. It wasn't grief that had stolen her appetite.

Perhaps it was guilt.

He walked back to the side of the bed and placed a fresh cloth on her forehead. She shuddered when he touched her.

He sat in the chair and tried to recall everything he knew about her. From her childhood and life growing up the pampered daughter of a marquess, to the last time she'd been seen in public. The day of Hunt's funeral.

Sam hadn't been there. He hadn't regained consciousness until weeks after Hunt had been buried. But every report he'd seen had noted that the Marchioness of Huntingdon held her composure remarkably well.

Hunt had once commented that her only interests were the latest styles of gowns and which balls they were to attend, but Sam knew that couldn't be all there was to her. The Hunt he knew would never have married anyone that shallow. He could never have tolerated anyone who wasn't a match for his intellect. And there'd never been anything to indicate Hunt regretted marrying her. Never.

So, how could she not mourn a man who loved her as Hunt had? Surely she cared for Hunt a fraction as much as he seemed to have cared for her?

Sam fought another wave of anger and turned his head when the door opened and Maude entered.

"I brought some broth."

"Set it on the table," Sam said.

Maude set down the tray, then picked up a glass and lifted the cool water to Lady Huntingdon's parched lips. Most of it ran down the side of her face, but a little of the liquid must have made its way into her mouth because he saw her swallow. Maude gently dabbed her bruised flesh with a soft cloth, then repeated the motion.

"Did she say anything while Bronnely was tending to her?" Sam asked

"You mean did she tell us why that blackguard attacked her? No, Major. It required effort enough for her just to stay alive."

"You know what they want, don't you?"

Sam focused his gaze on her, but she didn't answer, and he clenched his hands in frustration. "Why won't she give it over, Maude? She won't be safe until she does."

"You'll have to ask her that, Major. I'm sure she would if she thought she could. Evidently giving it over isn't possible."

Maude's words struck the nerve she'd intended. He sucked in a deep breath and slowly released it.

Maude gave Sam a sympathetic look over her shoulder. "I know what the mistress has is important to you, Major. But keeping it must be as important to her as it is to you."

They shared a look that hinted at an irreconcilable impasse, then Maude moved from the side of the bed and handed Sam the glass of water. "Make sure she drinks. Then try to get some of that broth down her if you can. I'll be back in a few hours."

Sam listened for the door to close, then took the glass and held it to her lips. He thought she swallowed a little of the water, but wasn't sure. Next, he tried to spoon some of the broth past her lips. On the first try, she turned her head and refused to open her mouth. He tried a stronger approach and forced her mouth open. She spit back most of the first spoonful, but swallowed the second, and the third.

"Just one more," he whispered when she turned her head away from him after the fourth spoonful.

"Please . . . no more."

He placed the broth back on the table by the bed and picked up the wine laced with laudanum. "Here. Drink a little of this. It will help with the pain."

She tried to shake her head, but the motion was barely noticeable.

"One swallow isn't enough to force you to tell me where you've hidden the necklace, my lady. It would take this whole bloody glass and more. Drink it. You aren't strong enough to survive much more pain and you know it."

She slowly turned her head on the pillow, and the raw pain in her eyes nearly took him to his knees. He'd never seen such helplessness. Or felt such a compelling need to protect. "One swallow," he demanded and held the glass to her lips.

She swallowed once. Twice. Then closed her eyes and sank back into the pillow. The effort it took to do that much concerned him. He straightened the covers around her, then sat back in his chair.

She labored for air, and he held her hand until her breathing returned to normal. And wished her small hand didn't fit so perfectly in his.

Chapter 4

The sun was high in the sky, the day nearly half gone. Sam had watched her toss and turn in restless slumber for hours. More than once he'd had to pin her to the mattress to keep her from tearing her stitches open or injuring herself further. More than once he'd had to assure her that she was safe. That her attacker was gone.

Twice he'd tried to feed her more of the broth, with little success.

He looked at the half-full bowl and decided to try again in a little while, when she was more awake.

Sam relaxed against the cushions, then bolted forward when she moved. Her chest rose with a gasp of air, and her hands grabbed fistfuls of the sheets covering her. Sam reached for her hands and held her tight while he whispered in her ear.

"It's all right. You're safe now. He's gone."

"No!"

"Yes, my lady. You're safe."

She struggled once more, then opened her eyes and stared at him. He knew the moment recognition dawned. She took a sharp breath, then released it.

He paused with her hand still in his. "Lie still. You don't want to tear your stitches open."

She relaxed, then turned her head toward the open window. "What time is it?"

"The middle of the afternoon."

She closed her eyes. "Where's Maude?"

"She went belowstairs to get you some hot broth."

"I'm not hungry."

"That hardly matters. You have to eat."

"I want you to leave."

She tried to pull away from him, but the pain from moving stole her breath. Instead, she clutched her fingers tighter around his hand and held on to him. "Go," she finally managed.

"Not a chance."

Her reaction was obvious, and she forced her pain-filled gaze to lock with his. "I want you . . . gone."

Sam felt a hitch in his breathing as he pulled his chair closer, still keeping her hand anchored in his. "Not until I have the necklace," he said without releasing her gaze.

"I can't give it to you."

A rush of anger and fury exploded like fireworks of bright light behind his eyes. Sam took several harsh breaths, waiting for his temper to abate. He searched for any conceivable reason she might have to keep the necklace. But all that came to mind was greed. The thought that Hunt had been so desperate to keep this woman's love that he'd risked his honor and integrity made Sam ill.

When he felt he at least had a small hold on his temper, he leaned forward in his chair and rested his elbows on his knees. "Do you know what you have, Lady Huntingdon? Do you know the value of the necklace you refuse to give up?" He took a deep breath as another wave of anger exploded inside him. "And I don't mean in monetary worth. I mean in human terms."

She closed her eyes as if she didn't want to hear what he was going to tell her. Well, too bloody damn bad! He wanted her to know what was at stake. What power she held in her hands. "The necklace your husband gave you is the tool we need to bring about a quicker end to the war. Having it will save thousands of lives. If you refuse to give the necklace over, you're as much as executing countless innocent young men."

She took a painful gasp of air, and the terror Sam saw in her eyes gave him reason to hope. Her next words killed it. "If I gave you the necklace . . . would you give it to Roseneau?"

Sam felt his temper rise. "Hardly, my lady. England has greater need of it. Roseneau is in part responsible for funding Russia's role in the Crimean War."

She turned her face from him, then pulled her hand from his grasp. The movement cost her much. She paled as she pressed her lips together in what he assumed was an effort to keep from crying out in pain.

Sam felt the rein on his temper slip. "The necklace doesn't belong to you. Your husband may have stolen it to buy your love, but once he knew what he had, he didn't intend for you to keep it. And he certainly didn't intend for Roseneau to have it back. He realized how important it was as a political tool. Both the necklace and the papers are invaluable."

Her bruised features froze. "Papers?"

"Yes. Papers he took along with the necklace. Surely you don't intend to withhold those?"

"I don't know . . . about any papers."

"Yes, you do. And I want them."

When she didn't answer, he bolted from his chair. "Your husband paid the ultimate sacrifice for those papers. He took a monumental risk and gave his life because he knew how valuable they were. I'll not let you destroy what he did."

Her face turned more ashen than before.

Sam braced his hands on either side of her and leaned close. "It is too late to undo all that has been done. Too late to bring Hunt back, but I want you to know this much. I will have that necklace. And when

I have it in my possession, I will hand it over to the British government. Perhaps something can be salvaged from the damage your association with Roseneau has already done. Perhaps some good can be realized from the noble deed Hunt tried to accomplish. But most of all, perhaps I will be able to understand how Hunt could love someone whose greed would allow her to betray every principle he stood for. Although I sincerely doubt it."

Sam pushed himself away from her and raked his fingers through his hair. Then he made the mistake of looking down at the bed. The Marchioness of Huntingdon—the object of his scorn and ridicule—had her eyes shut tight. But in the warm light from the sun filtering through the window, he saw her skin glisten as one tear after another streamed from the corners of her eyes.

Guilt assaulted him like a heavy weight pressing against his chest. Yet, he refused to take back his words. She, more than anyone, deserved his wrath and anger. By her refusal to help, she'd reduced Hunt's honor, and made his death a meaningless sacrifice.

Sam walked to the window and stared out at nothing. Hunt's face appeared as a reflection in the glass, so real and lifelike Sam had to hold back his hand to keep from reaching out to touch him. Instead, he looked over his shoulder toward the bed and stared at the marchioness's pain-ravaged face. When he could bear his guilt no longer, he made his way back to her bedside and reached for the laudanum-laced wine. "Here, drink one more swallow of this wine. It will help you sleep."

He tipped the glass before she had a chance to turn away from him. A small amount of the liquid made its way down her throat before she coughed, her body arching in pain. He laid her back on the pillows and wiped her face with a cool, wet cloth. When her breathing had slowed, he sat down beside the bed and waited for the drug to take effect.

Eventually, her features relaxed.

For a long time, he kept his vigil, watching her chest slowly rise and fall. He held her still when she thrashed in her delirium, and whispered comforting words when she moaned in her sleep. And when she cried out for help, he assured her he would keep her safe.

Finally, she fell into a deep sleep, where even her nightmares couldn't reach her.

Sam leaned back in his chair and closed his eyes. Praying he could keep his own nightmares at bay.

Hunt may have taken the necklace because he loved his wife, but he'd also thrown himself in front of the assassin's bullets to save Sam's life. With Hunt still cradled in his arms, Sam had vowed he wouldn't let his friend's death be for naught. He had four weeks to find the necklace and hand it over to the Foreign Office. Four weeks to discover the traitor's identity.

He owed Hunt for what he'd done. Owed him for saving his life.

One woman's greed was not going to destroy everything Hunt had stood for.

Chapter 5

"You're finally awake."

The concern she heard in his voice washed over her like a soft, gentle breeze. A breeze she knew could become a violent thunderstorm without warning. She closed her eyes and listened as he moved closer.

"Here. Drink this," he said. "It's just water." He lifted her head and pressed a glass to her lips.

Claire wasn't brave enough to look into his eyes. Instead, she stared at the long, muscular fingers that held the glass. She took a sip. The water was cool and felt wonderful going down her parched throat. She'd been so dry for so long. She drank greedily.

"That's enough for now." He took the glass from her mouth. "You can have more later."

He lowered her head and no longer touched her, but even without looking, Claire knew he hadn't moved. Knew he towered over her, waiting for her to look at him. She did, and it was the biggest mistake she could have made.

She looked over his shoulder. "How long has it . . . been?"

"Three days."

A rush of panic raced through her. Three wasted days she could have used to search for the necklace that would save her brother. His voice pulled her from her turmoil and back to the present.

"I thought perhaps you'd decided never to wake up."

"Are you . . . disappointed?"

His features hardened. "No."

"Where's . . . Maude?"

"She's resting. She hasn't gotten much sleep lately. I had a difficult time making her leave you even this long. I don't want to disturb her yet."

Claire closed her eyes.

"You don't have to worry, Lady Huntingdon. You're safe now."

Safe. Claire couldn't remember what being safe felt like. She couldn't remember her life before Hunt died and the threats started.

"Have you been here the whole time?"

"I helped Maude."

She sighed heavily. She could tell by the dark circles rimming his eyes he'd done more than help. She knew he'd left her side very little the past three days. That he'd gotten even less sleep. "Thank you."

"Here," he said, holding a bowl of soup close to her mouth. "Bronnely said to feed you the minute you woke up. You need to eat."

Her stomach rolled at the thought of putting anything in it. "I'm not hungry."

"That's hardly the point." He set the bowl back on the table and placed his arm beneath her shoulder. A sharp ache sucked the air from her, and she held her breath until he'd propped another pillow behind her.

"Just take a few deep breaths. It'll distract you from the pain."

"Is that . . . experience . . . talking?" she gasped.

He ignored her question and reached for the bowl of soup, then sat on the edge of the bed. "If I hold the bowl, can you feed yourself?"

"Yes, but I'm not—"

"Eat." He pushed a spoon into her hand and held the bowl closer.

Claire lifted the first spoonful, but her hand shook so that she barely got any of the broth into her mouth. The second spoonful wasn't much better. By the time she lifted the third spoonful, she was exhausted, and the spoon fell from her fingers into the bowl.

"Here. Let me."

"No. I've had—"

He ignored her again and filled the spoon and put it to her mouth. She had no choice but to eat what he forced into her mouth.

The soup was delicious and still warm, but it had been so long since she'd eaten anything, her stomach soon rebelled. "That's enough," she said and turned her head away from him.

He gave up and set the bowl back on the table. "Bronnely said you haven't been eating."

Claire wanted to laugh. Eating had been the furthest thing from her mind. Searching for the necklace had consumed her every minute since Hunt had died. She'd begun the second she'd received the first threat.

"Why? And don't tell me it was grief over losing your husband."

Her eyes snapped open and locked with his. The steel gray in his gaze was hard and calculating. His icy stare penetrated her like a rapier sword and ignited her anger. "How dare you."

He was too close. The heat from his body burned through the covers where he sat next to her. She wished he'd move. Wished he'd go far away and leave her alone.

For an eternity, neither of them spoke. But there were too many questions to which Claire needed answers. Too many contradictions between the man she knew Hunt was, the man she'd lived with for seven years, and what everyone assumed their relationship had been. Maybe, just maybe, the man who'd rescued her knew the truth. Maybe he'd known Hunt better than she had. Knew why everyone assumed she had the necklace. It was more than possible.

"Did you know my husband well, Major?"

A hollow smile crossed his face. "About as well as anyone, I imagine. Did you?"

His boldness stole her breath. "Obviously, not as well as I thought. How was it . . . we never met?"

"That was Hunt's idea. Being a spy for Her Majesty isn't the most respected occupation in England. Though I tried to keep my role with the government a secret, I wasn't always successful. Certain members of society knew I was a military advisor. I am a major, after all. As to any other role I play in the government, there is speculation, of course. But nothing that has been proven. Hunt thought if we were seen together overly much, people might link him to any covert operations of which I was a part. We couldn't afford to risk the exposure."

Claire closed her eyes and struggled to keep herself from crashing under the weight of this information. She'd lived with a spy for seven years, all the while pretending it had no consequences. But she could no longer ignore what he'd been.

The major turned on her as if he'd read her thoughts. "You have no right to judge him. He was invaluable to his country. His title gave him access to people and places the rest of us couldn't begin to infiltrate. He was a master when it came to living a dual role."

Claire wanted to laugh. Oh, he was a master at living a dual role, all right. As was she. Their public life had been totally opposite from the life they led behind closed doors.

"Tell me about France," she said, wanting to forget the way things had been. "How did Hunt get the necklace from Roseneau?"

Claire could see the frown deepen on his features. Could see the agitation in his movements. He rose from the side of the bed and stood by the window.

"I'm not sure it's necessary for you to know."

"Don't you? I was nearly killed because of . . . what happened there. I'd like to know . . . exactly what it is I'm . . . risking my life for."

The major clenched his teeth, then turned to face her. "Hunt and I were sent to France to retrieve jewels the Russian government intended to further fund the war. Roseneau was the middleman. The exchange was to take place sometime during the ball Roseneau was hosting."

A sense of disbelief washed over her. "The ball that Hunt and I attended?"

"Yes."

"You were there, too?"

"I was your driver."

She didn't want to believe him. She didn't want to know that Hunt would involve her in his work, would risk her safety along with his own. But he had. She'd been there with him. No wonder Roseneau was convinced she had the necklace.

"The jewels were locked in Roseneau's safe. We couldn't let the exchange take place. With the money the Russians would receive in exchange for the jewels, they could continue the war indefinitely. The cost in British lives would be unimaginable."

"And Hunt took the jewels?"

"Yes. As well as a necklace no one knew would be there. The Queen's Blood. An icon in Russian history. I believe Roseneau realized the war was close to ending and that this exchange would be one of his last. He must have taken the Queen's Blood either to ransom back to Russia, or to sell on the black market."

"Didn't he realize how dangerous that would be?"

Sam wanted to smile. "People involved in the ransom of jewels know the risks. And are willing to take them."

"But why did Hunt take the necklace if it wasn't one of the pieces you were supposed to steal?" she asked, her voice a weak entreaty.

He lifted his gaze and leveled her a piercing stare. "Why do you think he took it, my lady?"

The look in his eyes grew darker. More menacing. For the first time, Claire was frightened of more than the domineering powers he possessed. "I have no idea. I was hoping . . . you could . . . tell me."

"What if I told you he took the necklace for you?"

Claire felt the air leave her body. Nothing he could say would have shocked her more. "I'd call you a liar."

"Well, he did."

The major spat out the words with more vehemence than she was prepared to hear. His tone dripped with a bitterness that sank like a lead ball to the pit of her stomach.

"He took the necklace for you. Because he thought you were worth it." He swiped his hand down his stubbled face. "And for spite. Taking it out from beneath Roseneau's nose was a masterful coup. Considering."

Claire's breath caught while she tried to absorb what he was saying. What he was implying. "Considering what, Major? Are you assuming I withheld my love so my husband would lavish me with gifts? Is that what you think?"

"Perhaps. Or he was afraid he'd already lost your love and wanted to buy it back."

"You can't believe that."

"Can't I?" The major leveled her a harsher glare. "What if I told you I witnessed the display of affection you and Roseneau shared in the darkened corridor the night of his ball?"

Her heart stuttered in her chest. He'd seen her and thought . . . "That wasn't—"

"I know what I saw, Lady Huntingdon."

An ominous silence nearly choked her.

"Well, my conscience is clear, Major Bennett," Claire answered angrily. Why couldn't he just go away and leave her alone? "I'm surprised, given your opinion of me, you didn't let me die."

"I could hardly risk you dying before I had the necklace."

Claire fought the pounding in her head. What kind of person did he think she was? She saw the muscles in his jaw clench in anger. Watched as he rose menacingly from his chair and towered over her. She wanted to look away but couldn't. Wanted to be anywhere but in the same room with him, in the same city. In the same world. His next words frightened her.

"Roseneau will not give up until he has the necklace. You will never be safe as long as you have it."

"How foolish of me, then, not to give it to his henchman when he came for it."

The glare in the major's eyes was swift, his anger unmistakable.

"I see," she said, watching him through pain-clouded eyes. "You're trying to tell me I'd be safer if I gave it to *you* instead."

"That would be best for everyone."

She wanted to laugh. "It would have been best if my husband hadn't taken it in the first place."

She saw regret in his eyes even though the rest of his face revealed nothing.

"Why did you wait until now to come for the necklace?" She sighed through the pain. "Hunt's been dead for four months."

He hesitated. "I was detained."

He avoided any further explanation and busied himself by placing another cool cloth against her burning skin. His touch was gentle, but the tight clench of his jaw hinted at another emotion. When he spoke, his words caught her off guard.

"I know about your involvement with Roseneau, my lady. You may have fooled your husband, but I'm not so blind as Hunt."

"I don't know what display of affection you believe you saw," she said, unable to control her anger. "Nor am I involved with Roseneau in any manner. I do not know the man. Nor do I even like the man. He came upon me the night of the ball and tried to force his attentions on me. If you would have watched, as you say you did, you would have seen me push him away, then leave him." She stopped to catch her breath. "But you are obviously more interested in believing the worst of me."

The look on his face told her he didn't believe her.

"Roseneau's not going to win," he said. "I don't intend to leave your side until I have the necklace."

She sighed. "And if I refuse to give it to you?"

His hand lifted from the cut at her shoulder, and he leveled her a look so blinding it sent chills down her spine.

"I won't allow you to keep it," he said, his voice soft, deadly. "Representatives from Her Majesty will meet with French and Russian emissaries in in less than a month. I intend to see our government has the crown jewels."

"And the papers?"

"The papers will reveal the traitor. They'll give us the identity of the man receiving the jewels for military secrets, lead us to the British citizen who would trade our soldiers' lives for his own gain."

His gaze burned through her, his unrelenting hostility and determination a formidable force. She refused to be cowed by it. "What if you do not have the necklace?"

"I will have it."

Claire dropped her head deeper into the pillows and closed her eyes. She could never trust him. No matter how much she might want to give the necklace to him, or how desperate he was to take it away from her, she couldn't consider handing it over. Even if she had it. The major would never give it to Roseneau, and Alex would pay with his life. The British government had the other jewels to bargain with. The necklace was the only leverage she had to free Alex.

And she didn't even have that. Yet.

He walked to the window and braced his hand against the wood frame. "Have you considered, Lady Huntingdon, how you intend to live with yourself knowing you caused the deaths of thousands of innocent young men?"

Claire bristled. She fought the overwhelming pain slicing through her and the weakness sapping her. "I did not ask to be tossed into this game you and my husband were playing, Major. I was given no choice. Just as I have no choice now . . . but to play it out as I see fit."

He turned his head and looked at her over his shoulder. His eyes narrowed, making his threatening frown even more daunting. "I think not," he said, his voice soft and menacing. "Roseneau is not worth even one man's life. *You* are not worth one man's life."

"It must be wonderful to be so self-righteous."

"At least I am able to live with myself. Can you?"

"And if I told you . . . I didn't . . . have the necklace?"

"Then I would call you a liar and be right in doing so."

She glared at him through vision that was blurred. "What makes you so sure?"

Claire saw the scowl on his face deepen. Heard the disgust in his voice when he spoke. And his words were as painful as if he were driving a knife through her.

"Because your husband told me you did. Those were his dying words. He wanted to make sure you were safe. He thought he'd failed you. And he wanted you to know he loved you." He spun away and slammed his fist against the wall.

Claire wanted him to stop. She wanted him to take back his words. But he didn't. Instead, he repeated his damning accusation.

"*You* are the reason he took the necklace. And now he's dead!"

"Samuel. That's enough."

The room seemed to close in around her. She was barely aware of Bronnely's appearance in the doorway or his reproach. Barely aware of the hands touching her, or the water raised to her lips, or the cool cloth pressed to her forehead.

What the major had said consumed her thoughts. His words tore at her heart. How could she believe him—that her husband had loved her? That he'd stolen the necklace for her? Both were blatant lies.

Hunt didn't love her. He never had.

Chapter 6

"What the hell is going on, Sam?" Bronnely said, bending over Claire's pale, limp form. "If you want her dead, just take out your gun and put a bullet through her head. It will be more humane."

Bronnely held one hand over her brow and pressed the fingers of his other hand against her neck. Sam could see the rapid beating of her pulse at the small indent at the base of her throat. Her face was as white as it had ever been, and she struggled to catch her breath.

Sam walked over to the dying embers in the fireplace and slammed his fist against the mantel. Guilt ate away at him, gnawing deep inside his chest. He'd gone after her with all the accusatory bitterness he'd lived with since Hunt had been gunned down. And he was no closer to getting the necklace now than he'd been before.

He leaned down and threw two more logs on the ebbing fire. The room had taken on a chill. Why hadn't he noticed it before? He turned back to the bed and watched Bronnely toss another cover over Claire's trembling body. Then the doctor raised her shoulders and pressed a glass to her lips. Sam was glad it was the wine laced with laudanum.

"Has she taken any of Maude's broth?"

"A little. Not much."

Bronnely replaced the glass with the broth and lifted a spoonful to her mouth. "Just four spoonfuls," he said, sliding the first one between her lips. She swallowed, then coughed, but Bronnely didn't give up. He slid another into her mouth. Then several more.

"That's more than . . . four," she whispered on a gasp.

"So it is," Bronnely said, not bothering to hide his smile of satisfaction. "Now, let's see to your shoulder. You just close your eyes and I'll try not to bother you."

Sam watched Bronnely unbutton her gown and slide it over her shoulder. He tried not to look, but couldn't help but notice the rise of her breast that was partially exposed. She was a beautiful woman. Even if she was spoiled and greedy and unscrupulous. And she was brave.

Though he didn't want to, he had to admire her strength. Not too many men would have had the courage to stand up to his interrogation like she had. Not too many men would have been strong enough to fight off her attacker like she had. Not too many would have been able to withstand the pain she'd endured when Bronnely sewed her flesh together.

He didn't want to admire her. But he did.

He watched Bronnely remove the bandage and put a smelly salve on the wound before binding it in clean wrapping. She lay still and unmoving, her eyes clenched tight and her small, white teeth biting into her lower lip the whole while as Bronnely applied the salve. Even though she tried not to show it, it was obvious she was still in a great deal of pain.

Sam leaned his forearm against the wood at the side of the window and looked out at nothing in particular. He tried to forget the accusations he'd hurled at her, yet some of her answers came back to haunt him. *It must be wonderful to be so self-righteous.*

Is that truly what she thought of him? A wave of unease washed over him, yet he couldn't let her opinion of him matter. He couldn't let anything matter until he had the necklace. And yet . . .

. . . What if she doesn't have the necklace?

He turned his head and studied her. Didn't she know she wasn't safe as long as she had the necklace? Didn't she realize the Russians would only send someone else? Then someone else after that?

Sam raked his fingers through his hair. She could have died. She almost had because she wouldn't give it up. Could she possibly be that greedy? And yet . . .

. . . *What if she doesn't have the necklace?*

Sam tamped down the niggling doubt that reared its ugly head. Of course she had the necklace. Hunt's dying words confirmed she did.

He walked across the room and threw open the door. He had to get out of there. Had to escape the confusion warring inside his head. Had to come to terms with the possibility that things were not what he thought they were.

He walked out into the hallway and braced his hands on the oak railing overlooking the foyer below. He stood without moving until he heard the soft click of the door behind him. He knew Bronnely was there.

"Is she asleep?"

"Yes. Finally."

Bronnely walked up behind him and put his hand on Sam's shoulder. "Come down with me. I think we could both use a drink. I'll send Maude up to sit with her for a while."

Sam followed Bronnely down the stairs and went into the study while the doctor went to find Maude. Sam's first glass of brandy was half gone before Bronnely joined him.

"What was that all about, Sam?" Bronnely accepted the other glass from Sam and took a swallow.

"Nothing. I just—" Sam stopped, partly because he couldn't trust even Bronnely with anything concerning the necklace. And partly because he didn't know what he'd say if he could.

Bronnely lifted his glass and took a slow sip. "Perhaps she's not the villain you think she is."

"That remains to be seen."

"She's been through a great deal. More than anyone with her upbringing would have been able to handle. At least give her time to heal before you interrogate her like I just witnessed."

"I didn't mean to—"

"I know," Bronnely said, dismissing Sam's excuses with a wave of his hand. "Now . . ."

Bronnely gave Sam more instructions on the care of his patient, then left with the promise that he'd be back again tomorrow.

After he was gone, Sam went to his room to wash and shave and change his clothes. Then he walked down the hall to her room. He'd be better with her. Calmer. Not so intimidating.

But the minute he opened the door, he knew the damage was already done.

She was asleep, but her slumber was not restful. She was agitated. Maude stood over her, brushing her fingers across her skin and crooning soft whispers in an attempt to calm her.

Sam walked to the bed and caught Maude's worried glance before he focused on the small figure lying on the bed.

"She's terribly fitful," Maude said, shushing the marchioness as she thrashed her head from side to side. "She's been calling for Alex."

"Who's Alex?"

"Her brother. Alexander Linscott, Marquess of Halverston."

Sam stepped closer to the bed and took Maude's place holding Claire down. "Lady Huntingdon," he said, clasping her trembling shoulders. "Claire. Everything's all right. I'm here with you."

"Alex."

"No. It's Sam."

"No. Oh, Alex. I'm so sorry."

"Sh. It's all right. I'm right here. You're safe now."

She thrashed her head back and forth and flailed her arms as if trying to fight off the demons that haunted her. Her injured arm hit his shoulder, and he pinned her down when she cried out in pain.

Her movements became more agitated, and to keep her from harming herself, he picked her up in his arms, covers and all, and held her close.

"It's all right now, Claire. I've got you. No one can hurt you now."

"Alex."

"Yes. It's Alex."

"Are you all right?"

"Yes. I'm fine."

She cried out a small, helpless whimper and nestled against him, burying her face into his chest. Sam held her tight, then sat in the chair with her on his lap.

Maude pulled the drapes, shrouding the room in early darkness. She closed the door behind her when she left.

Sam kept Claire in his arms, watching her breathing slow and the worry lines on her forehead ease. Then she slept.

He held her far longer than necessary. But a part of him didn't want to put her down. A part of him wanted to hold her until she came to trust him.

So that when she woke, she'd tell him where she'd hidden the papers and the necklace, and this whole mess would be over.

Sam held her through the night and in the morning placed her back in her bed.

He sat back down in the chair and watched her, his arms feeling strangely empty.

Chapter 7

Claire swung her legs over the edge of the mattress and stood. It had been a week since she'd been attacked. A week of fighting the pain and weakness. Seven whole days in which she'd done little else but sleep and struggle with the nightmares that haunted her.

For the first few days, Major Bennett hadn't left her side. He was either stretched out in the chair at her bedside or standing quietly at the window, watching for any movement below. Then, three days ago, after Doctor Bronnely announced she was out of danger from a fever, he'd left. In his place, two burly officers stood guard outside her door.

Claire was thankful for the reprieve. Thankful he wasn't there to interrogate her. Thankful for the freedom to regain her strength away from his watchful eye. But most of all, she was thankful for the solitude so she could build up her endurance to fight the frightening emotions raging through her without his dominating presence there to confuse her even more.

Maybe the reason for her perplexity was due to all she'd endured since Hunt had been killed. Maybe it was her fear for Alex and the impossibility of her situation. Maybe it was her desperation to find the necklace everyone was convinced she had.

From somewhere inside her, a voice cried out a warning that it wasn't any of those things. It was him—the major. Without a doubt, she knew she had more to fear from *him* than she did from anyone Roseneau sent.

Not physically. Oh, no, he'd never harm her physically. The damage he could do would be much more devastating.

A strange and undeniable pressure wrapped around her heart, squeezing almost painfully until she sucked in a gasp of air. At first she'd refused to face it, this all-consuming mixture of need and desire and want and . . . fear that spread downward to the pit of her stomach and lower.

She'd never confronted such confusing emotions in her life. But ignoring them would only lead to disaster, or mask the threat until it was too late for her to defend herself. Because, whether she wanted to admit it or not, she had to fight herself as desperately as she had to fight the major. She had to fight with all the tenacity of a mother protecting her young.

She could never consider giving him the necklace. Even if it meant the war would continue. She had to be strong in her resolve. The desire to give in to him was overwhelming. One moment of weakness and she was doomed. And so was Alex.

She sucked in a fortifying breath and steadied herself against the bedpost, then pushed off, placing one foot in front of the other. Her progress was slow, but she was relentless in her attempt to recover before the major returned. It was the only chance she stood of saving Alex.

She made her way across the room, keeping her gaze focused on the far wall. She reached out and felt an immense sense of gratification the minute she touched it. She'd placed a chair there earlier so she could rest before making the trek back, but this time she wouldn't sit down.

She turned around when she reached her goal and took the first step back across the room. Then her second. And her third. She was halfway there.

"What the hell!"

Claire spun around in shock. He stood in the doorway, wearing a scowl as threatening as a black thundercloud.

She lost her balance and stumbled, her uninjured arm reaching out to break her fall. But before she hit the floor, his arms wrapped around her and pulled her close.

She wanted to push herself away from him, but she wasn't strong enough. Instead, she sagged against him. Her chest heaved from exhaustion.

He held her next to him, her head resting beneath his chin, her breasts pressed against his chest, her thighs touching his thighs. The feel of his body startled her.

She didn't want him to touch her. Didn't want to feel his arms around her, his strength envelop her. Such intimacy was totally alien to her, and more frightening than if he held a knife to her throat.

She rebelled against the strangeness of such closeness by placing her palms flat against his chest and pushing. He stopped her efforts by scooping her into his arms and carrying her to the bed.

"What do you think you're doing?" he asked, laying her down, then pulling the covers up around her. "You're hardly well enough to dangle your feet over the side of the bed, let alone be up and walking without anyone here to watch over you."

Claire sagged back into the pillow and closed her eyes. "I didn't expect you back."

"Today? Or ever?"

Claire's eyes snapped open and she stared up at him. "I hardly thought I would be so fortunate."

The scowl on his face darkened.

"Is it too much to hope that you've only returned to tell me good-bye? That you realize I don't want you here and have come to tell me you're leaving?"

"I've returned to get the necklace." He stood close to the bed and leveled her an intimidating glare. "You're running out of time."

An untenable chasm widened between them. He was the first to break the tension.

"Are you thirsty?"

"Please, leave me alone."

He ignored her request and propped a pillow behind her back, then filled a glass with water and handed it to her.

The water tasted good, and she drank nearly all of it before handing it back.

He reached for the clean bandages and salve Maude kept ready on the table beneath the window. "Bronnely sent word he can't come this afternoon to change your bandages."

"Then Maude can do it later."

"I'll do it now."

Claire felt a hitch in her breathing. She didn't want him to change the bandage. She didn't want him anywhere near her. "It can wait until—"

He didn't give her the opportunity to argue but sat on the edge of the bed. With deft movements, he unfastened the top buttons on her gown and pushed the material over her shoulder.

Although only her shoulder was uncovered, she felt strangely exposed and looked away. Ministering to her did not seem to bother him in the slightest. Not like it bothered her.

He removed the bandage from her shoulder with the same nonchalance as he might use to remove his hat.

Claire kept her gaze focused on the ceiling, making an effort not to look at the way his broad shoulders stretched the material of his white lawn shirt. Her blood thundered in her veins and bubbled like boiling water trapped in a kettle. Her face flamed with a searing heat, and she chastised herself again for letting him affect her like he did.

What was wrong with her? What more would it take to convince her that *he* was her most dangerous enemy? That to protect herself, the wall she'd so expertly erected must be firmly in place?

He'd removed his jacket and rolled up his shirt sleeves. She made the mistake of focusing on the bronzed skin of his exposed forearms. A strange swirling churned low in her belly that warmed her all over, and she squeezed her eyes shut. Oh, how she prayed he'd hurry.

"Bronnely did a good job. You're healing fine," he said, cleaning the wounds with a soft woolen cloth. "Has the pain lessened?"

"Yes. It's much better."

When he was satisfied the cuts on her shoulder and arm were clean, he opened the jar of salve Bronnely said was best for preventing infection.

"What do you suppose this is?" he said, lifting the jar and smelling it. "Or would you rather not know?"

The strong odor permeated the room and she wrinkled her nose. "I think I'd rather not know. In fact, I'm certain of it."

He concentrated on finishing, and Claire thought she saw a hint of a smile cross his face. She wished he hadn't smiled. It made him seem almost human. She preferred he remain cold and hard. And distant. That made it easier to remember that he was the enemy.

He finished in silence, then placed the salve and cloth on the bedside table and stood. He walked to the window and pulled the drapery open. His stance was rigid, his legs braced wide and his hands clasped behind his back.

Claire waited, knowing he had something on his mind.

"Do you know where I was before returning?"

He didn't wait for her to answer.

"I went to talk to your brother, the Marquess of Halverston."

Her heart stuttered. "Why?"

He slowly turned his head and glanced at her over his shoulder. "Because you called out for him in your fever. I thought perhaps you wanted to see him."

Claire's heart raced faster, each thud pounding against her ribs. "Did you find him?"

"No. No one's seen him for more than a week. Not even his friends at his clubs."

"You went to his clubs?"

He lifted the corners of his mouth in a grin that even in her wildest imagination could not be considered a smile. "Yes. Did you think they wouldn't allow me entrance?"

Claire felt her cheeks grow hot. "No. It's not that. I . . ."

"I imposed on my uncle's good name."

She stared at him, waiting for him to explain.

"The Marquess of Rainforth is my uncle. I'm the only son of his younger brother. Not titled—nor ever likely to be because of my cousin, Ross Bennett, Earl of Cardmall—but a relative nevertheless. Does that surprise you?"

"A little."

"The relationship is not widely known. I find it easier if few people know of my ties to nobility. It avoids talk and speculation concerning my political activities."

"Are you and your cousin close?"

"As close as I can get to anyone without risking exposing myself. My uncle and I share a certain closeness. Perhaps because he took me in after my parents died and assumed the only role of parent I knew growing up. Or, perhaps because I am not heir to the Rainforth dynasty. Therefore, nothing out of the ordinary is expected of me."

"The Earl of Cardmall and his father do not get along?"

"I'm sure in time they will. As soon as Ross assumes the maturity his father demands, and the sense of responsibility he will need to carry on the Rainforth name. What about you and your brother?"

"Alex?"

"Yes."

Claire sighed. "We are very close."

"Are there just the two of you?"

"No, I have another brother. But he's away at the moment."

Claire felt a wave of unease. She didn't want to talk about either of her brothers. The less the major knew of her family, the better.

"So Alex is the family you rely on most. I can see why you are so close."

Claire smiled. "As much as a sister can be. He was the heir and raised accordingly. His world growing up was much more diverse than mine."

"Did you resent that?"

"A little. It must be fascinating to have the experiences men take for granted."

"For example?"

"The freedom."

"You don't think you are free?"

"Not like you are, Major. I cannot come and go unescorted like you do. I cannot walk through the door of any establishment like you can. I am not expected to be able to carry on a serious conversation or express . . ." Claire dropped her head back on the pillow. "Well, there are many things a woman cannot do without causing a scandal."

"What mutinous thoughts. And all this time I thought you were the compliant daughter the nobility expects."

"None of us is exactly as we seem. You more than anyone should realize that."

"Yes, I should, shouldn't I? And it was quite shallow of me to assume you were nothing but an ever-so-docile wife to Hunt."

"I am hardly perfect, Major. If Hunt were here he'd tell you—"

She stopped short, then closed her eyes to conceal a multitude of emotions. Hunt wasn't here. Would never be again. She'd been far from the perfect wife. As he'd been far from the perfect husband.

"If Hunt were here, he'd tell me what?"

"Nothing," she whispered, trying to keep the regrets she lived with hidden. What good would it do now to wish things had been different? Or reveal the secrets Hunt had taken to his grave?

Claire squeezed her eyes tight and fought the confusion that haunted her.

"I hope you don't mind," he said, his velvety voice now coming from the other side of the room near the fireplace.

She hadn't heard him move, but that didn't surprise her. She could imagine him with his elbow propped casually against the mantel.

"I've made myself quite at home here. I took the liberty of spending a few hours in your morning room."

Claire's eyes shot open, her heart's rhythm increasing steadily.

"Why?"

"When I asked, one of your servants informed me that room is your favorite. The one in which you plan your busy schedule and do your correspondence. I thought perhaps I could find the necklace and this whole mess would be over."

"Did you find it?"

"No."

She wanted to cry out in relief. Instead she willed her breathing to slow and her nerves to calm.

"Do you know what I did find, though?"

She paused. Her heart thudded harder in her breast.

"I found your social calendar."

"Did you find it interesting?"

"There was nothing in it. Not one entry since the day your husband died."

"I am in mourning, sir. What did you expect? That I'd fill my days and nights making merry and attending every ball of the Season in celebration?"

"No. But it wouldn't be unseemly for close friends to call to share your loss. Or for you to attend a small, informal dinner with family after four months have passed. There isn't even mention of that. And the silver tray on the hall table is overflowing with cards and condolences that haven't been answered, my lady. Why is that?"

"I've been busy."

"Busy doing what?"

"That is hardly your concern, Major."

He turned to face her. "In your delirium you told Alex you were sorry."

Her heart fluttered. "Did I?"

"Yes." He stepped toward the bed until he towered over her. "What are you sorry for, Lady Huntingdon?"

Perspiration beaded on her forehead, and she willed herself to keep from wiping it away. She hated the way he interrogated her. Hated the scowl that deepened on his face when he talked to her, made even more obvious by the intensity in his voice and manners.

"For what do you have reason to be sorry, my lady?"

She swallowed hard and gasped for air. "I don't know. It must have been for some prank I played on Alex when we were children. Otherwise, I can't imagine what it might be."

"If you and your brother are as close as you indicate, don't you find it strange he hasn't been to see you yet? It's been more than a week already."

"He must be gone."

"Do you think so? He did not take his valet with him. Don't you find that strange?"

Claire clenched her trembling hands and she shook her head. "Perhaps he—"

"Nor did he take as much as a change of clothes. How would you explain that, Lady Huntingdon?"

Claire grabbed handfuls of soft covers in her fists and squeezed. "How should I know? Please. Leave me be."

She fought to keep the fear and terror at bay, but failed with every breath. Alex was suffering by the hour while she lay pampered and cosseted in her bed. And she was running out of time before Roseneau threatened to kill him.

She gasped for air as the room closed in around her. She needed to escape. Was frantic to get away from here. From him.

She threw off the covers and tried to sit upright. She slapped his hands away when he tried to hold her down.

When he refused to release her, she did the only thing possible . . .

She screamed.

Chapter 8

"What do you think you're doing?" he asked, releasing her, then stepping away.

Claire sat on the edge of the bed. Then stood. She lost her balance. He grasped her arms when she staggered, then lowered her to the bed.

For a moment, the room spun in dizzying circles. She fisted her hands to the mattress on either side of her and held on tight.

"I need to get up."

"You're not strong enough yet. You need to stay in—"

She shrugged off his hands and struggled to her feet, leaving him no choice but to help her—or watch her fall. He wrapped his right arm around her waist to steady her and reached his left in front of her to take her hand.

"Where do you intend to go?"

"I don't know," she gasped, making her way to the door. "Out of this room. Downstairs."

"You shouldn't be out of bed."

She ignored his argument and walked out into the hallway and toward the stairs. Tilly, the third-floor maid, came out of one of the rooms as the major picked Claire up to carry her to the first floor. The servant's eyes opened wide and she drew her hand over her open mouth to stifle a gasp.

"Your mistress needs a robe and some slippers," he ordered. "Bring them down at once."

"Yes, Major."

"Where do you want to go?" he asked when they reached the first floor. "The sitting room? The morning room? The blue salon?"

"The sitting room."

"Very well."

It struck her that he didn't ask directions; that he was familiar enough with her town house to know which room was the sitting room.

He walked down the long hallway, past the morning room facing east and the drawing room facing west. He didn't pause before the blue room on the right or the massive Huntingdon library on the left, but walked to the next door on the right. Timothy, one of her footmen, rushed to open the door and the major carried her inside.

"Build a fire," he ordered the footman as he walked with her to the settee closest to the fireplace. Timothy rushed to do his bidding and the major stood with her in his arms.

"You can put me down," Claire said, searching for her voice. She didn't want to be in his arms. Didn't want to be held next to him, to feel the heat from his body burn through her. Being held put her entirely too close. She wasn't used to the swirling deep inside her when he touched her. These feelings were wrong. She knew it. She'd never felt this way with Hunt. Not even at first when she'd tried to be a wife to him.

The major held her as if he hadn't heard her request, and watched Timothy build the fire. When Tilly rushed into the room with Claire's wrapper and slippers, he slowly lowered Claire to her feet. He didn't release her until he was certain she was steady.

"Hold on to me," he said in a low, soft voice. With a swift movement he reached out for the robe Tilly had in her hand and held it so Claire could slip her arms through the sleeves.

She gasped when he pulled the satin folds across her breasts then reached around her waist for the satin belt. Even through the material, the feel of him sent a shiver racing through her, and she staggered backward.

"Hold on," he issued again, then backed her to the settee and helped her sit. Without hesitation, he took the slippers from Tilly's hands and knelt at her feet.

Claire tucked her feet beneath the settee. "Tilly can do that."

"Tilly's going to bring us tea and ask Cook to make you something to eat," he said in a commanding voice. The second the shy maid glimpsed his intimidating gaze, she bobbed a swift curtsy and nearly ran from the room with Timothy on her heels.

"Please, don't do that," she said as he picked up her foot and held it in his hand.

"Do what?"

"Touch me so."

He arched his brows. "It's not necessary to play the innocent. You and Hunt were married for more than seven years, my lady. It's not as if you've never been touched by a man. Or that you cannot tell the difference between the manner in which I'm touching you and an intimate caress."

He reached for her other foot and held it in one hand as if proving his point, then slipped on her slipper. Claire pulled her foot out of his grasp as quickly as she could.

He ignored her discomfort and rose to his feet. "Put this over your legs," he said, placing a quilted coverlet across her lap. "If you get cold, let me know and I'll send someone for another cover."

"I'm fine."

But she wasn't fine. She was burning hot, and the heat had nothing to do with her recent illness.

"After I left your brother's home, I stopped by the Foreign Office." He looked up. "The Russian delegates will be here in a little more than two weeks."

Claire held his gaze even though she wanted to turn away from him. Her heart plummeted. Roseneau would be here before that.

"Everyone was busy making preparations for the meeting between Russia's delegates and Britain's foreign minister."

Claire watched the major step to the small table on the left side of the window. A porcelain figurine of an elegant lady with tiny pearls in her golden hair and an evening gown of emerald green sat on a tatted doily. He picked up the figurine and examined it closely, then carefully set it on the floor before swiping his fingers carefully over the table.

The table had a narrow drawer in the front that opened by pulling a small, round ivory knob. He opened it and sifted through the contents before closing it and tipping the table to search the underside for any other hidden drawers or compartments. When satisfied that whatever he was searching for wasn't there, he set the figurine back on the doily and lifted his gaze to hers.

"I was tempted to assure them that they'd have in their possession something that would give them an advantage in the negotiations. But of course I didn't."

Her heart thundered in her breast, the blood pounding against her ears.

"I knew if they even got a hint at what you're hiding, you'd be residing in one of London's renowned prisons before you had time to throw a gown in a valise."

She fought the urge to look away from him. His piercing glare dared her to fight him. She didn't. She knew it was a battle she would lose. How could she match his wit and determination when she could barely think straight watching him search her home?

She'd gone over this room more than once in the weeks following the first threat and hadn't found anything. But what if she'd missed it?

What if she'd overlooked where Hunt had hidden the necklace and the major found it?

He moved to the matching table on the other side of the window and repeated the process. This figurine's hair was dark and sprinkled with tiny diamonds, and her gown was of deepest gold. He picked it up. Examined it.

Claire followed his movements as if in a trance. She couldn't think past the roaring in her head. All the time she prayed he wouldn't find the necklace. Because he'd never give it over to her. Never. She was more convinced of that than ever. And Alex would—

"Your tea is getting cold," he said, pointing to the tea Claire didn't realize had been delivered. She reached out with trembling hands and picked up the cup and saucer Tilly had brought. Her hands weren't steady enough to bring it to her lips. She could barely breathe while he moved from the small side tables dotting the room, to the matching china cabinets in two corners, to the narrow bookcase between the windows on the east, and finally to the gilded escritoire against the far wall.

"Did Hunt discuss the trip to France when you returned?" he asked, lifting the two elegant Chinese vases on each corner of the mantel and looking inside them.

"No."

He picked up the small tinderbox at the rear of the mantel and lifted the lid. "What did you think of Roseneau?"

Claire tried to focus her thoughts. "He was very charming. But that was before you and my husband emptied his safe."

The major's hands stopped midair, and he glanced over his shoulder. His gaze locked with hers for a brief moment before he resumed his search. "Did Hunt know about you and Roseneau?"

Her heart leaped in her breast. "Know what?"

"How close the two of you were?"

"Regardless of what you think, we were hardly close, Major. We barely knew each other."

"Really."

He said the word not as a question, but as a statement of fact. He'd seen her with Roseneau and believed the worst. For some reason she couldn't explain, she didn't want him to. "Monsieur Roseneau attended an informal dinner party at our home less than a year ago. I found him very charming. That's why I didn't think anything was out of the ordinary when we were invited to his home in France. He and Hunt seemed on quite good terms."

"I'm sure they were. Hunt obviously didn't know of your feelings for the Frenchman."

"There was nothing to know," Claire said, her temper rising.

"You'll excuse me if I don't believe that little lie," he said, the look on his face hard. Accusing. "You forget. I happen to know differently."

Claire watched him skim his hands between the cushions of the furniture scattered throughout the room. She tried to swallow, but her mouth was too dry.

"He may possess *you*, my lady," he said, looking up from the chair he was searching, "but he will never possess the necklace."

The breath caught in her throat and the room shifted around her.

"I'd like to go back upstairs," she said, clutching the cushions on either side of her. She couldn't take any more of his accusations. Every nerve in her body was stretched tight, the pounding in her head growing more painful with every minute.

"Of course." He walked to her and took the cup and saucer from her lap. He set them on the table. "You didn't eat anything."

"I wasn't hungry."

"Then you'd best tell yourself when you wake up from your rest you're going to be exceedingly hungry. I'll have both our dinners served in your room. I am confident you will eat everything on your plate. Is that understood?"

She leveled him a serious look. "I prefer to eat alone."

"People under house arrest are hardly allowed the freedom they desire. Be thankful you are permitted to leave your room."

"You can't be serious."

"Can't I?" Without giving her time to answer, he scooped her into his arms.

She thought she was prepared, thought her anger would keep her from feeling anything when he pulled her against his muscled chest. But it didn't. Every muscle in her body tightened, and she held herself stiff to keep from falling against him. He looked down at her with a frown on his face.

"What's wrong? Are you in pain?"

"No. Please, put me down."

He ignored her request and strode across the room and down the hall. She didn't look at him while he carried her up the stairs, or when he placed her in her bed.

"I wouldn't try to get up if I were you," he warned her from the doorway. "I've given your servants orders to check on you every few minutes to make sure you're resting."

"And you think they'll report to you if I'm not?"

He smiled. "If they value their freedom, they will."

Claire turned her face toward the wall. She knew her servants were loyal, but she didn't want to put them in a position where they'd be forced to lie for her.

She listened as he made his way across the room, and sighed in relief when the door closed firmly behind him.

She was alone. She squeezed her eyes tight, fighting to keep the tears from escaping. But lost the battle.

He wasn't going to let her out of his sight. From now on she wouldn't even be able to move around in her own home without him watching her. Even if she was the one who found the necklace, he'd take it the minute she recovered it. And Alex would die.

Claire lay in the quiet room and stared at the ceiling. The shadows lengthened as the sun began its descent. Eventually, she closed her eyes and fell asleep knowing what she would do. Knowing the only choice left to her.

⁓

Claire placed another bottle back in the rack and leaned her forehead against the cool wall in the wine cellar. She didn't know how long she'd been in the cold, damp underground, but knew it had been hours. Perhaps three. Maybe four. And she couldn't stay much longer. It would be dawn before long and the house would begin to stir.

Cook would be the first to rise, to mix her dough and bake her biscuits and bread for breakfast. Next Timothy would rise to light a fire in the dining room. And later Tilly would come to her room to help her rise.

And *he* would come to see how she'd slept.

Claire pushed herself away from the wall and searched through another row of wine bottles. Her head spun and she reached out to steady herself. She'd stayed up far longer than she was used to—far longer than her body was strong enough to handle, but she had no choice. She had to search for the necklace while everyone slept. Had to look for it while he wasn't aware of her every move.

She thought of the hours she'd spent with him last evening. He'd been true to his word and had their dinners served in her bedroom. He'd evaluated every bite she put in her mouth, then ordered her to eat more when she told him she was finished. And for at least a puzzling moment or two, she thought he was truly concerned about her.

Even after they'd finished, he'd sat with her for the rest of the evening. They didn't talk about anything important, but more than once he gave her the opportunity to tell him where she'd hidden the necklace.

Of course she couldn't, and the frown on his face deepened as the minutes stretched on. In the end, he gave up and went downstairs.

When he was gone, Claire let Tilly help her into bed, then lay there until the house grew quiet. Eventually she heard him come upstairs. Then she waited another agonizing hour longer until she was sure he was asleep before she got out of bed and put on her robe.

She'd chosen to search the wine cellar first because she hadn't been down there yet, and because it was farthest away from the rest of the house, therefore the least likely that anyone would hear her. When all was quiet, she'd crept down the servants' stairway and opened the door with the housekeeper's key to begin her search. She'd said a quick prayer that she would find the necklace in time to save Alex's life and pulled the first of the hundreds of bottles off the rack.

That had been hours ago. Now, Claire's shoulder ached and the cold seeped through to her very bones.

She shivered as she opened one of the crates sitting on the floor and sifted through its contents. Finding nothing, she lifted more bottles off the rack and checked to make sure they contained only wine.

She thought of the major sleeping upstairs, and her stomach rolled nervously. She'd never been so frightened in all her life. Never felt so alone. If only she could trust him enough to ask for his help to free her brother. But she couldn't. He'd never think Alex's life was more important than the necklace.

And, he thought there was a connection between her and Roseneau.

She walked around a rack that reached nearly to the ceiling and tried to ignore the daunting task before her. Each slot contained another bottle of the fine wines Hunt had been so proud of. She remembered how much he'd enjoyed serving the rare vintages. Recalled the pleasure he'd taken in stocking his cellar with only the best wines.

She did miss him. She'd been so very comfortable with him. Even though many aspects of their marriage left a void filled with disappointment and regret, there were parts of their life together she would always cherish.

Such as the hours they'd spent in each other's company and the lively conversations they'd enjoyed. Hunt often told her she was his best critic as well as his best verbal sparring partner.

And for seven years she'd told herself she was satisfied with what they shared. But it had never been enough.

And a part of her hated him for what he couldn't give her.

Claire reached for another bottle and a sharp pain jabbed through her shoulder. She clutched her hand to her arm and waited for the pain to abate. Her knees trembled from weariness and she was so exhausted she could barely stand any longer. It was time to quit. Tomorrow night she would be stronger. Tomorrow night she'd be able to last until sunup. But not tonight.

She blew out all the candles but one and took the single taper with her. No one heard her as she made her way up the back stairs. When she reached her room, she quietly closed the door behind her and crawled into bed. She was so cold; so tired.

She pulled the covers up around her throbbing shoulder and fell asleep.

Chapter 9

Sam leaned back against the blue velvet cushions of the plush chair angled near the settee where Claire sat in the drawing room and watched her pour the tea he'd insisted be served. He couldn't tamp down the niggling fear building inside him as he watched her. Something was wrong. Instead of improving, her health seemed worse each morning when she awoke.

It had been three days since he'd caught her out of bed. Three days for her to gain back more of her strength and for her health to improve. Instead, she barely seemed able to keep her eyes open, let alone lift the floral china teapot. It took every ounce of his willpower to hold himself back from reaching out to take the pot from her trembling hands.

Outwardly, he saw slight improvements. The bruises on her face had faded to various shades of purples, greens and yellows, and the wounds on her shoulder and neck were healing remarkably well.

As the discoloration and swelling lessened, she should have taken on a hint of her former healthy glow. But her coloring was pale and sallow, while the black circles rimming her eyes grew darker by the day. There was also a vacant look in her eyes that frightened him, and her lethargic movements evidenced an underlying illness. Most of the time it was obvious that she could barely hold on to consciousness.

Sam took the cup she handed him and leaned back in his chair. "Do you feel all right?"

Her gaze remained fixed on the cup and saucer in her lap, as if looking up required too much effort.

"Yes. Fine."

"I think I'll have Bronnely look at you anyway."

"No." Her gaze shot up and she issued him a defiant look. "I'm fine."

He rose to his feet. "You don't look it. You've lost even more weight, if that could be possible, and you have about as much color as this napkin." He held up a white linen Tilly had brought in with the tea, then wadded it in his fist. "I've seen soldiers coming in from battle who look better than you."

"And whose fault is that?" She dropped her cup and saucer on the table with a clatter and bolted to her feet.

Sam moved to let her rise. This was the strongest he'd seen her react in days.

"How do you expect me to improve when I've been placed under house arrest and accused of hiding a necklace that will result in the deaths of thousands of men? When you watch over me every minute of the day, evaluating my every move? When I am forced to stand by while you search my home room by room, floor by floor?"

"You don't have to watch."

"It's my home!"

"Perhaps you are only concerned because you're afraid I'll stumble onto the necklace while you aren't around and you'll lose the slim chance you have of giving it to Roseneau."

"How dare you! You don't know—"

"I know Hunt loved you. I know Hunt took the necklace and he gave it to you."

"You don't know that!"

"He told me! His last words were that he loved you. His marchioness. That *you* had the necklace."

Her face paled even more, and Sam reached out to steady her when she staggered. Her knees buckled beneath her, and she sagged against him.

"Sit down," he said, lowering her to the settee. He sat beside her. He tried to pull her against him, but she stiffened and turned away.

"He didn't . . . say that," she whispered, her voice thick.

"Yes, Lady Huntingdon. Your husband's last thoughts were of you. He said to tell you he was sorry. That he loved you. And that I was to get the papers from you."

She looked up at him, her eyes wide with panic. "He didn't give them to me."

Sam stiffened and pulled away from her. Anger rose in him like an active volcano. "How long do you think you can play this game? How long before I find them and make you pay for what you've done?"

She tried to move away from him, but the arm of the settee trapped her close. He refused to move. For several long seconds he watched her struggle to keep from crumbling under his domineering scrutiny. Finally, he gave in and rose to allow her to escape his confinement.

"I think you've been up long enough. You need to go back to your room to rest."

"And while I'm locked in my room, what do you intend to do, Major?"

He leveled her a knowing gaze. "Begin my search of the guest bedrooms. I can do at least one before I lose the light."

He watched her struggle intensify. A part of him regretted how cruel he'd been to her. She was, after all, Hunt's widow. A woman who'd evidently been the perfect wife to her husband. A woman who'd been an ideal match for someone as virile as Hunt was reputed to be.

Sam remembered the rumors that had followed Hunt before he and the marchioness married. Rumors concerning a certain actress Hunt had kept for years. A mistress no one thought Hunt would ever give up. But he had.

The biggest shock of the Season had been when Hunt had married the lovely daughter of the late Marquess of Halverston, Lady Claire. Everyone doubted there was a woman who could keep the Marquess of Huntingdon satisfied. But Lady Huntingdon must have been just such a woman. Not once in the seven years they were married did even a hint of scandal or impropriety touch Hunt and his marchioness.

Sam turned his hardened gaze on her as she rose from the settee, then reached out to steady her when she swayed. She shrugged away as if his touch burned her. As if being near him was more than she could bear.

"If you intend to search my bedrooms, then by all means, let us begin." She lifted her chin and pasted a smile on her drawn face. "It's getting late. I'd hate to think you'd lose a minute of daylight in your quest to see me hanged."

She grabbed a handful of her black bombazine mourning gown and swished it away from him, then stormed past him, her shoulders high, her back ramrod straight.

Sam followed on her heels. When they reached the first guest room on the second floor, she swung open the door and entered the room. "Where would you like to start?"

"I'll search the room. You can sit in that chair and wait. Unless, of course, you've changed your mind and would like to go to your room and lie down. You look like you need the rest."

"Thank you, Major. I'm always so flattered by your compliments. And no. I wouldn't think of forcing you to do such an unpleasant task by yourself." She walked toward the large wardrobe against the far wall. "I'll start here, if that's agreeable with you."

"As you wish," Sam said, watching her stalk away from him. She lost her balance and staggered. She was not well. Perhaps it was the strain of having him here . . . of losing her husband . . . of having her world change so completely. But he didn't think so.

If she was no better tomorrow, he'd send for Bronnely whether she liked it or not. Then he'd confine her to her bed so he could search the rest of the house without her interruption. He had to find the necklace and the papers that would tell him who the traitor was.

And he had to find them soon.

Sam stood out in the garden behind the Marquess of Huntingdon's house and listened to the quiet sounds of the night. There was something disquieting about this time of the day, the hours long after midnight, yet well before sunrise. The hours where all one's thoughts and worries grew larger and more insurmountable than in the light. Where no solution seemed to be in sight for the problems that loomed so monumental.

Perhaps that was why he couldn't see this clearly. Why the niggling doubts wouldn't go away. Why his mind kept telling him she had the necklace and the papers, while something deeper inside told him she might not.

He knotted his fingers into a fist and brought it down against the sturdy rock wall he was leaning against, then took another swallow of the brandy he'd brought with him. He knew the answers to his questions even if he didn't want to admit it.

He wanted to believe her.

He didn't want to think she'd done what the evidence told him she had. In his heart, he wanted to believe Hunt *hadn't* given her the necklace or the papers.

But Sam knew he had. Hunt's dying words proved it.

He swallowed the rest of his brandy and turned to go inside. The minute his gaze hit the outline of the house, his steps halted and his breath caught. Light streamed from Hunt's library. A light that hadn't been lit before.

He made his way to the house and crossed the terrace in long, angry strides. He stepped through the open glass-paned doors, then softened his footsteps so she wouldn't hear him. He wanted to surprise her. Wanted to catch her either getting, or hiding, or moving the necklace and papers. Wanted to prove to her he wasn't the fool she thought he was—that he'd known all along she had the jewels.

Sam stepped through the terrace doors to Hunt's study, then down the darkened hallway to the library. He reached for the knob. She may have used her body to charm Hunt into betraying his principles, but Sam wouldn't let her do the same to him. He was immune to her strength, to her spirit. He knew her lying, deceiving ways and intended to expose her. He turned the knob and threw open the door.

He expected to find her hiding the papers in a new, more secretive place. Or perhaps even strolling around the room with the necklace draped around her neck. But she wasn't. She was crumpled in a heap on the floor with piles of open books scattered about her. She was asleep.

Sam closed the door with a muffled click and walked over to her. She was dressed for bed, her pale peach satin robe fastened over her nightgown. Her hair was bound back in a long plait that hung over one shoulder, and her slippered feet were tucked beneath her. Her head was tilted to the side and rested against the leather spines of a row of Hunt's rare books. Her relaxed posture exposed the fading bruises on the left side of her face.

He reached down to lift the book from her lap. Long, wispy lashes rested seductively against her cheeks, and her hands lay limp in her lap as if they'd fallen there from exhaustion. She didn't stir, dead to the world.

He looked from her to the ladder she'd used to reach the higher shelves, then to the open book in her lap. And he knew. Knew without a doubt what she'd been doing.

She'd been searching for the necklace and the papers, just as he'd been doing. She'd been searching the house room by room in hopes of finding them before he did. The reason could only be that she didn't have them. And that meant she'd been telling the truth all along, while he'd refused to believe her.

What if she doesn't have them?

Sam felt his knees weaken and a heavy weight press painfully against his chest. Why had Hunt told him he'd given them to her if he hadn't?

He looked down at her sleeping so peacefully and felt an uncomfortable stirring. Hunt's widow was truly beautiful, but with a beauty that surpassed the obvious. She had an inner strength that allowed her to go on even after she'd nearly been killed. An intelligence that was the match of anyone he'd ever met. And an unyielding determination that gave her the ability to battle him on equal footing. But that didn't answer the question of why she was so intent on finding the necklace before he did. Or whether or not she'd give it over if she did.

He reached down and picked her up in his arms. He thought she'd awaken, but she was so exhausted that even being lifted from the floor didn't rouse her.

Now he knew the reason for the dark circles that rimmed her eyes. For her pale complexion and emaciated look. Instead of sleeping, she'd spent every night searching for the necklace. And she'd watched him all day long to make sure she was close by in case he found it.

He walked to the maroon velvet sofa angled before the fireplace. He intended to lay her down so she could sleep more comfortably, but he lost the desire to be separated from her when she breathed a sigh that wafted like a gentle breeze against the bare skin at the base of his throat.

He knew he didn't want to put her down when she snuggled closer to him and nestled her head in the hollow beneath his chin. Then, when she looped her small arm around the back of his neck in a graceful, yet intimate gesture, he couldn't have let her go if he'd been ordered to.

He sat in one of the oversized wing chairs scattered throughout the room, and held her in his arms.

He was sure she'd wake, but she didn't. Not completely. Just the slightest stirring, as if something warned her everything was not as it should be.

She absently threaded her fingers through the hair at the nape of his neck. She didn't open her eyes, but Sam could see by the small frown on her face that the feel of him against her registered in small degrees. It wouldn't be long before reality forced her to wake.

He watched her intently. One arm supported her back as she wound herself around him. His other arm lay loosely over her torso. His hand kept her hip pressed snugly against him.

He hadn't intended to react to her nearness but lost his battle early on. Her long, thick lashes fluttered as she slowly woke and attempted to open her eyes. Her fingers continued to thread through his hair as if she enjoyed the feel of it. It was all he could do to ignore the uncomfortable heaviness in his groin. There was nothing more arousing than watching her wake.

He knew the moment her predicament registered. Her eyelids flew open, and she jerked upward.

"Just lay still," he whispered. "You're all right."

She wanted to bolt from his lap. He could tell it by the way she tensed in his arms and from the rapid heaving of her chest as she fought for air. But she didn't. Her only concession to the embarrassment of waking atop him was the release of her fingers from his hair and the slow sliding of her arm from around his neck. Her arm fell to her body and she tucked her hand awkwardly against her middle, making sure she kept it far enough away that it didn't touch him. And she said nothing.

For several long minutes, they both looked at each other, her gaze indicating there was nothing to say; she had no excuses to make for why she was searching Hunt's library that she thought he wanted to hear. Or that he would believe.

Sam dropped his head against the back of the chair and closed his eyes. For an eternity he just held her, not moving even one finger. Partly because he was afraid what her reaction would be. Mostly because he was terrified of his own. When he spoke, his words weren't a question, but a statement of fact.

"You don't have the necklace."

"No."

"Nor the papers."

"No."

"What game was Hunt playing? What did he mean when he told me you did?"

Her silence told him she didn't have an answer.

He was back to the beginning. No closer to finding the necklace and possessing the papers than when he'd barged in on the Russian who'd come after them.

Sam wanted to be angry with her but knew he didn't have the right. She'd never lied to him. From the start she'd told him she didn't have what he wanted. And that had been the truth. But someone had them. Or they were hidden somewhere in this house. In some secret hiding place that only Hunt knew about. Sam vowed he'd find both the necklace and the papers if he had to take the house apart brick by brick.

Chapter 10

Sam stood on the ladder and searched the books on the top shelves while Lady Huntingdon took the bottom shelves. They removed each book and opened it, looking for any secret hiding place Hunt might have hollowed out on the inside of the book, then checked the back of the shelves for any secret compartments that might be concealed in the wood. So far neither of them had found anything, and they'd been working side by side for three hours. Three very uncomfortable hours.

"Do you remember what Hunt did when you returned from France?"

Sam had asked her questions all morning, forcing her to recall every aspect of their trip to France. Especially the evening of Roseneau's ball. He could see her frustration grow with each new question, but she answered each of them in more detail than he expected.

She placed the book she was inspecting in her lap and stared into space as if trying to recall. "Nothing out of the ordinary. We returned late in the afternoon and I went upstairs to change and rest for a while. We ate a light dinner and Hunt spent the rest of the evening in here. He might have worked all night because when I woke the next morning, the door was still closed."

"He didn't come to your bed that night?"

Sam could see her cheeks darken from where he stood on the ladder. She busied herself with another book and answered with a soft, "No."

"What was your marriage like?"

Her gaze flew up to him and she glared at him with a sharp, disbelieving look. "That is hardly any of your business, Major."

"But it is." Sam took a step down the ladder. "Were you and your husband close enough that he'd confide in you about the necklace and the papers when you returned from France?"

Sam watched her hands clench in her lap. "I didn't know about the necklace until I received the first threat."

"When was that?"

"A month or so after Hunt's death?"

"Who was it from?"

"I don't know. It was just a demand for the necklace and instructions where to leave it."

"What did you do when you received it?"

"I began my search for the necklace. I thought perhaps I'd find it among Hunt's papers. When I didn't find it, I considered that the demand was a hoax. Until the night that man broke into my house."

His hands tightened to fists. Bloody hell. Didn't she realize the danger she was in?

He leveled her a glare filled with warning. "Whatever your relationship with Roseneau, he's not worth the risk you're taking. When this is all over, he's going to be lucky to escape with his life. If the Russians don't make him pay for what he's done, the traitor will kill him to keep his identity a secret."

Her face paled. Her eyes filled with terror at the mention of Roseneau and the lengths everyone involved in this would go to protect themselves. "Are you trying to frighten me, Major?"

"If you're smart, you're already so frightened that nothing I say can scare you more. I just want you to realize I won't allow you to give the necklace to Roseneau."

There was a noticeable lift to her shoulders, and Sam felt an invisible wall go up between them.

The two of them had come to somewhat of a silent agreement the previous night. They would both search for the necklace and the papers. When they found the papers, he had no doubt she would willingly give them up. But when they found the necklace, he would have to take it from her. And he would. He just wanted to know what was so bloody important about possessing the necklace.

The closed look on her face was interrupted by a soft knock at the door. Watkins stood there with an expectant expression.

"Excuse me, my lady, but you have a guest. Lord Barnaby has returned and would like a moment of your time."

"Barnaby," she whispered softly, but Sam couldn't miss the affection in her voice when she spoke his name.

Sam watched the transformation in her with amazed interest. Her fingers flew to her mouth as if stifling a cry and she jumped to her feet.

"Yes, Watkins. Tell Lord Barnaby I'll be right there."

She made a move to leave and Sam stopped her with a raised hand. "Show Lord Barnaby in, Watkins."

"No. I need to—"

"Lady Huntingdon will receive him here," Sam ordered again. Watkins turned to his mistress, then with a look of regret, nodded and left the room.

Sam ignored the hostile expression on Lady Huntingdon's face and watched the doorway, waiting for the man who'd come to see Hunt's widow.

Sam knew from her reaction the two of them were close. Just how close remained a mystery. From the expectant look on her face when

Watkins announced him, she anticipated that this Lord Barnaby would rescue her from all her threats. Especially him.

Every warning alarm he'd perfected from his years in the service screamed. He readied himself to be on the alert, but even that wasn't enough for the shock when the door opened and Watkins announced their guest.

The stranger entered the room, and stopped. A frown deepened across his forehead. It was obvious he was confused by Sam's presence. And resented having him here.

Sam met the stranger's gaze and studied him. There was something vaguely familiar about him, but Sam couldn't place where he'd seen the stranger before. He was obviously close to Lady Huntingdon. The look of relief—even adoration—he saw on her face gnawed in the pit of his stomach. Her reaction left him feeling unexplainably irritated.

The hopeful anticipation etched on her every feature coiled a knot deep inside him. Sam turned back to the man called Lord Barnaby.

"Major Bennett," Lady Huntingdon said softly, "I'd like you to meet—"

"The major and I have already met," Lord Barnaby interrupted, his gaze not leaving Sam's.

Lady Huntingdon looked surprised. "Oh, I didn't realize."

"Yes. The major and I have a mutual acquaintance," Lord Barnaby offered, a look of satisfaction on his face. "Although I don't often see you in your cousin's company, I recall having seen you with him."

Sam was confused. Why didn't he remember this meeting?

"You are acquainted with my cousin, the Earl of Cardmall?" Sam asked, trying to decide if there was any reason to question Lord Barnaby's connection to his cousin. "And how is Ross?"

"He was fine when last I saw him. But that was quite some time ago. I've been out of town for several weeks."

Sam studied the visitor with a discerning eye. With a warning that prickled the hair at the back of his neck, Sam realized Lord Barnaby was studying him with as much intensity.

Sam guessed Lord Barnaby's age at approximately his own, nearing thirty. There was something about him that told Sam Lord Barnaby was used to taking command of every room he entered.

"You were a friend of Lord Huntingdon's?" Sam asked, stepping aside to allow Lord Barnaby to enter. Lady Huntingdon's guest moved forward, but didn't take his evaluative gaze off Sam, a trait Sam found more than a little disconcerting.

The stranger's hair was dark blond and a little longer than was in fashion. He sported a shadowy beard that evidenced the days he'd spent traveling. The fact that he'd come to see Lady Huntingdon before even seeing to his own needs gave Sam cause to question exactly how close the friendship between them might be.

The man was dressed in an expensively tailored jacket and pants, and his demeanor was every inch that of nobility. Not until Sam walked to where Lady Huntingdon stood did Lord Barnaby's gaze rest on her for more than just a glance.

Sam watched the expression on his face change. Saw the muscles of his jaw knot and his fists clench.

Lady Huntingdon's face had improved much; the swelling had gone down and the bruises had gone from purple and black to faded greens and yellows. But the dark circles rimming her eyes only made her pale complexion seem sicklier.

The look on Lord Barnaby's face went from concern to outrage and he reached out his hand to turn her face for a closer look. "Claire?"

Claire? Sam took note of the familiarity.

"It's all right, Barn. It looks much worse than it is." Lady Huntingdon cast them both a nervous glance. Out of instinct, Sam moved closer to her. Lord Barnaby did the same.

"What happened?"

"Someone broke into the house last week."

"Are you all right?"

"Yes. Major Bennett came to my rescue."

"You have to get out of here. I'll take you—"

"Lady Huntingdon's not going anywhere," Sam interrupted, unable to conceal his fury.

Sam saw Lord Barnaby's physical reaction, saw his shoulders rise and his back straighten. Saw the muscles in his jaw knot and his hands clench to fists. The large man, who Sam was sure would be quite formidable in a fight, moved forward as if he intended to go on the attack.

Lady Huntingdon stopped him with a raise of her hand. "I can't go anywhere, Barn. Not until we find the necklace."

"Did you tell the major you don't have it?"

Sam was shocked. "You know about the necklace?"

"Yes. And you can't think Claire has it."

They both looked at Lady Huntingdon.

"I'm afraid he does," she answered for Sam. "Or at least he did. Is that right, Major?"

Sam nodded.

"I don't believe this."

"It's all right, Barn. It seems just before Hunt died, he told the major he'd given me the necklace."

"But he didn't. Why would Hunt say such a thing?"

"I don't know," Lady Huntingdon said almost as a whisper.

Sam watched the expression on her face turn from masked confusion to outright fear. Lord Barnaby must have seen it, too.

"Claire can't help you, Major. It's stupid to keep her here where she's in danger."

"No," Sam argued. "It's essential she remain here. She may remember something that will help us locate the necklace. As for her safety, I have a small army of men guarding her. She's safer here than anywhere else."

"I can see how well you protected her, Major."

Sam took a warning step forward, struggling to keep his temper in check. Lord Barnaby closed the distance with an equally determined step.

"That's enough," Claire said, raising her hand. "Arguing will accomplish nothing. Besides, the major's right, Barn. I can't leave. Not until we find the necklace."

"Are you sure, Claire? I could take you—"

"She'll stay here. No harm will come to her."

Sam kept his voice soft but maintained an unyielding tone. The two men faced off, Lord Barnaby's piercing glare a warning Sam had no trouble interpreting.

"See that it doesn't. Or you'll answer to me."

The man Lady Huntingdon had familiarly called Barn gave Sam another deadly look. He then looked back to her as if to give her another chance to change her mind about staying. When he was assured she thought herself safe enough with Sam, he bade her farewell with the promise to return.

When he was gone, Sam had the strangest feeling that he'd just been threatened by a man who wouldn't hesitate to carry through on his threat.

Chapter 11

The mantel clock struck midnight as Claire raced across the flagstone terrace and descended the three brick steps. She ran down the garden walk, taking the side path past the cherub fountain, then around the white lattice gazebo to the cluster of stone benches. She could travel this way in her sleep, she knew it so well. She'd spent many an hour here since Hunt died. Thinking. Wondering. Questioning. But never coming up with any answers.

She pulled her skirts close to her so they wouldn't get snagged on the thorns of the rose bushes that lined the walk, and raced toward her destination.

It was a beautiful summer night, clear and crisp, with a gentle breeze blowing and not a cloud in the sky. The moon was full, lighting the path as she made her way around a bed of azaleas.

Now she would not have to battle the major by herself. Barnaby was back, and she could lean on him when the overwhelming confusion the major caused became too intense. She would have Barnaby to keep her mind focused on finding the necklace that would save Alex, instead of the niggling whispers of her conscience that told her the necklace should be used for a greater good than saving only one man.

But that one man is Alex. How could she live with herself if she didn't do everything in her power to save him? How could there be any greater good?

She pushed such traitorous thoughts aside as she turned to the right. She took three short steps. Then stopped.

"Claire?"

She clasped her hands to her mouth and cried out his name, then raced into his waiting arms.

His arms wrapped around her, enfolding her to him like a shelter in a raging storm. For a few minutes he held her and let her lose herself in his strength. She was never so grateful for anything in her life.

When she calmed, he placed his finger beneath her chin and tipped her face upward. Claire knew the bright moonlight would reveal more of her bruises than she wanted him to see. She lowered her gaze and studied the deep V of his open shirt. Ever so gently he ran his finger over her cheek and across her jaw.

"I never should have left you alone."

"You had to." Claire's stomach knotted. "You didn't find it?"

"No. I searched Hunt's two country estates. It wasn't there."

"Oh, Barn. Where is it?"

"I don't know."

Barnaby placed his finger beneath her chin and tilted her head back. It gave him a better view of her face. "Are you sure you're all right?"

"Yes, fine. The major took excellent care of me." She smiled. "Mostly because he wants the necklace." Claire pulled away from Barnaby and clamped her hands around his upper arms. "Barn, they've got Alex."

Claire's brother stepped back as if he'd been struck. "What did you say?"

"Roseneau's got Alex."

"Bloody hell! How do you know?"

"The man Roseneau sent to get the necklace told me."

"But the major said he was Russian."

"He was. Anyway, his accent indicated he was. But Roseneau sent him."

Claire saw the hard look in Barnaby's eyes. "What did Roseneau's man tell you? Every word, Claire. What did he say?"

"He said they had Alex and would kill him if I didn't hand over the necklace." Claire swiped at the tears that ran freely down her cheeks and she choked back a sob. "Roseneau is scheduled to arrive in England in a few days, if he's not already here."

"Is there any chance Major Bennett's found it and is just playing with you?"

Claire shook her head. "He doesn't have it, Barn. He's as desperate to find it as we are." Claire swallowed past the lump in her throat. "Oh, Barn, what are we going to do? The major thinks the Russians sent the man who came after the necklace. He believes I want to give the necklace to Roseneau because we're lovers."

"The bastard," Barnaby whispered.

"If the major finds it first, he'll never use it to free Alex."

Barnaby reached for her hands and held them in his. "We'll get Alex, with or without the necklace."

Barnaby released her, then paced the small walk. He stopped suddenly and turned to face her. "Does the major know Roseneau's got Alex?"

Claire shook her head.

"You don't trust him, do you?" He paced a few feet in front of her. "Why?"

Claire felt a cold chill race down her spine. "Oh, Barnaby." She fisted her hands at her side. "I'd trust him with my life and be glad he was there to help me. But I'm afraid to trust him with Alex's. There aren't any gray areas with the major. Everything is either black or white. He sees the necklace as the only way to bring an end to the war. Except I can't give the major the necklace. If I don't give it to Roseneau, he'll kill Alex."

"Then we'll have to get Alex without the necklace."

"But how?"

Barnaby sat down with her and held her close. "I don't know. But don't worry. You and Alex are the only family I have left. I'm not about to lose either one of you."

Claire let Barnaby hold her for a while, then pulled away and looked at him. "Barn, tell me something. And please, no lies. What was the connection between you and Hunt? Are you spying for the government, too?"

Claire watched Barn mask his expression. "Are you?" she asked again.

A sad smile lifted the corners of his mouth and he rose to his feet. "I'm not nearly as good as Hunt was."

An icy coldness washed over her. "But you do the same work? Risk your life to steal jewels and papers and information?"

Barnaby halted with his feet braced wide and his hands locked behind his back. "I'm a second son, Claire. Not the heir like Alex. I don't have his responsibilities. And I've always had a penchant for the military. It was Father who refused to buy me a commission. You know what an expert he was at manipulation, how little he cared what any of us really wanted. He didn't want to risk something happening to me until Alex had provided him with an heir."

He turned to stare up at the stars. "I think Hunt sensed what I really wanted. A few years ago he asked me if I'd be interested in helping him obtain some 'private' information. I jumped at the opportunity, even though I didn't realize at the time that I was gathering covert information for the government."

Barn turned his head to look at her over his shoulder. "He was phenomenal, Claire. He could ferret out information without anyone even realizing he was interested in what they were saying. He could walk through a room and when he left he knew more gossip and intelligence than anyone who'd been there all evening."

"And you were his pupil?"

Barnaby laughed. "He was my tutor. I tried to learn everything I could from him."

"What about Major Bennett?"

Barnaby's smile faded. "He's good. Maybe even better than Hunt, but in a different way."

"How?"

"He's more dangerous. Hunt was a negotiator, a man with a wealth of finesse. The government sent him in first when they didn't want to dirty their hands. But, if Hunt's technique didn't work, they sent in Bennett. He wasn't afraid to use force, to go in and clean up a mess without leaving any evidence behind."

Barnaby's words echoed in her head. "You mean he wasn't afraid to kill."

"If he had to," Barnaby said almost in a whisper.

Claire remembered how quickly and easily he'd killed Roseneau's man. A part of her was glad the major was ruthless. It was honest. He was so unlike Hunt, whose ruthlessness consisted of lies.

"Then why did they need you?"

"Not long after I started working with Hunt, he told me he wanted out. He said he was tired and there were things in his personal life that needed taking care of."

"Do you know what they were?"

"No. Just that he wanted out and the Foreign Office needed someone who could infiltrate Society. Bennett didn't have my pedigree, plus he didn't want to leave the field. So Hunt chose me. Who better than the brother of a marquess?"

"Is that why you were at Roseneau's ball?"

"No. I was there to protect you."

Claire's eyes opened in surprise.

"Hunt wanted me there in case something went wrong. I was to make sure you got out safely." Barnaby hesitated, staring up at the stars. There was a gentle breeze that moved his full-sleeved white lawn shirt. Then he broke the silence and asked, "Were you happy with him, Claire?"

She felt her cheeks warm and lowered her gaze to her hands in her lap. "I wasn't unhappy, if that's what you're asking."

"No, that's not what I mean. I know you weren't in love when you married. I just hoped that in time . . ."

Barnaby stopped and Claire gave the only answer she could. "We grew very comfortable with each other."

"No one could believe it when you agreed to marry Hunt. You were so young and he was so much older."

"Not that much."

"Nearly fifteen years."

Claire laughed. "What you mean is that no one could believe that Hunt agreed to marry *me*. I was hardly sophisticated enough for someone with Hunt's reputation. Hardly the one to catch the Marquess of Huntingdon." She looked into Barn's eyes and saw a sadness there. "I knew his reputation. Everyone did. I knew about the mistress he kept. The mistress everyone said he'd never give up."

"Why did you agree to marry him so easily?"

She sighed. "Because Father gave me little choice in the matter. He and Hunt's father had already drawn up a marriage contract. Oh, Hunt was vehement in his refusal. It's the only time I was afraid of him. He and his father had a terrible fight. He didn't want to marry. Especially me. Then something changed his mind."

Claire stood so she didn't have to face Barnaby. "I think his father had some hold on him and he blackmailed Hunt into marrying me."

"To the world, you seemed the happiest of couples. It was all an act, wasn't it?"

Claire couldn't bring herself to tell her brother the truth. No matter how much she wanted to expose Hunt to a man who'd always idolized him, she couldn't bring herself to admit their marriage had been a lie. To admit to her brother how adept they'd both been at playing the charade. But most of all, she was embarrassed that anyone might find out how impossible it had been for Hunt to love her.

"Our marriage wasn't so bad. We were quite compatible. Over time we even became friends."

"Bloody hell, what did Father do to you?"

"Only what he thought best."

"Best for whom?"

Claire smiled, remembering the argument she'd had with her father, begging him not to force the marriage. Knowing how much her betrothed detested the thought of taking her as his bride. Hunt had even threatened to leave England rather than marry her. But none of that mattered.

Her father wouldn't listen. His angry words still stung. That a woman's only worth was in the match she made, one that brought the best advantage to her family. And there wasn't a better advantage, as far as her father was concerned, than for his daughter to marry the Marquess of Huntingdon. So, she'd lived in harmony for seven years with a man who couldn't love her.

"My marriage to Hunt was best for all concerned." Claire swiped her damp palms against her skirt. "But that's not what's important now, Barn. It's Alex. What are we going to do?"

Barnaby hesitated, then clasped his hands on her shoulders. She could tell he'd made a decision, and she was glad to let him. She was so tired of shouldering the worry and responsibility alone.

"You're going to go back to bed and get some rest. I'll do some checking and see what I can find out. In the meantime, keep looking for the necklace. It's got to be here somewhere."

"Barn, if I gave you the necklace, you'd give it to Roseneau to free Alex, wouldn't you?"

Claire waited for her brother to answer. She needed to hear him say he wouldn't make the same choice as the major. But his silence lasted too long.

"You wouldn't let Alex die, would you?"

"No, Claire. I won't let Alex die. I promise. I won't let Alex die."

Claire breathed a deep sigh and let her brother hold her tight for a little while longer before she stepped out of his arms.

"I'm so glad you're here," she said, kissing him on the cheek. Then she picked up her skirt and made her way back up the path.

"Claire."

Barnaby's voice stopped her.

"Be careful of Bennett."

Claire frowned. "I'm not afraid of him, Barn."

"You should be," Claire heard him say, and he was gone.

Sam stood next to the window in a dark third-floor bedroom. He'd watched Lady Huntingdon race down the path and throw herself into her lover's arms, then sit with him on the stone bench with his arms wrapped around her. He wondered if Hunt knew how often his wife had been unfaithful to him. If perhaps that was the reason he'd taken the necklace. To woo his wife back to his bed. To win her back at any cost.

The thought made him angry. Sam knew something had been bothering Hunt. He'd even hinted that he was going to retire; that he'd already begun training a new agent to take his place. Now he knew why. He was desperate to fix what was wrong with his marriage.

Sam raked his fingers through his hair and watched Hunt's widow with the man she'd called Barn. From the looks of them in each other's arms, Sam was afraid nothing could have fixed Hunt's marriage.

He wondered who he was. How long she'd known him. Certainly long enough for the man to be overly concerned about her welfare. And certainly intimately enough to call her *Claire,* as he had this afternoon.

Sam fought the strange anger roiling inside him. He refused to give a name to the emotion. What he felt was better off ignored. It was more important to figure out the dichotomy of the woman he watched in the garden.

How could the woman Hunt had described be so different from the woman Sam had gotten to know? She wasn't shallow. Nor was she interested only in parties and balls and more gowns to add to her wardrobe. She was intelligent, with a keen mind and a strong sense of purpose.

And her purpose was to find the necklace before he did so she and her lover could live the remainder of their days in luxury. Well, he'd be damned if he'd let her.

He stormed across the room and out into the open hallway. He walked with no purpose, yet his footsteps seemed to have aim. He was drawn to Hunt's study, to the room where a small part of Hunt still lived.

He opened the door to the study and stepped inside. The room still had a masculine scent, the faint smell of cigar, the rich pleasant odor of leather and brandy and burning wood. It was all part and parcel of the man Hunt had been.

Sam walked over to a small table and lifted a crystal decanter. He filled a glass to the top, needing the mind-numbing relief of expensive brandy and dark brooding.

He drank the first glass, then refilled it and walked to a large wing chair in the corner and sat. The room was dark, the blackness burgeoning with silence.

He drank Hunt's brandy and remembered the man who had saved his life. The man he doubted Hunt's wife even cared was gone.

Chapter 12

Claire slowly made her way back to the house. How had her life become such an entangled mess? How could she have lived with Hunt for seven years and realized so little about him? How could he have embroiled both her brothers in the same underworld that had killed him?

She made her way across the flagstone terrace. When she reached the house, she opened the door to Hunt's study and stepped inside, then quietly closed the door behind her. She let her eyes adjust to the darkness before she wound her way around the furniture scattered throughout the room. She was nearly to the door when his voice stopped her.

"Were you searching for the necklace in the garden, my lady?"

Claire's hands flew to her mouth to muffle the scream that rose to her throat. She spun around and focused her gaze on the shadowed corner of the room.

"I . . ."

She felt him rise more than saw him, felt his presence engulf the room. He walked to the window behind Hunt's desk and drew back the drapes. Bright moonlight filtered through the room, casting him in black shadows that fell across him like a looming threat.

She saw him clearly then. Saw his towering presence, his broad shoulders accented by the full-sleeved white lawn shirt glowing bright against his bronzed skin. But mostly her gaze was drawn to the foreboding frown that drew his dark, angry brows together. He anchored one hand against the side of the window as if concentrating on something outside, and lifted a glass to his mouth and drank.

"Did you enjoy this pleasant evening?"

"Yes. Quite."

He took another swallow and turned to face her. "It's rather late to be wandering out in the dark, don't you think?"

She saw him set the glass down on the table and take a step toward her. She backed away. "I couldn't sleep."

"Yes. I can understand that. One's conscience can be very annoying at times."

Claire wanted to answer his caustic remark, but stopped when he took another step. And another. She kept pace in the opposite direction, not wanting to let him come too close. His nearness was intimidating.

"Do you have that problem often?"

"No."

Claire needed to separate herself from him. She placed her hand behind her and reached for the door.

"Did Hunt know, do you think?"

She froze with her hand on the knob. "Know what?"

"About you and your lover? Do you think he knew he was sharing his bed with another man?"

The air left her body, her head spinning in circles. "I don't know what you're talking about."

"Don't you?"

He closed the distance between them in slow, deliberate movements.

She inched away from him but found her back pressed against the door with no place to run.

He leaned closer, the smell of fine brandy on his breath. "Keeping a lover a secret from Hunt was quite a feat. Especially satisfying a lover *and* a man as—how would you term it? Attentive, perhaps—as Hunt?"

Claire felt her cheeks burn. Her heart thundered in her chest while the blood pounded against her ears. "I don't have—have never had—a lover."

"Oh, really?" The major leaned closer, propping his left hand on the door to the side of her head and sliding his left leg between hers. "That's not what it looked like tonight."

Her heart skipped a beat. Dear God, he'd seen her with Barnaby. Seen her and thought—

"It's not what you think."

"It's not?"

"No. I wasn't—"

The firm pads of his fingers brushed down the side of her face and across her lips. "Your bruises are fading."

"That wasn't my lover. That was my—"

He cupped her cheek in his hand and leaned his forehead against hers. "Is he the reason you want the necklace? I thought it was for Roseneau. But I was wrong, wasn't I?"

"No. Oh . . . No . . ."

He brushed a kiss on her forehead, then another against her cheek.

Claire couldn't catch her breath. Her skin was on fire. His touch ignited her flesh and burned as if she was standing in a flaming inferno. She couldn't do this. She had to stop. She turned her head away from him. "Don't. Please."

He turned her face back with a finger beneath her chin. "Why? You seemed to enjoy it earlier."

"No. No, I didn't. I wasn't—"

He lowered his head until his face was nestled in the crook of her neck. His mouth touched her skin just beneath her ear. A thousand spikes of fire spiraled to the pit of her stomach.

She placed her hands on his chest, knowing she should push him away. But she couldn't. She was drawn to him, like a dying man to his last gasp of air. Her palms felt on fire, as if the skin beneath his shirt was alive with heat.

When had the wariness she harbored for him been replaced by a desire so intense her mind no longer functioned? When had the threat he presented been overpowered by a hunger she needed to satisfy? When had her resolve weakened to the point she could not find the strength to keep her desires from consuming her?

He pressed his body closer to her. Every inch he touched burned with a fiery heat. He wrapped his arms around her and lowered his head until Claire could feel his breath whispering against her skin. He was going to kiss her. She knew he was. Just as she knew she shouldn't let him. As she knew she was powerless to stop him.

She looked into his eyes and drowned in the raw emotion she saw. He ground out a harsh sigh before he covered her mouth with his own.

His lips were warm and firm, his touch demanding. He kissed her as if he wanted her, as if he were desperate to possess her. And at the same time as if he'd lost the battle to protect himself from her.

He deepened his kiss, his mouth moving over hers with greater intensity. His lips parted over hers, and his tongue skimmed the seam between her lips until she opened to him.

On a loud moan, he kissed her again. His tongue intensified its assault, then entered her mouth in search of some treasure.

The feel of him against her, inside her, touching her, holding her, caressing her, drove her to a wild frenzy she couldn't battle. She'd never felt so possessed. Never given herself to another man like she was surrendering herself to this man, the man who'd saved her from the attack, who'd taken care of her afterward. Who'd sat with her night after night and held her when he thought she might die.

Her insides burned from the affect he had on her, and she wrapped her arms around his neck and held tight. Her breaths came in violent gasps, and he kissed her again, moving his lips over hers. His kisses were all-consuming, his desperation increasing. And Claire couldn't have stopped him if her life depended on it.

He cupped her breast, and she arched into him as heat and passion and desire ran rampant. Her legs weakened beneath her; her body flamed where his hands touched her. She knew she should make him stop, but every part of her ached for his touch.

Then, with a movement so sudden it left her reeling, he lifted his mouth from hers and stepped back. He sucked in a harsh breath and dropped his arms from around her, then stared at her with a look that changed from confusion to contempt. An icy-cold emptiness washed over her, and she reached out her hand to steady herself.

Barnaby had been right. Samuel Bennett was even more dangerous than the man Roseneau had sent.

A shiver wracked her body. How could she have been so foolish? Hadn't she sworn she would never open herself to such heartache again? No matter how often she'd hinted that she wanted to be a wife to Hunt, he'd refused her at every turn. The remorse in Hunt's eyes had torn at her heart. He didn't want her, and the guilt she saw was a barrier that kept them apart. Hadn't she vowed that she would never suffer those same looks of regret from any man ever again?

The desire she felt for him—if desire it was, for surely there couldn't be any real feelings between them—was a traitorous emotion she vowed she would never give in to again. She could never survive something so painful. Never survive the embarrassment she'd lived with for seven years. Or the ugly truth that even though she was a pretty package with all the ribbons and bows—an enviable pedigree, a pristine reputation, an unbelievable dowry—inside she was unable to be what a man desired in a woman, what a husband needed in his wife. As Hunt had found out on their wedding night and since then had kept secret from the world.

She stumbled to one of the chairs angled before the fireplace and dropped to the soft cushion. The world around her ceased to exist as she stared into the lifeless grate. Her chest heaved as she tried to catch her breath, but it was so hard. His kiss had taken so much from her, had forced her to face regrets she thought she'd never have to confront again.

She clutched her hands together as she tried to regain control. The major's next words were nearly her undoing.

"Was Hunt aware of your lover before he died? Is that why he was considering retiring?"

Claire darted him a venomous look.

"The man I met in the garden isn't my lover. He's my brother."

His eyebrows arched, and the corners of his mouth lifted in a sinister smile that said he didn't believe her.

"His name is Barnaby Linscott, Lord Barnaby, second son of my late father, the Marquess of Halverston. He is two years my senior."

Surprise was evident on his face before his expression turned hard.

"Believe what you want," she said, making an effort to rise. He stopped her with a look and an intimidating step in her direction.

"Why didn't you introduce him as such this afternoon when he arrived?"

"I started to, but Barnaby interrupted and kept his identity to himself. I don't think he trusts you."

A frown deepened the major's already formidable expression.

"I sent for Barnaby after the second threat arrived. I didn't know what else to do. I had no one else to turn to."

"So he ran off and left you to manage on your own?" The major raked his fingers through his dark hair, pushing the stray strands of coffee-rich hair off his forehead with a none-too-gentle swipe. "Why didn't he stay here to protect you?"

Claire shook her head. "He wanted to, but I thought Hunt might have hidden the necklace at one of his country estates. I sent Barn to look for it."

"And you stayed here alone? Even after you'd received more than one threat?"

Claire sighed. "I didn't take them seriously. Why should I? It was the necklace they wanted, not me." Claire rubbed her fingers against her temples. "Do you have any idea what it's like to find out you've lived the last seven years with a stranger? A man whose main interests should have been taking care of the estates his father had turned over to him, caring for his tenants, and running a very profitable Huntingdon Shipping?"

Claire sank back against the upholstery and closed her eyes. "When in reality, I find out his long absences were due to covert missions he was performing for the government. Now some very dangerous people think I have a necklace he stole."

Unable to stay seated any longer, Claire rose from the settee. She felt his eyes on her as she walked to Hunt's desk and fingered the cool wood on the top of his desk.

She stared at the papers Hunt had been working on the day he died and ran her finger over the paperweight he had a habit of rolling in his hand when he was thinking. She touched the black leather ledgers sitting on the corner. She hadn't moved any of his things. Hadn't been able to bring herself to come into this room, other than the night she'd been attacked. It reminded her too much of the man she'd lived with, cared for, disappointed, her whole married life.

She leaned against the corner of the desk and fought the heavy weight pressing against her chest, pushed back the tears that threatened to surface. Tears she had yet to shed over a man who'd been incapable of loving her.

"Why do you want the necklace?" he asked, the threat in his voice plain.

"My reasons are personal."

"You know I can never let you have it," he said as a statement of fact.

"Not even if it is a matter of life and death?"

"It is already a matter of life and death. The life or death of thousands of innocent young men."

There was no compromise in his tone, no understanding in his words. Her heart plummeted. How could she justify using the necklace to save only one life?

But that one life is Alex's.

How could she live with herself if she gave up the necklace and Alex died? How could she live with the guilt if she didn't, and thousands of innocent young men died in his place?

He stepped into the center of the room and clasped his hands behind his back. He faced her squarely, his legs braced wide and his head tilted just enough for her to feel his threat. "I received a message from my uncle, the Marquess of Rainforth. He is hosting a small, informal dinner party this evening. You and I will be in attendance."

Claire glared at him, determined to make a stand. "No. I am in mourning yet and—"

"Society's rules don't apply here. This is important. Roseneau will be there."

Claire felt the floor shift beneath her. "I . . ." She shook her head. "No. You can't make me go."

"You don't have a choice. Our presence has been commanded. You are, as my uncle put it, 'the guest of honor.'"

Claire felt the room spin around her. She couldn't face the major. Roseneau was probably the one who'd killed her husband. He *was* the one who'd sent someone to attack her. And, he'd kidnapped and threatened her brother. She clenched her hands at her side and glared at him. "I don't want to go."

"I'm surprised. I thought you'd be eager to see Roseneau again."

Claire's temper flared. She wanted to reach out and slap the smug expression from his face. Instead, she spun away from him and clutched her arms around her middle. She looked out the window and saw nothing but blackness.

For a long time, he let their silence consume the room. Claire broke the tension with her question. "Why do you think he wants me there?"

"Other than to see you again? He's giving you an opportunity to hand over the necklace."

"I don't have it."

"But I want you to convince him we do."

She turned to face him. "Why?"

"Let's just say it raises the stakes. Letting him believe we have the necklace puts your friend in a much more precarious position. And perhaps, if we're fortunate, in his desperation he will make a mistake and reveal our traitor."

Claire stared at him, unable to hide her confusion. "If Roseneau and I are the close acquaintances you assume we are, how do you know you can trust me?"

"I don't. But I'm willing to risk it."

"Then there's no need for me to go in person. I can just send him a message informing him—"

"No. You will go in person."

His plan didn't quite make sense. Then suddenly she understood. Her blood turned cold. "You don't want me to go because of Roseneau, do you? You want to use me as bait. You think there's a chance that the traitor will show his hand if I am there and he believes that I have the necklace. You want me to draw him out."

The unreadable mask on his face didn't give a clue to his thoughts. His subtle silence let her draw her own conclusions. With slow, deft movements, he walked over to the side table and poured some of Hunt's brandy in his glass. He took a small sip, then placed the glass back on the table. When finally he spoke, there was a coldness in his voice that matched the hardness in his words.

"The dinner was Roseneau's idea, but probably at the traitor's insistence. There's a good chance he'll be there. Until we find the papers, this is as close as we're going to get to finding him."

"How is your uncle connected?"

"Roseneau and my uncle have been friends and business associates for years. Roseneau requested my uncle host a dinner party to give him an opportunity to see all his English friends while he is visiting. Your name was at the top of the list. My uncle is only an unwitting accomplice."

Claire felt a chill race down her spine.

"You have to attend. It's important that Roseneau thinks we've found the necklace and you're waiting for an opportunity to get it away from me. It's even more important the traitor is convinced I have the papers."

"But he knows you don't or you'd have arrested him."

"No. He'll assume he hasn't been arrested because I haven't broken the code that identifies him."

"How will he learn that?"

"That will be your responsibility, my lady. It shouldn't be hard, considering your past association with Roseneau."

"But I don't know who the traitor is."

"You don't have to. All you have to do is tell Roseneau I'm close to breaking the code. He'll tell the traitor. And once the traitor knows I have the papers, he'll have to come after them."

"And you'll be waiting for him?"

"Something like that, yes."

Claire considered what the major was telling her.

If she told Roseneau they were still searching, he might give her more time in which to find it, time she desperately needed. Or, maybe he'd realize since they didn't have the necklace, holding Alex hostage wouldn't do him any good and he'd let him go.

If only she had something Roseneau might consider taking in exchange for the necklace. Something he desired but that was beyond his reach. A shiver raced down her spine, and Claire slammed her mind shut on the thought taking form.

That left the major's second option. To tell Roseneau the major had the necklace but refused to give it over. If she could convince him that she was no longer in control, and that holding Alex wouldn't benefit him any longer, maybe he'd release him. Then negotiations for the necklace would focus between Roseneau and the major, and Alex would be safe.

Or, she could offer him something he would consider in exchange for Alex. Something—

Her thoughts refused to go further. Oh, how she wanted to trust the major. Wanted to believe everything would work out as he planned. But she couldn't.

Claire turned toward the window and stared out into the darkness. A lead weight pummeled to the pit of her stomach at the thought of facing Roseneau. She sensed the kind of man he was, had known it when he'd cornered her at the ball. When he'd trapped her in a dark corridor and refused to let her leave. When he'd touched her and held her and made improper advances even though she'd done nothing to encourage him.

He was manipulative, a man used to getting what he wanted. A man who thought money and power gave him liberty to do whatever he wished. And this was the man with whom the major thought she was having an affair. Knowing what he thought made her as sick as when Roseneau had kissed her. She'd been able to escape his unwanted attentions only because they'd been interrupted by Barnaby and his friends.

Claire didn't want to think what would have happened if they hadn't come upon them. Roseneau was one of the most self-confident, aggressive men she'd ever met. He was nearly as old as Hunt, but it was almost as if he'd defied the passing of time. The years had been very kind to the handsome Frenchman, even though his reputation as a connoisseur of fine wine, lavish entertaining, and beautiful women was renowned.

A rush of dread raced through her veins. There was a third option open to her. An option she hadn't wanted to consider before, but one that lurked on the edge of her sanity. An option she no longer had the luxury of ignoring.

Alex had done nothing to deserve being thrown in the middle of this nightmare. If there was anything she could exchange for her brother's life, she had no choice. And she possessed only one thing Roseneau might want. Something she would offer only as a last resort. Something it would take every ounce of her courage to give.

She turned to face the major with a heart incapable of feeling anything more.

"What time am I to be ready?"

"We will leave at eight."

"Very well. I think I'll go to bed now, if you don't mind. It's been a very long day."

He nodded, then moved to open the door. She walked past him with the same resolve that had gotten her through the last four months. At least she knew what few options were left her.

Too much had been taken from her. So much more would be demanded from her before this was finished. She would do what she had to do, and survive with what was left.

Chapter 13

Sam helped Claire into the carriage, then sat on the leather-cushioned seat opposite her. He tapped the roof with his walking stick and the Huntingdon carriage lurched forward. He enlisted Lieutenant Honeywell to act as their driver, although the Marchioness of Huntingdon didn't seem to notice. Just as she hadn't seemed to notice much of anything from the time she'd come down to leave.

She'd walked into Hunt's study where Sam had been waiting, and his breath had lodged in his throat. She was absolutely stunning. Her gown was a rich shade of purple satin, so deep it was nearly black. The shiny material molded to her exquisite form, and it shimmered with each step she took.

Her shoulders were covered just enough to hide the bandage over her wound, while the bodice was cut low in front to reveal the creamy white rise of perfect breasts. Not exactly the gown he thought she would choose since she was still in mourning, but one that drew the attention where she intended and suited the situation perfectly. A single strand of pearls was all the jewelry she wore. It was all she needed.

Her hair was done up in cascading ringlets drawn back loosely from her face and allowed to fall to the center of her back. Tilly had wound a matching purple satin ribbon through Claire's golden curls. Sam envied the ribbon, wishing it were his fingers wending through her silky hair.

She wore just the right amount of face powder to hide her telltale bruises, and in her hand she carried a fan made of black lace. He had no doubt the fan was intended to hide any of the bruises her face powder had failed to conceal. All that was missing was a hint of life in her eyes—any expression other than the dread he glimpsed for just one second before she so expertly hid it.

Sam had seen this reaction from soldiers before battle. The ones who didn't hide their terror behind robust laughter, gay singing, and all the liquor they could hold shut themselves away in a private world where outside horrors couldn't reach them. They turned distant and quiet, as if they could separate themselves from the danger they were about to face.

Claire was doing just that. Separating herself. Preparing for whatever she was forced to confront. Resigning herself to accept the consequences.

Sam wanted to reach over and hold her hand. He wanted to comfort her, although giving in to the unfamiliar emotions coursing through him wasn't a risk he was willing to take. Never before had he felt such a pull as he did when he was near her. Never before had he battled such raging desire, as if she were his to care for.

He tamped down this intense reaction and pulled himself back to the present.

"All you have to do is convince Roseneau I have the necklace and the papers," he said as their carriage rumbled through London's narrow streets.

She blinked once, then focused on him with the sharp intelligence he was used to seeing. "Perhaps you should tell me exactly what message you want me to relay, Major. There will obviously not be a better opportunity."

Sam sat back against the squabs. The woman he counted on to face her enemies was back. The strong, determined warrior who'd refused to give up her fight to get the necklace for herself stared at him across the carriage. The woman who'd refused to succumb to the physical pain of her attacker; who hadn't backed down even once from Sam's relentless demands, when any other woman he knew would have buckled under the pressure in a heap of satin and lace and hysterics. That woman now faced him with unyielding resolve. And for some reason, her intractable determination bothered him. As if she wasn't facing Roseneau because he'd ordered her to. But because meeting him would bring about something she wanted.

Something was not right. For several minutes he couldn't understand why he was bothered by her unflinching determination. By her reserve. Then, as if a light illuminated the problem, he realized the source of his concern was Claire's initial reaction to his demand that she meet with Roseneau. It was totally wrong. What he'd seen hadn't contained even the slightest hint of eagerness at the possibility of meeting with her lover, but dread.

Why had she put up such a fight when he'd told her what he wanted her to do? If she and Roseneau *were* lovers, why had she adamantly refused Sam's request that they attend his uncle's dinner? And what made her change her mind when he unveiled his plan to deceive Roseneau? She was guarding another secret he would have to unveil. Sam wondered what danger she was in that she wasn't sharing with him.

He studied her impassive expression as she waited for him to answer. He would have to watch her closely tonight. If she intended to betray him, he couldn't allow her efforts to go unchecked.

"It is not a message, exactly. It is more an *impression* you should leave with him."

She raised her narrow eyebrows and tilted her head in a most becoming manner. Sam was struck by how exceptionally lovely she was. But her face was an unreadable mask he couldn't decipher.

"I want Roseneau to realize that you aren't in control. That I am. That I've been working on the papers I found in the pouch with the necklace."

She waited. When he didn't add any more information, she looked out the window. She appeared very calm and relaxed. Too calm and relaxed. Except for her hands clutched tightly in her lap, she gave no sign this evening was any more difficult for her than any other.

"Can you handle that?"

Her eyes locked with his. "Don't worry, Major. I'll do what has to be done."

Sam squelched the uncomfortable impression that hinted at a hidden meaning to her words, but he didn't have time to comment further. Their carriage slowed in front of the Marquess of Rainforth's town house, then stopped. "A warning, my lady. Tell Roseneau only what you've been instructed. No more."

"Your trust in me is reassuring, Major."

"Trust is not the issue. The danger Roseneau presents is. Don't forget. I'll be close by, should you have need of me."

"I doubt that will be necessary. If I'm to play my part and relay your message convincingly, I'll need some degree of privacy. Besides, I doubt Roseneau will attempt anything amid the crowd your uncle has invited."

"Don't underestimate him, Claire. And don't underestimate me."

She lightly rubbed the cut across her shoulder that he knew still pained her, then answered almost beneath her breath, "I am well aware of the threat you present, sir. The lengths to which both you and Roseneau are willing to go is never far from my mind."

Her remark caught him off guard, but the carriage door opened before Sam had an opportunity to think further on what her words might mean. Sam exited first, then turned to help her down. She took his hand with that familiar air of cool detachment Sam found irritating, and stepped to the street. Why did she portray such aloofness? Was this the face she put on in public? Or was this how she was to her husband, too?

"Keep the carriage as close to the entrance as you can," Sam told Honeywell, looking for the nearest open area. "And be ready to leave quickly."

"Yes, sir," Honeywell said, indicating a spot on the opposite side of the street where he intended to park the carriage.

"Are you expecting trouble, Major?" she asked as they made their way up the cement walk to the Marquess's town house.

"No. I just don't want a long wait when we're ready to leave."

She glanced at him with a look that said she didn't quite believe him, but she didn't question him further. They were already at the door and Rainforth's butler, Pittingsworth, was there to take their hats and cloaks.

"The guests are assembled upstairs in the small ballroom," the butler said, taking Sam's cloak. "Franklin will show you and the lady up, sir."

"That won't be necessary, Pittingsworth. I know the way."

"Very well, Major."

Sam held out his arm. When she placed her hand on it, he realized she was trembling. A knot formed low in his gut when he looked down at her pale face. She was terrified. Even though she tried to mask her fear with that all-too-familiar unapproachable demeanor, he saw through her air of indifference.

He covered her hand with his and gave her fingers a gentle squeeze. He held her gloved hand as if he could take away her apprehension. Her surprise was evident, and she pulled on her hand, intending to remove it. He held tight and wouldn't let it go.

"Don't forget—I'll be right here," he said before they entered the room. "Don't leave my sight."

Sam stopped at the top of the stairs that led down to the ballroom. There were at least fifty people gathered there already, with more undoubtedly coming.

"I thought you said this would be a small dinner party."

Sam looked around the room, searching for familiar faces. Searching for Roseneau. "That's what I was led to believe."

"Do you see him?"

"Who?"

She breathed a shaky sigh that said she had no intention of answering him.

"No. Not yet." He scanned the room again, then led her down the steps and into the crowd. There was no opportunity to reassure her again before his uncle, the Marquess of Rainforth, came bustling forward.

"Samuel, it's so good to see you. And Lady Huntingdon." Rainforth clutched her hand. "Allow me to express my deepest condolences on your loss and thank you ever so much for attending."

Claire accepted Rainforth's words with a slight nod. He beamed, then rambled on as Sam took her hand back and looped it through his arm.

"I can't tell you how grateful I am Samuel persuaded you to attend tonight. I know coming back into Society cannot be easy for you."

"No. But necessary, nevertheless. Thank you for inviting me."

"Nonsense. It's my pleasure. Have you had a chance to meet our guest of honor, Monsieur Roseneau?"

"No, my lord. We have both just arrived."

Sam saw her look into the crowded room and knew the instant her gaze found Roseneau. She stiffened, and her fingers dug into his arm. She swayed unsteadily beside him. He wanted to pull her against him, but couldn't. Instead, he stepped closer, hoping his nearness would be enough.

Rainforth cast a glance over the crowd. "Oh, there he is." Rainforth waved him over. "I know he's very anxious to meet you again. He and your husband were quite good friends, were they not?"

"They were business acquaintances," Lady Huntingdon answered, her voice calm and controlled, her fingers digging deeper into his arm. "I could not say as to the degree of their friendship."

Roseneau was in the midst of a conversation with at least six of the influential guests Rainforth had invited. The second he spotted Lady Huntingdon, he stopped his conversation and turned to face her.

Sam felt the tension between the two thicken, and for a second he was convinced that there was more between Lady Huntingdon and Monsieur Roseneau than the necklace. And whatever it might be, it was more adversarial than affectionate.

Sam wondered if it was possible that he could have been wrong about the connection between Roseneau and Lady Huntingdon.

Sam looked down to where Claire had a tight grip on his arm. Her chest rose and fell as if she'd exerted herself. The pulse at the base of her throat beat rapidly.

"Just stay where I can see you," he whispered, but he wasn't sure she heard him.

"Claire?" he repeated a little louder.

She shifted her gaze from Roseneau and glanced at Sam for just a moment. What he glimpsed startled him. Not the look of affection he expected, but unadulterated hatred. A bitterness more intense than he'd ever imagined he'd see in her eyes.

Chapter 14

Claire's blood boiled. Her body trembled in anger at seeing the man who'd caused her so much pain.

He was just as she remembered him, as handsome and distinguished as before. And she wanted to kill him.

She wanted to take his life as she was certain—whether directly or indirectly—he'd taken Hunt's. She wanted to make him pay for embroiling Alex in this mess. She wanted to cause him pain equal to the pain he'd caused her. A pain that would never go away. Instead, she lifted her gaze and greeted him as was appropriate her station.

"Lady Huntingdon. What a pleasure. And Major Bennett."

Roseneau gave the major a challenging look, then turned his attention back to her. He lifted her hand to his mouth and kissed the air above her fingers. Oh, how she wanted to pull her hand away from him and slap his face. How she wanted to let him know how much she detested him.

But she didn't. She couldn't. He had Alex. Until Alex was free, she couldn't do anything but follow her plan.

"Monsieur Roseneau. It's a pleasure to see you again."

"Lady Huntingdon. You cannot imagine how devastated I was to hear of your husband's death. Lord Huntingdon and I had conducted many business dealings together. He was a most admired associate as well as a dear friend. He will be greatly missed."

"Thank you, Monsieur Roseneau."

Roseneau stepped back and let his gaze move in slow perusal. "May I compliment you, my lady? You look stunning."

Claire fought the shiver of revulsion as his eyes slowly undressed her. The seductive smile on his lips made her feel dirty.

He hesitantly released her hand and said, "I was afraid perhaps you would not come."

Claire lifted her eyebrows. "Oh, really. And why is that?"

For a second, Roseneau looked a little nonplussed, but recovered quickly. "Because of your recent loss, of course."

She looked him squarely in the eyes, not giving him the opportunity to doubt her meaning. "Yes. Well, there are times when matters of importance take precedence over personal preferences."

"That sounds very serious, my lady."

"It is. The tragedies in one's life are often pushed to the background under light of such matters." She paused for effect. "I have made certain discoveries that demanded I attend tonight."

A slow, euphoric smile lifted the corners of his mouth. "I'm sure I will find anything you have discovered most worthwhile, Lady Huntingdon. Perhaps we could discuss this further after dinner."

A gleam of victory shone in his eyes. He was like a cat ready to pounce on his prey.

Claire fought a chill that made her shudder. If Roseneau was the cat, she was the mouse he was about to devour. The thought scared her to death, and yet . . . Roseneau had Alex. She had no choice but to make whatever sacrifice was necessary to free him.

She lifted her head and then spoke the last words she wanted to say.

"I'd be delighted."

Sam pushed his way through the crush of people crowding the small ballroom after dinner, and reached for a glass of brandy from one of the small refreshment tables scattered throughout the room. As he brought the glass to his lips, he moved his gaze from the spot where Claire talked with a group of women on one side of the room to where Roseneau held court with a group of status-seeking members of the *ton* on the other. It wouldn't be long before Roseneau made his move. Claire's comments had enticed him enough to guarantee he'd seek a moment alone with her. Sam didn't want to be too far away when their meeting took place. The room was too crowded to risk losing sight of either of them.

He took another sip of brandy and ignored the small orchestra playing softly in the corner. Numerous clusters of sofas and chairs dotted the room, all of them filled with guests intent on some topic of conversation or another. Those who couldn't find room to sit, stood together in little groups.

Sam let his gaze sift over the crowd, trying to memorize every face there. One of them was undoubtedly the traitor. And whoever it was, they possessed enough influence that they were privy to top military strategies. The problem was that there were a dozen or more here tonight who fit that requirement.

Sam's thoughts were cut short by his uncle's interruption.

"There you are, my boy," the Marquess of Rainforth said, striding up to him with his usual exuberance. Sam always thought his uncle moved with the forcefulness of a thunderstorm, showering countless blessings, or wreaking willful destruction on everything in his path. He was no different tonight.

"Have you had a chance to talk with Ross?"

Sam shook his head. "He's been quite busy fighting off his crowd of female admirers," he said with a smile. "I haven't seen him alone all evening."

"Well, when you do, I would like to ask a favor."

"Of course. What trouble has my cousin gotten into now?"

"No trouble, really."

"Ah. Then he has been remiss in some area and you think it will have a greater impact if *I* remind him of his duties."

Rainforth smiled. "I never could put anything over on you. You get that from your father. He always knew what I needed before I asked. Sometimes it was quite exasperating."

Sam smiled while letting his gaze take in the crowded ballroom. Claire was still in sight, as was Roseneau. He turned his attention back to his uncle.

". . . and you always manage to bring him around to do what's expected of him."

"And just what is it you'd like me to discuss with him?"

"I want an heir, Samuel. Ross is turning eight and twenty, and I'm not going to be around forever. I want the Rainforth title secured before I die."

Sam tried to hide the smile that lifted the corners of his mouth. To his uncle, the Rainforth title and the considerable fortune that went with it were of the utmost importance. Sam only wished his cousin felt the same. From all the rumors he'd heard, Ross Bennett, Earl of Cardmall, went through money as fast as his father could give it to him.

Sam checked again to make sure Claire was in sight. She was. "Is there anyone in particular you want me to suggest as a future daughter-in-law?"

"Now, don't laugh at me, boy. But what kind of father would I be if I hadn't put at least a little thought into the kind of female who'd make the best countess for Ross? And since he isn't putting any effort into finding a wife himself, I feel I have to."

"He looks like he's doing pretty well to me," Sam said, nodding to where Ross seemed to be the central attraction for at least a half-dozen single ladies of the *ton*.

"Pshaw! That's all for show. There isn't one female in that gathering who'd be a suitable countess. He's playing the ladies' man simply for my benefit, to make me think he's making an effort. But I know differently."

"I see. And on whom have you decided as your first choice for your future daughter-in-law?"

Rainforth nodded to the opposite side of the room where a group of five or six pretty young women stood talking and laughing. "The one in green. Lady Caroline, the Earl of Penderly's daughter. Excellent breeding, exceptional dowry, and pretty eyes."

Sam nodded his approval at his uncle's first choice. She was lovely.

"Or, the one by the window, in blue. Lady Penelope, Baron Renfroe's daughter. Her father doesn't have quite the pedigree I'd prefer, but her mother was the Duke of Ashtonbury's daughter. Excellent family, you know."

"Of course," Sam nodded, trying to hurry his uncle's conversation.

"Then there's the Marchioness of Huntingdon. I know she's still in mourning, but special allowances can always be made for a young widow alone."

Sam's gaze flew to where Claire stood talking to a group of friends. He suddenly wanted to remove her from the room. Wanted to take Claire out of his uncle's sight. He didn't want anyone considering her as a marriage prospect. Bloody hell! He didn't even want anyone looking at her with that on their mind. "I'm not sure Lady Huntingdon is in the market for a husband, my lord."

"Nonsense, Samuel. Every lady is hunting for a husband. Marriage to Ross would be an enviable match. Everyone knows that. And they're of a similar age."

Sam turned his gaze to the circle of men where Roseneau had been standing. He was gone. Sam searched the room while his uncle continued down his list of reasons Ross should settle down with a wife. Roseneau wasn't anywhere.

"Are you listening, Samuel?"

"Yes, Uncle." Sam looked to the spot where Claire had been. "I'm listening."

She was gone, too.

"And you'll talk to Ross?"

"Yes, of course. Now, if you'll excuse me. I see someone I need to speak with."

Sam pushed his way through the crowd, searching for Claire and Roseneau. His heart raced as he realized they weren't in the room. That somehow they'd left without his notice.

Damn his uncle and his trivial worries. Damn Ross and his irresponsible ways. But Sam knew he had only himself to blame. He'd let her get away when he'd sworn to keep her in view.

Sam walked the perimeter of the room, searching every alcove and secluded spot. When he was sure they weren't in the room, he headed toward the stairs. Perhaps Roseneau had taken her to Rainforth's study, or the library, or—

"I say, Sam," his cousin Ross said, grabbing Sam by the arm to stop him from rushing past. "What's the hurry?"

"Not now. I've got to—"

Sam brushed Ross aside and turned to search the other side of the room. Ross's words stopped him from taking another step.

"He not here."

"Who?"

"Roseneau."

Sam spun around to face his cousin. "What makes you think I'm looking for Roseneau?"

"A guess."

"Actually, I was looking for Lady—"

"Stay away from him, Sam."

Sam lifted his eyebrows. "Is that a warning, Ross?"

Sam studied his cousin's face. Ross's easygoing expression was gone, the look in his eyes as serious and menacing as the tone of his voice. Sam took note of the change and decided to feign ignorance. "But he's your father's friend and a guest, Ross."

"You know exactly what he is, Major. I only wish my father did. He thinks the sun rises on him."

Sam stared at his cousin, trying to evaluate the message he was sending. How could Ross know about Roseneau? How could he know about anything?

Sam struggled to find an answer.

"Don't underestimate him, Sam. He's not as harmless as—" Ross stopped, as if he realized he'd said too much.

"As what, Ross?"

"Just be careful."

Before Sam could say more, Ross threw the remainder of his brandy to the back of his throat and handed the empty glass to a passing footman. "Oh, look. There's Pinky. I have to offer him my sympathies. I hear he's betrothed to Lady Eunice Quigham, though it seems he's quite happy about it."

Ross took a step away from Sam and stopped. When he turned around, there was a happy smile on his face. "If you're looking for Lady Huntingdon, I believe she's out on the terrace."

The Earl of Cardmall walked away, laughing gaily, as if their serious conversation had never taken place.

Sam watched him go, then made his way to the double French doors that led out onto the terrace. The same gut-wrenching unease he felt before every battle roiled deep in his belly.

And a greater fear as Ross's words echoed in his head.

Chapter 15

Claire kept her hand on Roseneau's arm as he led her out into the cool night air.

"Do you need a wrap, my lady?" he asked, his concern a practiced art. It meant absolutely nothing to her tonight.

"No. I am fine."

He placed his other hand over her gloved fingers and walked with her to the far side of the terrace, to a secluded spot where they couldn't be seen or overheard. When they reached their destination, Claire turned to step away from him. But Roseneau clamped both hands around her upper arms to stop her.

"You'll be warmer if you stay close, Claire."

Claire stepped back, deliberately breaking his hold. She wanted to slap him, wanted to rake her fingers down his face and leave him scarred and bleeding. She wanted to see the fear in his eyes when she pulled the small pistol she'd hidden in a pocket of her skirt and pointed it at his chest. But she couldn't do any of that. Not until Alex was free.

"I'm far from cold, monsieur," she said with the gentlest of smiles on her face. "I rarely am. And . . ." She took a step away from him, then another, while slowly tracing her fingers over the low cement balustrade. When she was a safe distance from him, she turned her head to look at him over her shoulder. ". . . I didn't realize we were such close acquaintances that you felt at liberty to use my Christian name?" She smiled seductively. "Yet."

His eyebrows arched, then his smile broadened. And he laughed. "Am I correct in assuming this enjoyable banter is leading somewhere?"

"Perhaps."

"Then, *perhaps*, you would like to enlighten me."

Claire turned around to face him, her expression as relaxed as she could make it. "I want my brother released."

He stepped closer. "Then I presume you brought me the necklace."

"Can I presume you have already released my brother?"

Roseneau smiled. "How thoughtless of me. If I would have anticipated you having the necklace, I certainly would have. Do you have it, Lady Huntingdon?"

"No."

"Who does?"

Claire tried to sound in control. Tried to make the lie believable. "Major Bennett. He's keeping it until the Russian representatives come the end of next week."

"And the papers?"

"Papers?"

"Don't play the fool, my lady. You know what papers I'm talking about. If you have the necklace—which you do—then you also have the papers. Where are they?"

Claire shrugged, as if his accusations meant nothing to her. "Major Bennett's working every hour of the day and night to decode them. I think it won't be long until he knows the traitor's identity. I'm sure all of England will take great pleasure in watching such a man hang."

Roseneau was quiet. When he spoke, Claire felt a greater fear than she thought was possible.

"If you do not have what I want with you, then there is nothing for us to bargain with."

"And there's no need for you to hold Alex. Keeping him hostage can do you no good."

"Can't it? I want that necklace and the papers, Lady Huntingdon."

"I already told you. I don't have them."

"Then get them!"

"You know as well as I that Major Bennett will never trade them for Alex's freedom."

"That's very unfortunate, my lady. Your brother was sure you would come to his aid."

Claire's blood ran cold. "Don't hurt him. Please. None of this is his fault. He isn't involved in any of it."

"But you are. And I want that necklace."

Claire's heart raced. The blood thundered in her head. She couldn't breathe, couldn't think. She had no choice. Alex would die unless she could help him. Unless she . . .

"What else will you take in place of the necklace?"

His eyes turned hard and black and dangerous. For a long time he only stared at her, his gaze angry and hostile. Then understanding dawned, and the glint in his eyes frightened her more than before. "What else are you offering, my lady?"

Claire swallowed hard. She couldn't do this. She was going to be ill. She clutched her hands at her side, making tiny, painful fists. "Anything I have that you want."

He stepped closer until he was so near her she could feel the heat of his vile body next to hers. The corners of his lips curled upward. His eyes gleamed with a greedy, eager look.

Claire forced herself not to run when he touched his hand to her bare flesh. She forced herself to stand still when he ran the fingers of one probing hand along the low bodice of her gown.

"How interesting."

His eyes ogled the flesh that was exposed to his gaze as he ran his fingers back across her skin. With each passing, he dipped lower over her breasts, his long fingers reaching deep beneath the material, so deep he nearly touched her nipples. She swallowed hard.

He smiled. Then he leaned close and Claire knew he intended to kiss her.

"Lady Huntingdon," a voice said from somewhere behind them.

A small gasp of relief escaped from deep inside her. Roseneau stiffened. "How unfortunate," he murmured against her ear, then turned to face their intruder. "Major Bennett, what a surprise. Did you also come out to enjoy this nice evening?"

"There was a matter I needed to discuss with Lady Huntingdon and couldn't find her. Thank you for seeing to her welfare," the major said, crossing the terrace until he stood next to her.

Claire watched the two men evaluate each other, heard the unspoken threat, felt the undeclared challenge. They were both formidable enemies. Both dangerous, threatening men. But one she would trust with her life.

"The pleasure was mine." Roseneau lifted her hand and brought it to his lips. "We had a very enlightened conversation, Major. One you would have found quite interesting."

"Then I regret I did not seek the lady out sooner."

"Your loss was my gain." Roseneau turned so his gaze bore into her. "If you will excuse me, my lady. There are many friends inside I have yet to greet. I bid you a pleasant good night."

He turned to go, then stopped. "Thank you for your generous offer, Lady Huntingdon. I'm not sure I can be persuaded to exchange one treasure for another, but one never knows. The offer is tempting indeed." Roseneau shrugged his shoulders. "Whatever I decide, you will know my answer shortly."

Claire watched him go through the double French doors, then spun away and clutched her arms around her middle. She couldn't stop shaking. Couldn't find enough air to fill her lungs. Couldn't keep her small cries from echoing in the darkness.

She felt herself sway. The major's arms came around her, turning her, pulling her close to him.

"What the hell was that all about?"

"Hold me," she whimpered, her voice a weak whisper, her words jagged fragments. "Please . . . Oh, please."

Claire nestled against him and buried her face against his warm chest. There was nothing sexual in the way he held her; nothing sensual, and yet . . . she'd never experienced such complete surrender as she did at that moment. She wrapped her arms around his waist and clung to him. Twice he'd saved her. Twice he'd come when she'd needed him. Twice he'd held her in his arms.

His hand traveled up and down her spine, comforting her. Soothing her. His lips touched the top of her head. She could feel his muscled strength, smell his clean, masculine scent. He held her until she stopped shaking. Until her breaths could fill her lungs. And he held her even longer.

Finally he placed his fingers beneath her chin and tilted her face. He was angry. She could see it in his eyes. They blazed hot, the gray as intense as she'd seen the night he killed Roseneau's henchman. Some of his anger was directed at her, she knew. But most of it was directed at Roseneau.

"Why did you come out here alone with him?"

"How else did you expect me to deliver your message?"

"Not out here where no one could see you. Not alone!"

"What would you have had me do? Conduct our conversation in front of fifty people?"

"No, but I couldn't find you. He could have—"

He stopped. She saw the concern in his eye and waited for him to finish. He did not. He only looked at her. "Are you all right?"

She nodded and gave him a shaky yes. "Please, take me home. I want to go home."

"Very well."

He wrapped his arm around her waist and escorted her through the crowd still drinking the Marquess of Rainforth's excellent and never-ending supply of liquor. They said a quick farewell, and the major got their cloaks while Claire waited by the door. She couldn't wait to leave. Couldn't wait to get away from Roseneau.

The major came back with her cloak and wrapped it around her shoulders, then led her out of the house and down the steps.

When Honeywell saw them exit the town house, he pulled the carriage away from the curb and crossed the street to get them. Before it came to a complete stop, the major had the door open. He lowered the step, and Claire took her first shaky step up.

"My lady! Lady Huntingdon! Wait!"

Claire turned around as one of Rainforth's servants came running toward them. "This is for you, Lady Huntingdon," the maid said, holding out a narrow, oblong package. "Monsieur Roseneau said to make sure you got this before you left."

Claire shook her head and pulled her hand back. She didn't want anything he had to give her. Didn't want any gifts from him.

The servant's happy smile turned to perplexed agitation, and she glanced from Claire to the major, looking for instructions as to what to do.

"But he said to make sure you received it, my lady."

Claire pulled back even further. It must have become obvious to the major she wasn't going to take it. He took it for her.

"Thank you," he said to the relieved servant. "Tell Monsieur Roseneau that Lady Huntingdon received it."

"Yes, sir. Thank you, sir."

The servant bobbed a quick curtsy, then raced back to the house. Major Bennett followed Claire into the carriage. "Do you know what it is?" he asked when the carriage was rolling down the street.

She shook her head.

"Why would Roseneau give you a gift?"

"I don't know."

But she did know. It was the answer to her proposition. An answer she didn't think she was brave enough to discover.

Claire huddled in the corner of their carriage as it rambled through the streets. Her teeth chattered and her whole body trembled from her encounter with Roseneau. She'd never been so frightened in her life. Never been so physically sick with dread. The box was the size a necklace might come in. What if he had accepted her proposition? What if he hadn't?

She wrapped her arms around her middle and tried to keep her teeth from chattering. She couldn't.

"Bloody hell, Claire," she heard the major whisper. He placed Roseneau's package on the seat and moved beside her. He pushed her skirts aside to make room for his large frame.

She made the mistake of looking at him. His eyes still brimmed with fury; his mouth was pressed to two tight lines. The only term that could describe the expression on his face was *murderous*.

He slid close beside her, and with infinite tenderness wrapped his arm around her shoulder. She turned into him when he pulled her close, as if that was where she belonged. She buried her cheek into his chest and slid her arm around his middle, feeling the strange warmth of his flesh beneath his linen shirt.

"Do you think Roseneau believed you when you told him I had the necklace and the papers?"

She nodded, unable to get the words out.

For a long while they sat in silence. Then he asked the first question she knew she could not answer. "What generous offer did you make him?"

He spoke through clenched teeth, his words short and clipped. She could hear the anger in his strained voice. She could feel the bridled fury in the tenseness of his muscles. Every part of him seemed stretched taut, ready to snap.

"What?" he repeated.

"It was nothing," she lied.

"What did he mean when he said he wasn't sure he could exchange one treasure for another?"

Claire pushed herself away from him, moving as far into the corner as she could. "I don't know. Please, leave it be."

"I can't and you know it. What treasure was he talking about? What did you offer him, Claire?"

His voice echoed in the closed carriage, his anger a palpable thing. He turned to face her, his enraged face looming closer to her in the dark shadows.

"What?"

"It was nothing! I did what I was supposed to do. I told him you had the necklace and had no intention of giving it to him. And I told him you were close to discovering the traitor's identity. Now leave me alone!"

Claire clenched her fists in her lap. Damn him! They had less than one week to find the necklace, and she didn't have the slightest idea where Hunt had hidden it.

"What deal were you attempting to make?"

Claire was ready to shout her denial when the carriage stopped. The major jumped down to the street, then turned to help her. She didn't look at him. She couldn't. She knew he expected her to confide in him. Expected her to play the part he'd assigned her, then yield to his better judgment when any decisions had to be made. But it wasn't *his* brother Roseneau was holding hostage. It wasn't his life that had been destroyed.

She felt his hands at her waist, touching her, helping her, and she ignored the strange swirling in the pit of her stomach.

The second her feet hit the ground, she spun past him and raced to the house. She needed space. Needed to be alone so she could think. So she could search the house more thoroughly.

Oh, she wished Barnaby were here. Wished things were different and she could confide in the major. She was desperate to give her problems over to him.

Claire sped up the short walk, then through the open door Watkins held for her. The major was close on her heels. She knew it even though he hadn't made a sound.

It was strange how she felt his presence. Even Hunt's nearness hadn't been this powerful. But Hunt had never held her like the major had. Hunt had never comforted her the way the major had. And Hunt knew what the major hadn't discovered yet. Hunt had found out what the major would never know.

She didn't stop to hand Watkins her cloak, but walked across the entry room toward the stairs.

"Claire."

She continued on her way up the stairs.

"Claire. Stop."

Claire halted, then turned to face him.

He was close. Not close enough to touch her, but close enough that she could see the fire in his steel-gray eyes. Close enough to feel the power that radiated from his towering strength.

She held his gaze, daring him to question her further. Her mind was made up. She would do this on her own. She would battle Roseneau with the only artillery she had. With the only means at her disposal. There was nothing the major could do to help her except give over the necklace. And she knew he wouldn't if he had it.

"I'm tired." She started to turn away from him, but the lift of his hand stopped her.

"Open it."

He held the package the servant girl had brought out to them. A pretty little box wrapped in gold paper and tied with a deep burgundy ribbon. She didn't want it. Maybe tomorrow she could face the gift

Roseneau intended her to have. The first of many gifts she would receive for services rendered. But she didn't want to see it tonight.

"Open it!"

She gave him her most defiant look, then snatched the package out of his hand. She pulled at the ribbon, whipping it free. It fell to the floor. She tore at the gold paper with little care. It fluttered down with the ribbon. When the long, flat box was unwrapped, she looked him in the eyes, then tossed the lid in the air and held the box out to him.

She didn't want to see what Roseneau had given her. Didn't want to see what value he put on what she'd agreed to do for him. So she kept her gaze focused on the major's face.

His reaction was unmistakable, but not the one she anticipated. He did not look at the contents of the box as if he was impressed or amazed, but as if he were shocked. Puzzled. Repulsed.

"Claire?"

He reached for the box, taking it from her hands. It was almost as if he wanted to hide it from her. She looked down. Looked at the scrap of cloth she knew had once been ivory linen with the letters *AL/MH* embroidered in the corner. One of a matching set of three handkerchiefs she'd given Alex last Christmas with the initials *AL/MH*, Alexander Linscott, Marquess of Halverston. The handkerchief was lying in the bottom of the box, soaked in blood.

"No!"

Claire clamped her hands over her mouth to muffle the scream she couldn't stop. Her legs threatened to go out from beneath her while her body trembled like a leaf blowing in a gale storm. The major put down the box and held her, but Claire was oblivious to his arms around her or his hands caressing her.

She had Roseneau's answer. She'd failed. If she didn't give him the necklace, Alex would die.

Chapter 16

"Claire!"

Sam guided Claire to the base of the stairs, picked her up in his arms, and carried her to the nearest room. Watkins rushed ahead of him and opened the door to the downstairs study. Sam stepped inside and placed her on the nearest sofa. She trembled and gasped for air. Sam was suddenly frightened for her.

"Claire."

He reached for her hand and held it. Her fingers shook in his; her lips were pressed tight and colorless.

"Claire, what is it? Whose handkerchief is that in the box?"

She looked up at him. Her face was as pale as fine porcelain, her eyes filled with terror. "It's Alex's. Oh, God help him. It's all my fault."

Sam turned to the butler. "Bring me a glass of brandy." Watkins raced to get the brandy. "What does your brother have to do with this, Claire?"

"The handkerchief is his. His initials are on it—Alexander Linscott, the Marquess of Halverston."

Sam mumbled a harsh curse as Watkins handed him a glass. "Here, drink this," he said, lifting the brandy to her lips. She looked at it as if she'd never held a glass of brandy before, as if she had no idea what to do with it. He tipped it and let her swallow.

"Tell me what's happened. Everything."

Her tears flowed freely now, streaming down her cheeks as her body trembled. "He has him. Roseneau has Alex," she said through her sobs. "He told me tonight he wouldn't release him until I gave him the necklace."

Sam tried to absorb her words. *Roseneau has her brother.* This was why she was so intent on finding the necklace. Why she couldn't let anyone else find it. Why hadn't he realized that greed wasn't the reason she wanted it?

She twisted her hands in her lap. "I never should have lied to him. I should have told the truth so he knew we didn't have it and couldn't give it to him."

"It wouldn't have made any difference."

She flashed him a hostile glare. "How do you know? It might have."

"Roseneau isn't that benevolent of a man."

"But if he knew we didn't have it, maybe he would have agreed to my bargain and let Alex go. Oh, God! What have I done?"

Sam's heart skipped a beat. "What do you mean, maybe he would have agreed to your bargain?"

She pounded a fist against her thigh as she rocked back and forth on the settee. "Nothing. It doesn't matter. That's why he sent the handkerchief. To tell me he wouldn't agree to anything I offered."

Every nerve in Sam's body snapped. She'd tried to make Roseneau an offer. But what did she have that he might want? She didn't have the necklace. She didn't have the papers. She had nothing except—

"Bloody hell! You offered to trade places with your brother. What the hell were you thinking?"

"I was trying to get my brother back!"

"Why didn't you come to me? Why didn't you tell me Roseneau had your brother?"

"Because you couldn't help me. No one could. Not without the necklace."

Sam looked at her and knew why she hadn't come to him. Knew that he'd made it plain he wouldn't give the necklace up just to save one man. Even if that man were was brother.

"Watkins. Go find Lieutenant Honeywell."

"Yes, Major."

"Take one more sip," he said to Claire, lifting the glass to her lips.

She did and nearly choked on the swallow.

Sam waited for her to catch her breath, then dabbed at her tears with a handkerchief he had in his pocket. She lifted her gaze to meet his, her eyes filled with pleading, with fright. "Please, help me."

Sam nodded and set the glass on a nearby table. When he turned back to her, he unclasped the linen frog at her neck and slipped her cloak from her shoulders. "How long has Roseneau had your brother?"

"Since I was attacked. The man Roseneau sent told me they had him and wouldn't release him until I handed over the necklace."

Sam whispered a muffled oath while he slipped her gloves from her quivering hands. "Does Barnaby know?"

"I told him when he was here last night."

Sam got up from the settee and paced the room. "Where is Barnaby now?"

"I don't know."

"Did he say what he was going to do?"

She shook her head and tried to answer, but her voice broke when she tried to speak. But he'd heard the fear in her words. Seen the trepidation on her face.

He raked his fingers through his hair in frustration and walked across the room. With one arm braced against the fireplace, he stared into the flickering flames. Bloody hell! They only had a few days.

"Roseneau won't kill your brother until he's certain we won't ransom the necklace for him. This was a warning. His trump card. He'll wait now for us to answer him."

"How?"

Sam was saved from having to lie to her when Honeywell burst through the door.

"What is it, Major? Watkins said—" Honeywell's eyes grew wide when he looked at Claire.

Sam turned back to Claire. "We need to find your brother, my lady. Does he have a town house here in London?"

"On Kensington Square."

Sam issued Lieutenant Honeywell an order. "Go to Lord Barnaby's place on Kensington Square, Lieutenant. See if he's there."

"Yes, sir. And if he's not there?"

"Go to Roseneau's town house on Berkely Square. See what you can discover. Be careful, though. Don't let anyone see you."

"Right, Major."

The door closed behind Honeywell before Sam could bring himself to face her. He knew what he'd see on her face. The pleading look that said she wanted his promise to hand over the necklace if they found it. A promise he could never make.

"Why don't you go upstairs and lie down for a while? I'll send someone for you when your brother arrives."

"I'm not tired. I can use the time until Barnaby gets here to continue our search."

"You're exhausted. What good will you do anyone if you become ill?"

She bolted from the settee and glared at him. "What good will my resting do Alex? If *you* need to rest, feel free to do so, Major. I intend to look for the necklace."

Sam held his breath and forced his temper to cool. She wasn't thinking clearly, wasn't in any condition to know what was best for her. She'd gone through too much in the last few weeks. That must be it, or she wouldn't have tried to handle everything on her own. She would have come to him a long time ago.

"You and Roseneau were never lovers, were you?"

She turned on him with the most blatant anger he'd ever witnessed. "I loathe the man."

"And at his ball? When I saw you in his arms?"

The look of surprise on her face was genuine. "Roseneau caught me unawares. He made advances that"—she paused and took a breath—"that I was unable to stop. Luckily, Barnaby was keeping an eye on me and interrupted us before things went too far."

Sam swiped his hand across his face and thought of all the times he'd accused her of being unfaithful. Of having an affair with Roseneau. "Why didn't you tell me?"

"Tell you what? That there was nothing between Roseneau and me? That finding the necklace was a matter of life and death? That I couldn't let you have it when we did find it?" She clenched her hands at her sides. "I did!"

With a lethal glare, she stormed across the room. They were in Hunt's study, the room that most reminded them of Sam's friend, Claire's husband. The two side walls were lined with books, the shelves running from ceiling to floor. The back wall was made up of tall, multipaned windows that looked out onto the garden behind the house, a garden that, if it were daylight, would boast well-tended flowers in full bloom.

A door took up the middle of the front wall, the empty spaces on either side of the opening decorated by two huge paintings, one of which Sam was certain was a Gainsborough original. This whole room represented the Marquess of Huntingdon's life, from the books on the shelves to the paintings on the wall to the maps and charts on a table in the corner. This was what his friend's existence had consisted of.

Sam felt a pang of regret and loss. Then he wondered what he would leave behind if something happened to him. And whether or not his death would matter to anyone.

Even Hunt's presence, in time, would be of little consequence. Once the people whose lives he'd touched were no longer here to remind the world of his existence, what would be left behind to tell future generations of the man he'd been? Hunt had left no legacy. No children. No heir. Even his name would be extinct after Lady Huntingdon was not alive to carry it. Or when she remarried and forsook the Huntingdon title to take on her new husband's name.

Sam felt a stab of anger that things had turned out as they had. That Hunt's life had yielded so much—yet so little. But was his own life any different?

He looked at the woman sitting on the floor, opening each book in search of the necklace. She'd been Hunt's wife. Had known him better than anyone. But what did that matter when she was left alone with nothing but her memories?

Sam realized how little he really knew her. How wrong he'd been about her. And how much he admired her.

The need to be with her and protect her intensified. He'd never had these feelings before. Never wanted to let anyone get close enough to be a part of his life. Not like he wanted Claire to be a part of his.

He suddenly realized these feelings for her had been growing for a long time. From the second he'd found her after Roseneau's henchman had hurt her. When he'd sat at her bedside hour after hour and cared for her. When he'd comforted her and held her in his arms. And later, when he'd kissed her.

If he would have allowed his heart to speak instead of his mind, he would have known then that he wanted her. Even though he knew how impossible it was for him to ever have her. He was a bloody spy. The same as Hunt had been.

He mentally shook himself, facing head-on a dilemma that had only one outcome. No matter how he looked at it, the situation both he and Claire had been thrown into could end only one way. He had a duty to perform, for both his fellow man and his country, and that duty was to do whatever it took to bring about a quicker end to the war. He could never let his feelings for Claire get in the way of what he had to do.

With every ounce of his will, he concentrated again on the task before him. "When you and Hunt returned from France, what did Hunt do?"

"I told you already," she said, thumbing through another book. When she finished, she put the book back on the shelf. "We returned home late afternoon. We changed, ate a cold supper, then Hunt came in here. I didn't see him for the rest of the evening. When I came down the following morning, he was still working in here. I don't think he'd slept all night." She pulled another book from the shelf and opened it.

"Did he say anything? Anything at all about the necklace? Or the papers?"

She shook her head, then put the book in her hands back on the shelf and reached for another. "I sent a tray in to him because he hadn't joined me for breakfast. About an hour later he had his valet pack a bag and he left."

"Did he say where he was going?"

"He said he had estate business he needed to take care of."

"How long was he gone?"

"A month. Maybe longer. I can't remember."

"A month? He left you here alone for a month?"

"He did that often when he had estate business. Now I know that excuse also included work he did for the government."

"Did he say anything at all before he left?"

She shoved herself to her feet and moved to the other side of the room. "No. But that was not uncommon. He rarely did."

Sam watched her pull out a book, look inside, and shove it back with more force than before. He knew he shouldn't ask her more, but he had no choice. Time was running out.

"He rarely did what? Inform you where he was going or when he would return?"

"Both, Major. Does that surprise you? Hunt told me very little of his business dealings. He spoke even less of things that mattered to him. His purpose was obviously to keep me in the dark regarding anything in which he was involved. It was only when we were in public, when the two of us were on display and he had to act his part, that he pretended we were the perfect couple. Now are you satisfied?"

Sam stood in shock, his feet rooted to the floor. He watched her whip books from a shelf, open them with an angry flip, then shove them back in place.

Sam knew she'd passed the point of exhaustion long ago. She was frantic with worry. And desperate. Perhaps that was why she said what she just had. Had exposed certain pieces of her personal life she normally wouldn't have revealed.

"This isn't Hunt's fault," Sam said, as if he knew how angry she was with Hunt.

She slammed a book against the floor. "Isn't it? Then whose fault is it?"

Sam didn't have an answer for her. He wasn't even sure why he'd said that, other than he'd felt a need to defend Hunt.

"He loved you, Cl—"

"Don't!" She held out her hand to stop him. "You can say a lot of things. But don't tell me my husband loved me. I don't care what you thought he said. He—"

She clamped her hand over her mouth and hissed through clenched teeth as she took a deep breath. When she spoke again, her voice was laced with bitterness.

"Just. Don't."

Sam watched her continue searching through the books. How could her marriage to Hunt have been anything like what she was describing? Hadn't Hunt's dying words been that he loved her?

"I don't understand what you're telling me," he said, watching her open another book.

"Don't try, Major. It's not important."

"Maybe I think it is."

She glared at him with a look that left no room for debate. "Perhaps I don't consider my relationship with my husband anyone's business but my own."

Her face was pale, her lips drawn tight. Sam knew she was on the verge of collapse. He stared at her as she turned to continue her search. She staggered, and Sam bolted forward to catch her. He wrapped her in his arms.

She allowed him to hold her long enough to gain her balance, then tried to push away from him, but he refused to let her go. "You can't keep this up for much longer," he whispered in her ear.

"I don't have a choice. I have to find the necklace. Roseneau's going to kill Alex if I don't."

"We'll find him first."

Sam kept her in his arms, moving one hand over her back while running the fingers of his other hand through her thick, golden hair. He cradled her head in his palm and nestled her close.

She snaked her arms around his waist. Not out of instinct, or maybe it was, but more than likely it was because she didn't know where else to place them. She pressed her palms flat against his back and leaned closer. It was as if she needed him to hold her as much as he wanted to have her in his arms. "Tell me about your marriage to Hunt?"

She shook her head. Her body stiffened against him. The subject of her marriage to Hunt was obviously off-limits.

He rubbed his hand over her again until she relaxed in his arms. He'd never felt such consuming fire when he'd been with any other woman, and he'd had more than his share in his nearly thirty years of bachelorhood. But none of them affected him like she did.

He tried to ignore the fiery heat that spread through his body. Told himself in a dozen different ways that he shouldn't hold her like this, that he shouldn't think the thoughts he did when she was near. But none of his warnings mattered. None of the rules he'd set down for himself seemed to have any substance when she was in his arms. He knew she felt it, too.

She kept her body pressed against him, her thighs touching his, her torso next to his, her breasts moving against his chest with each labored breath she took. It was magical, the heat that spread from her body to his, from his body to hers. He needed to have her, to taste her. To feel her melt in his embrace.

Sam held her tight with one hand and moved the other over her shoulder and down her arm. Her waist was narrow and he spanned it easily, then worked his hands up her torso until his fingers grazed the underside of her breasts. He wanted to touch them, to feel their heavy weight in the palm of his hand.

She took a deep breath, as if she realized the danger they were in. Her arms dropped from around his waist and skimmed up his chest, palms flat, fingers splayed. And she pushed against him, gently at first, then with more force.

"Don't. Please. We can't—"

Sam halted her words by placing his finger over her lips. Her face was tilted upward, her eyes wide, filled with wonder, her lips slightly open as if searching for an objection that would fight her desire. And Sam couldn't wait any longer. He lowered his head and caught her sigh in a kiss.

Chapter 17

He was going to kiss her.

Claire started to push him away, then stopped. She was unprepared for the pleasure of his kiss. She had never felt such pull, such warmth spread through her body. It reached every part of her. Waves of desire swirled low in her stomach. Her need to be touched and held grew in intensity.

She knew she shouldn't let him do this. Shouldn't allow him to touch her, hold her, kiss her. But Heaven help her, what he did to her was nothing short of earth-shattering.

She felt so safe in his arms, so alive and wanted when his hands touched her, when his fingers moved over her. It was almost as if she could begin again, as if he were showing her what it could be like with someone who desired her. As if this time . . .

He deepened his kiss. Hot, fiery spirals swirled deep in her belly. Her mind rushed in confusion.

She tried to match Sam's efforts, amazed that she'd never known a man's kiss could have this effect.

She'd never dreamed a man's touch could be so consuming. Hunt's kisses had been quick, cold, unfeeling. His lips pressed to her forehead. Or her cheek. But never to her lips.

Memories of Hunt's avoidance of intimacy struck her full force, filling her with a desperation to experience what she'd lived without every day of her marriage.

Sam's mouth moved over hers, tasting her lips, drinking from her. Her legs weakened beneath her; her whole body tingled with a sensation she didn't understand. Her stomach churned as if she'd been thrown into a raging whirlpool.

With shocking clarity, she realized she wanted this. She desired this. She didn't want to live another minute without knowing what it felt like to be held and kissed by someone who cared for her.

Time ceased to exist. Everything ceased except Sam's lips moving over hers, his hands holding her, and his body pressed against her. With a desperation she didn't understand, she moved her hands over him, feeling the corded muscles across his shoulders and down his arms. It was as if she couldn't touch enough of him, as if she suddenly realized how empty and lacking her marriage had been. She was being given a glimpse of the wonders Sam's kisses promised, and she was desperate to experience more.

He kissed her again, drinking deeply, then broke their kiss and lifted his mouth from hers. She didn't want him to, and she pulled him closer.

"Sam?"

"Someone's coming," he said without releasing his hold.

His breathing was heavy and labored, and hers was no different. She listened to the commotion at the front door and struggled to regain her composure before they were found out.

She stepped out of Sam's arms as Barnaby threw open the door.

"Claire? Are you all right?"

Barnaby crossed the room and grabbed her by the shoulders. He held her at arm's length and looked at her as if he feared the worst.

"It's not me, Barn. It's Alex. Roseneau sent me one of the handkerchiefs I embroidered for him last Christmas. It's all bloody." Claire clamped her hand over her mouth. "Oh, Barn. They've hurt him."

"Sh," Barnaby said, pulling her close. "It'll be all right."

Major Bennett stepped toward them. "I'm glad Honeywell found you."

"He was just leaving Roseneau's home," Lieutenant Honeywell volunteered. "From the back."

The major's brows arched, which only emphasized the frown on his forehead. "What were you doing at Roseneau's house?"

"Paying a visit."

"I hardly think so. Roseneau isn't home."

The major waited and finally Barnaby answered, "A perfect time, then."

"Perfect for what?"

"To look for anything that might tell us where Roseneau has Alex."

The major's body stiffened as if he couldn't believe what he'd heard. He finally spoke. "Did you find anything?"

Barnaby reached into his pocket and pulled out a sheet of paper. He handed it to Sam.

"What is it?" Claire asked, her heart pounding faster. She moved to the desk where the major had taken the paper and was reading it beneath a lamp. She stepped closer and looked over his shoulder.

"It's a sheet from Roseneau's ledger. There's an entry to a Clyde Biggins, made just before Alex was kidnapped. It's for rent on a warehouse in Southwark."

Claire looked up at Barnaby. "Is that where you think they've got him?"

He shrugged his shoulders. "It's a place to start."

The major folded the paper and put it in a drawer in Hunt's desk. Next, he opened a side drawer and took out a gun. He checked to make sure it was loaded, then put it in his pocket. He closed the drawer, then turned to Barnaby. "Stay here with your sister. Lieutenant Honeywell and I will see what's there."

Claire saw Barnaby's shoulders tense, saw his eyes turn black with fury.

"You, Major, can go to hell. It's *my* brother who is possibly in that warehouse and *I'm* going to get him out. If you insist on coming with me, that's your choice, but I'll not stay behind like some pampered dandy."

"Your sister needs—"

"Then *you* stay with her. You've spent little time elsewhere the last two weeks."

"Stop it! Both of you." Claire wanted to shake them. "No one needs to stay with me. But someone needs to get Alex. He's hurt. He might even be—"

Claire stopped. She couldn't say the words. Couldn't even allow herself to think the thought.

"Honeywell," the major ordered. "Stay here and guard the house."

"Yes, sir."

"Watkins, have someone bring the carriage round back. We might need it to bring Lord Halverston back. And tell them to hurry. It will be dawn in a couple of hours. We've got to be in and out of that warehouse before it's light."

"Yes, Major," Watkins said and ran from the room.

Claire watched as the major opened another drawer and took out a knife and another gun. Neither of these was Hunt's. The major must have put them there when he moved in.

When he was ready, he turned to Barnaby. "Do you have a gun?"

Claire saw her brother smile, then pat the inside of his jacket. The major nodded, then walked to the door. "Do you know how to use it?" he said when he passed Barnaby.

"Sometimes I get lucky, Major, and hit what I'm aiming at."

The major ignored Barnaby's sarcasm and walked across the room. Her fear must have shown because Barnaby placed a hand on her shoulder and squeezed. "Don't worry, Claire. Nothing will happen to either of us."

"Or Alex. I want all of you to come back safely. I'm not sure I could go on if anything happened to any of you."

She didn't want to look at the major when she said that, but she did. It was as if her gaze was drawn to his.

In answer to her words, his eyes slowly moved to her lips. His message was clear. He knew their kiss had meant something to her.

He gave her a final look, then issued her butler an order on his way out. "Watkins. Have a room ready in case the marquess needs one."

"Of course, sir. We'll have everything he needs."

And the major was gone.

Barnaby gave her a quick kiss on the cheek before he followed the major from the room. The carriage was waiting at the back, and Barnaby opened the door and climbed inside while the major climbed atop and took the reins.

Claire watched until they were out of sight.

"You'd best go inside, my lady," Honeywell suggested as he scanned the street.

She slowly went back into the house. She told Watkins to have plenty of hot water and bandages ready, and to wake Maude in a little while and tell her they might have need of her.

Lieutenant Honeywell stood guard at the door while Claire walked back into the room that had been Hunt's study and continued her search for the necklace.

Chapter 18

Sam stopped the carriage close to the warehouse and jumped to the ground. Barnaby was already waiting for him.

"How do you want to handle this, Major?"

Sam breathed a sigh of relief, happy he didn't have to argue with Barnaby Linscott. He'd been afraid Claire's brother would insist on taking control.

Sam looked at the old wooden structure in one of the seedier parts of London. It was a single-story building that looked like it was about to collapse in on itself.

A large double door took up most of the front, with high windows on either side. The windows might have allowed sunlight to penetrate the interior of the building had they not been so caked with dirt and grime. A narrow alley separated the building from a neighboring building, which didn't appear to be in any better condition.

This wasn't a building Sam thought many people might even notice unless they had a specific reason to search it out. A perfect spot for Roseneau to hide the Marquess of Halverston.

"There are probably two entrances. I'll take the back and you watch the front. If your brother's here, he's more than likely in the back."

"Maybe we should stay together, then."

"No. I don't know how many guards there are."

Sam pulled his pistol from inside his jacket and checked it. Then he reached for his knife. "We can't let anyone escape to tell Roseneau his prisoner is gone. With any luck, he won't find out for a few days."

"And by then, the Russian representatives will have arrived?"

Sam's gaze darted to Barnaby. "How do you know about that?"

Barnaby shrugged. "It's a matter of being in the right place at the right time. Or knowing the right people. For instance, who would ever have guessed the esteemed Marquess of Huntingdon was a spy? Or that the two of you worked so closely together?"

Sam studied Lord Barnaby and fought the niggling questions that consumed him. "Yes. Who?"

Claire's brother was a mystery. And Sam hated mysteries to which he didn't know the answers. He gave Barnaby another look, then took off his jacket and threw it in the carriage. Removing one's jacket was a trick Hunt had taught him. It made moving in a fight much easier.

Sam slipped his knife and gun into the waistband of his pants where they would be in easy reach. When he finished, he turned to discover Claire's brother had done the same.

Another coincidence Sam found unsettling.

"Give me about five minutes to get inside, then be ready. Don't let anyone get past you."

"Yes, Major," Barnaby said. "Good luck."

Sam took one step and stopped. "You know, there's a good chance they've already moved him."

Barnaby nodded. "I know. I would have if I were Roseneau. He can't chance us finding Alex until he has the necklace."

Sam felt the weight of Barnaby's words. As much as he wanted this to be over, he knew the odds weren't in their favor. He gave Barnaby a final nod, then checked the gun at his waist and walked away.

He stayed in the shadows as long as he could, then crossed the street. They still had an hour or so until they no longer had the advantage of darkness. That would be more than enough time. Unless something went wrong.

When he reached the warehouse, he stepped around the corner of the facade. A long cluttered alley stretched the length of the building and Sam hugged the rough wood until he came to a back exit. Two dirty four-paned windows were high off the ground on either side of the door. Sam moved a barrel beneath one so he could look inside.

A faint light burned from a lantern inside about halfway down the length of the cavernous room. Two men rushed about, gathering their belongings and stuffing supplies into a burlap bag. It was obvious they were preparing to leave.

A makeshift bed lay in the corner of the room, but in the darkness, Sam couldn't make out whether or not anyone lay beneath the heap of blankets. A gnawing lump in the pit of his stomach told him that even if the Marquess of Halverston were there, he may already be dead.

The fact that the men were cleaning up to erase any evidence that they'd been there could indicate that they were preparing to move the marquess—or his body. If so, he'd arrived just in time.

Sam tried the window, praying it wasn't locked. It was. He moved the barrel to the other window and pushed. The window moved—not far, but enough to indicate it wasn't locked. Sam pushed harder. It opened just far enough that he could squeeze through.

He looked below him to the spot inside the building where he'd land. Boards and boxes and a pile of debris Sam couldn't distinguish in the dark cluttered the floor. He pulled his gun from his waistband. The element of surprise would be gone the minute he vaulted through the window. There was no way he could fall without being heard.

Sam pushed up the window a little farther to keep assessing the situation. This wasn't going to be easy, but he had surprise on his side.

He hefted his body to the sill of the open window. With his gun in his hand, he leaped through the opening. He landed hard on the floor and immediately rolled to the side.

The man closest to where he landed spun around and fired. Sam heard the bullet whiz past his head. He dodged in the opposite direction as another shot echoed in the long, empty building.

He had hoped to startle them enough to get closer, but he wasn't so lucky. An uneasy feeling shot through him as the second man spun toward him with a gun in his hand and fired.

Sam felt a burning pain in his upper arm and dove to the ground. The first man lunged forward and Sam rolled to the side as the long blade of the man's knife swiped downward.

Sam leaped to his feet and rammed a fist into the first man's face, then went after the second gunman. But that man was ready for him, and Sam had to back up a step when he circled him with the expertise of a back-alley fighter.

An empty box prevented Sam from moving freely and he paused to kick it out of his way, then pulled his knife from his waist and brought it in front of him. The man stepped back, as if evaluating Sam's skill. Sam saw a wariness in his gaze that bordered on respect; then a broad, malevolent smile showed a toothless mouth when the man noticed the blood darkening the sleeve of Sam's shirt. He growled loud enough for Sam to hear, then moved to attack Sam's injured side.

Sam avoided one onslaught after another, knowing he had to choose the perfect time to strike. And it had to be soon. He'd lost too much blood already and couldn't waste the little energy he had left.

Sam spun to the side and slashed his knife downward. This time he hit muscle and flesh. The man moaned and lunged forward, knocking the knife from Sam's hand. Before Sam could reach for it, the man grabbed him from behind and pulled Sam's arms back. His knees buckled beneath him as spikes of red-hot pain shot through him.

Sam took a deep breath, then jerked free and threw his elbow back, catching the man in the gut. The man doubled over in pain. Sam spun around, knowing this was his only chance to take him down. He brought his fist up beneath the man's chin and punched him with all his strength. The man fell to the floor, his head cocked at an unnatural angle.

Sam spun around to fight the other man but before he could attack, the man caught Sam across the shoulder. A searing pain sucked the air from his chest and he fought to stay on his feet.

Sam sagged to the side, then dove for the closest weapon. He knew he probably wouldn't make it in time, but he refused to give in without a fight. He reached, grabbed the knife, and spun around. Then stopped short. The man stood in front of him with a pistol aimed at the middle of his chest.

"You're a dead man," the man whispered, and then squeezed the trigger.

Sam dove to the side as a shot echoed in the empty warehouse. But he felt no pain. Instead, the man in front of him stared in wide-eyed amazement, then sank to the floor.

A small black circle of blood on the man's back grew larger, and his open eyes stared in sightless death.

Sam lifted his gaze to focus through the murky darkness to the place where Barnaby stood with a pistol in his hand.

"Are you all right?" Barnaby took a step toward him and looked at his arm.

"I'm fine," Sam answered, trying to ignore the burning pain that ran down his back. "But we need to get out of here."

Time was of the essence now. Three gunshots wouldn't go unnoticed for long.

He cast a glance to the pile of blankets in the corner of the warehouse. "See if your brother's here."

Barnaby gave him little more than a cursory nod, then raced past him. Sam followed, keeping his arm as immobile as he could. He watched Barnaby hunker down and pull back the covers. Sam didn't need to look to see that the makeshift pallet was empty—Barnaby's vile oath confirmed it.

"We're too late. He's gone." Barnaby bolted to his feet and kicked the blankets with his foot. "The bastards have moved him."

Sam ground his teeth together, both from the pain as well as regret. He'd so hoped they'd be in time. For Claire as much as anyone. But he should have known when Roseneau sent the bloody handkerchief that he'd move him.

Sam stepped past Barnaby and knelt beside the blankets. "Feel this," he said, moving so Barnaby could put his hand where Sam indicated.

"Bloody hell! It's still warm. That means we only missed them by minutes."

"It also means your brother's still alive."

Barnaby's chest heaved. "We have to find him."

"We will," Sam said, lifting the closest blanket. "Get that lantern."

Barnaby brought back the lantern from the other side of the room.

"Hold it closer."

Barnaby moved the lantern to shine directly overhead, and Sam leaned down to get a closer look.

"What is it, Major?"

"Blood. Fresh."

"Ah, hell."

Sam lifted the blankets one by one and shook them out. Something heavy clattered to the floor. Sam picked it up and handed it to Barnaby.

"It's Alex's. His ring. He always wore it."

Sam struggled to his feet, ignoring the blinding pain shooting through his arm and shoulder. "He left it to tell us he was here. Now we'll just have to figure out where they took him."

"You make it sound easy."

Sam grimaced. "Nothing's ever easy, so we'll have to rely on help."

"From whom?"

"From Roseneau himself. We're going to let Roseneau lead us to your brother."

"How are we going to do that?"

Sam braced his hand against the small wooden table in the center of the room. "Roseneau still wants the necklace. He knows he's a dead man without it. As long as he thinks we have it, your brother's safe. We'll have to let him think we're prepared to give it to him."

"But we don't have it."

"Then we'll have to stall until we do. The Russians are scheduled to arrive in England next Thursday. Roseneau will want the necklace in his possession by then."

"And you intend to make sure Roseneau doesn't go unpunished for the role he played, don't you, Major?

Sam leaned heavier against the table as an uncomfortable tension stretched between them. "He deserves to pay for the lives he's taken. The same as our traitor."

"What about Claire?" Barnaby asked on a sigh.

Sam thought of how desperate Claire was to save her brother. She thought they had a choice. But they didn't. Not getting here in time to rescue her brother took away all their options.

Unfortunately, if Barnaby Linscott sided with his sister, Sam would be fighting a much more complicated battle. He needed to find out before he took another breath. He braced himself, trying to ignore the pain that was worsening, and faced his adversary squarely. "Are you of the same mind as your sister?"

The grim set of Barnaby's features evidenced a regret that was bone deep. He shook his head. "Alex would never allow even one brave soldier's death to be on his conscience. Let alone thousands. But Claire's a woman. And she loves Alex. She'll do whatever she believes she has to do to save him."

"Then we'll have to be certain she isn't put in a position to make such a decision." Sam shoved himself away from the table and took a step toward the door. "You and I know she wouldn't be able to live with herself no matter which choice she made."

Sam walked across the empty warehouse, his boots thudding heavily on the rough wooden floorboards. An uncomfortable weight pressed against his chest. Somewhere in the back of his mind he wondered if he'd be able to live with the decision he knew he had to make—the decision that might cost Claire's brother his life.

Barnaby followed him out of the warehouse and down the alley to the waiting carriage. Sam was thankful they'd brought it to take the Marquess of Halverston home. At least he wouldn't have to try to stay atop a horse.

"How badly are you hurt?" Barnaby asked as he opened the door and helped Sam inside.

"I'll be better when Bronnely gets me sewed up."

Barnaby moved his gaze to Sam's shoulder. "Let's get you home," he said, the frown on his face darkening.

The carriage rocked when Barnaby climbed atop, and Sam sank back against the cushions as they took off down the street. He closed his eyes and tried to block out the pain. Just as he tried to block out the disappointment he knew he'd see on Claire's face when they arrived without the Marquess of Halverston.

Maybe it was the pain. Maybe it was the disappointment of finding the warehouse empty and knowing they were no closer to finding Halverston now than they'd been before. But Sam couldn't stop reliving the night Hunt had died in his arms. What the hell had he meant when he'd said she had it? When with his dying breath he'd told Sam that Claire had the necklace?

Sam swiped the film of perspiration from his forehead and dropped his head back against the cushion. Even though she didn't realize it, Claire must have the necklace. And the papers. Hunt must have hidden them before he left. Or after he returned home. Otherwise he wouldn't have warned Sam to protect Claire. It had to be in the house somewhere.

Sam ground his teeth as another stab of pain shot through his shoulder. Roseneau had barely gotten Halverston away in time tonight. He wouldn't be so careless again. Nor would he give them another chance to get so close to rescuing him.

They were running out of time.

Chapter 19

Claire paced in front of the window, waiting for the carriage to arrive. The sun was just beginning its rise above the horizon, but the streets were still deathly quiet. None of the nearby homes showed any activity. It was far from fashionable for any of the nobility to be up at this hour of the day. But Claire didn't care about anyone else. She only cared about the carriage that would bring her brothers and Sam home to her.

She looked down the street again and her heart raced in her chest. A carriage turned the corner. She gave a little cry when the carriage slowed. Then she raced toward the front door when it stopped and Barnaby jumped down from atop.

"They're here!" she cried to Watkins. The servant opened the door, then rushed out to help Barnaby. Claire ran out onto the portico and stopped at the top of the stairs. Barn and Watkins were helping someone to the ground.

The major.

Her heart thundered in her chest and she turned around to a waiting footman. "Go for Doctor Bronnely. And hurry, James!" She turned to the few servants who had refused to go to bed until they knew if the marquess was safe. "Go ready the major's room," she ordered. "And bring up plenty of water and towels."

The servants scurried to do her bidding. Claire rushed forward as the major walked through the doorway. His left arm hung limply at his side and a dark circle stained his shirt. A sheen of perspiration covered his face and his lips were stretched taut in a grimace against the pain.

Claire reached out to steady him. "How badly are you hurt?"

He took a shaky breath before he answered. "Not bad. I may need Bronnely though."

"I've already sent for him," she said. "He should be here soon. Can you make it up the stairs?"

He nodded and kept his feet moving.

Claire walked beside him, then moved closer to him when she realized how badly he'd been injured.

"We were too late," he said. He reached for the railing with his uninjured hand. "Roseneau had already moved him."

Claire glanced back at Barnaby. There was a serious look on his face.

"He's alive, Claire. At least we know that."

Claire nodded and took each step with the major. His breathing was increasingly labored. Claire knew the inordinate amount of effort it took for him to stay on his feet. The minute he reached the room, he staggered, and she and Barn struggled to catch him before he fell.

"Hold steady, Major," Barn said, loosening the top button on the major's shirt. He then took his knife and slit the material down the front. When he'd removed the major's shirt, he lowered him to the bed. "Bring up some whiskey, Watkins," Barnaby ordered, then he grabbed one of the towels a servant brought.

"Press this cloth hard against his back and hold it, Claire. Can you do that?"

Claire looked at the blood-soaked shirt and swallowed hard. "Yes."

The major groaned when Barnaby pushed against her hand to indicate how much pressure he wanted her to apply. He stepped aside, and the wounds on the major's shoulder and arm were exposed.

A knot clenched in Claire's stomach when she looked at the bruised, gaping flesh. She sucked in a breath before increasing the pressure on the worst part of the wound where blood still seeped out. She heard a soft moan and knew she'd hurt him.

"Harder, Claire."

Claire pushed harder.

"Harder!"

Beads of perspiration covered her forehead as Claire held the cloth to the major's back. "It's not stopping, Barn."

"Yes, it is. Just keep pushing."

Claire leaned forward and pushed so hard the muscles in her arms ached. And she kept pushing. Until Doctor Bronnely walked through the door.

"What have we got here, Sam?" he said, setting down his bag and pulling back the cloth Claire had been holding so tight.

"A scratch," the major answered through clenched teeth. "What took you so long?"

"I was having tea with the Queen and hated to leave." Bronnely cleaned around the edges of the wound at the major's shoulder, then said, "I'll need some water and some brandy."

Claire ran to the washstand and brought back a pitcher of water while Barnaby handed him the bottle Watkins had brought up. Bronnely poured a healthy measure into the glass and gave it to the major. He drank it in one long swallow.

"That is what *you* were supposed to do, my lady," the major said.

"So it was, Major. Would you like some more?"

She didn't wait for him to answer but took the bottle from the doctor, put more in the glass, and handed it to him. He swallowed it as fast as he had the first.

"I'm not nearly as brave as you," he whispered, his words not slurred half as much as she'd hoped they'd be.

"I doubt that, Major," Claire said, brushing back a strand of hair that had fallen over his brow. Her fingers paused at the side of his face to feel the rough stubble on his cheek and the hard angle of his jaw. He was so magnificently handsome that Claire's heart skipped a rapid beat.

Her hand reached for his. A blazing warmth spiraled downward through her body to settle low in her belly when his fingers grasped hers. Their grip was neither weak nor harsh. But binding.

Claire held his gaze as long as she could, until his eyes delved too deeply, possessing too much of her. The bond that held them together was startling. For a second, it frightened her. She thought he felt the same. Thought she saw it in his eyes.

God help me. When did this happen?

"Let's get this started," Bronnely said. "Help the major lie down."

Claire thought to pull her fingers away, but he wouldn't let go of her hand. And she didn't want him to. She settled in a chair Barnaby had pushed close to the bed and stayed there with Sam's large, powerful hand clasped in her smaller one.

She reached for a damp cloth and wiped the perspiration from his brow, then turned to see what Bronnely was doing. He had a bottle of liquid in his hands and was about to pour it over the major's shoulder and arm.

"This is going to burn like hell, Sam. But it'll keep out the infection."

"I'll be fine."

The major breathed in a harsh and jagged breath, as if preparing for the pain.

"Hold him," the doctor ordered Barnaby when he had the bottle over the wound. He waited until Barnaby had a solid hold, then poured the liquid up and down the major's shoulder.

The major bucked at the first wave of pain.

Claire sucked in a breath and held it. She prayed the pain wouldn't last long, but it seemed to last an eternity. The muscles twitched at his jaw and he ground his teeth in agony. But he didn't utter a sound. He held stoically still, with his hand clamped around hers.

"Done," Bronnely announced, and the major sagged in relief. Claire wiped the cloth down the side of his face, then brushed away the tears that streamed down her own. Tears for Alex. Tears for a man who'd nearly given his life to help her.

"All that needs doing is to sew you up," Bronnely said, threading a needle. Claire wasn't brave enough to see the metal point weave in and out of his torn flesh. She focused instead on his gaze, willing him to take as much of her strength as he wanted. Willing him to take whatever he needed from her. Except her heart. That she could give to no man.

She knew the instant the needle pierced his skin. His muscles tensed and his grip tightened. But he didn't cry out. She knew how desperately he wanted to. She remembered from what she'd gone through. Remembered how she'd tried to occupy her mind with anything except the needle pricking her skin and the pain. When he spoke, she knew he was trying to do the same.

"You said Hunt locked himself in his study when you returned from France, then left. Do you have any idea where he went from here?"

She shook her head. "I asked his valet if he'd given him any hint as to where he was going, and Watkins, too, but neither of them knew."

"Barnaby," he said through clenched teeth.

Barnaby stepped closer to hear him.

"Have Lieutenant Honeywell take you to a man called McCormick—"

"I won't need Honeywell's assistance, Major. I know how to reach McCormick. Honeywell's presence will be better served here. What do you want me to tell McCormick?"

The major stared at Barnaby a long time, then shook his head as if trying to clear it. As if trying to understand something. He opened his mouth to speak but closed it on a gasp and clenched his fingers tighter around Claire's. She knew the pain was becoming unbearable.

"Explain to him about your brother and the . . . necklace. But don't mention the papers. Tell him not to let Roseneau out of his sight. Roseneau's got to . . . make contact with the men who have your brother soon. Then—"

He stopped and shook his head, then gasped. Doctor Bronnely was sewing through the center of the wound, the part that was the deepest and looked the most raw.

"This is important," he continued. "Have him send more men here . . . to guard your sister. She's not safe. Roseneau might . . ."

Claire could hear the desperation in his voice and tried to reassure him. "I'm fine, Major. Barnaby's here and Lieutenant Honeywell. And it won't be long before you're well enough, too."

He was groggier, his words more slurred. "You can't take any . . . chances, Claire. Roseneau's running out of . . . time."

"I know. I'll be fine."

She looked at him and tried to fight the worry eating at her. His face was as pale as the sheet beneath him and his words barely louder than a whisper.

"Be careful, Claire. Just . . . be—"

He gasped once before his head lolled to the side, and he lost consciousness.

"Finally," Bronnely said, shaking his head. "He's the most obstinate, bull-headed man I've ever met. I had enough laudanum in that glass he should have gone under long ago. Serves him right for not cooperating."

"Will he be all right?" Claire said, staring at his pale face and the long, jagged cut down his back.

"He'll be fine. He's too stubborn not to be."

Even though Bronnely had assured her that the major would sleep all day, he hadn't. Only now, as the sun was beginning its descent, did he finally lose his battle to stay awake. At long last, Claire felt confident enough to leave him for a few minutes. She followed Barnaby out of the major's room.

"It's getting late, Claire," Barnaby said, walking down the hall at her side. "Why don't you rest for a while. You haven't left Bennett's side all day."

"I'm fine." Claire stopped in the middle of the hall. "I need to check with Lieutenant Honeywell to see if he needs anything. Did you contact McCormick?"

"Yes."

"Is he the man you and the major answer to?"

Barnaby smiled. "He's the head of the Foreign Office."

"Is that who Hunt answered to also?"

Barnaby wrapped an arm around her shoulder and led her down the hall and into her room. "Hunt didn't answer to anyone, Claire. Except himself. That's what made him so invaluable. He never worried about orders. He could do what he wanted."

"And the major?"

Barnaby took her to the other side of her bedroom, where a large cushioned chair was placed at an angle before the fireplace. After she sat, he threw a quilt over her, then squatted down in front of her.

"Be careful of Bennett, Claire," he said, cradling her hands in his. "He's not what you need right now."

Claire studied her brother's handsome face. "And just what is it you think I need?"

Barnaby pushed himself to his feet and stepped to the fireplace to put another log on the dwindling fire. "Something more than you had with Hunt. Something better that what I observed the seven years you were married."

"There's no need to wonder any longer what was wrong with my marriage. Hunt is dead."

"But you're not."

"And just what does that mean?"

"You're looking for something, Claire. But Bennett can't give it to you."

She lifted her gaze. "You're wrong, Barn. I'm not looking for anything. My marriage may not have been anything like I thought it would be, but the years I spent with Hunt taught me a valuable lesson. A lesson I don't intend to repeat."

"I'm not sure I understand."

"No. I'm sure you don't. And it's just as well."

"I just want you to be happy, Claire."

She tried to smile but wasn't sure she succeeded. "How do you judge happiness, Barn? I had more gowns than any woman needs in a lifetime. I had servants to see to my every need. I entertained lavishly and was courted by some of the most powerful people in Europe, including our Queen. What more could I want?"

"Someone to love you. Love you with all their heart. Someone to give you a home filled with laughter and children. Someone on whom you can shower all the emotion you've kept stored inside you your whole life. That's what you need. And Bennett can't give it to you."

She knew he meant well, but she wasn't ready to deal with it right then. Not when all she wanted was to do exactly what Barn was warning her not to do. To go back to the major's room and sit at his side. To hold his hand like he'd held hers. And talk to him like he'd talked to her. But she couldn't admit any of that to Barn. She could hardly admit it to herself.

Nor did she want to face the reason her heart raced in her breast every time she saw him. Or the reason her heated blood pulsed through every part of her body when he stood close to her. Or the reason she ached to have him touch her; or pull her into his arms; or press her up against his muscled strength. No, she didn't want to try to understand any of this, let alone explain it to Barnaby.

For seven years she'd suffered in a marriage that had left her with a gaping void. For seven years she'd lived with an aching loneliness that went bone deep. But no matter how desperately she wanted to find relief from the pain, she knew giving in to the desires she felt for Samuel Bennett wasn't the answer. Just like her marriage to Hunt hadn't been the answer, either.

"Don't worry, Barn. I have no delusions concerning Major Bennett. I know exactly what he can offer."

"Then you know how capable he is of hurting you?"

"Only if I let him," she said, then tried to make the smile on her face seem sincere. "Which I have no intention of doing, Barn. Now, I think I'd like to sleep for a while."

Barn leaned over and kissed her on the cheek. "Do you want me to send Tilly up?"

"No. I'm fine."

"Good night, then."

"Good night, Barn."

"And don't worry, Claire. We'll bring Alex home safely."

Claire bit her lower lip. "I know. The major says Roseneau won't risk harming Alex until he has the necklace."

"He's right." Barn gave her a reassuring smile, then left.

Claire sat before the blazing fireplace for a long while, watching the flames do their fiery dance. She knew she should go to bed. Knew she should get some rest while she could. But she wasn't tired. All she wanted to do was go back to where the major slept and be with him. Even if he didn't know she was there.

Claire gathered her blanket in her arms and carried it with her across the room. She walked down the hall and stood outside his door with her hand on the knob.

The major. She couldn't allow herself to think of him any other way. Not as Samuel, or Sam, like she'd heard Doctor Bronnely call him. Or as Bennett, as Barnaby did. Only as "the major." It was a more distant title.

It put their relationship in the right perspective. Kept him at a comfortable distance. Where she needed him to be. Where she would be sure to keep him. Because Barn was right. He was dangerous. Just how dangerous was clear every time her body reacted to him the way it did.

As if she couldn't stop herself, Claire turned the knob and stepped inside. The room was dark, with only one candle lit on the bedside table and a small fire in the grate. Shadows danced against the wall and before her on the hardwood floor. She walked across the room until she was beside his bed.

He lay on his right side, sleeping soundly. A large white bandage covered his left shoulder and wrapped around his back and over his chest. The covers she'd placed over his shoulder earlier had slid down to his waist, exposing as much flesh as she'd seen of him. She was glad he wasn't on his back, where she'd have a clear view of his chest and stomach, and even lower.

She wasn't sure what, if anything, he wore beneath the sheet, and her gaze moved to his exposed flesh. She couldn't help but study what she could see of him. Couldn't stop her gaze from staying riveted on the unknown. He was truly a magnificent specimen of masculinity, all hard, bulging muscle, and formidable strength.

A pool of heated lava moved to the pit of her stomach, causing her knees to weaken. This was not the reason she'd come here. This was not what she wanted to experience.

She clutched her hands into the folds of her skirt until her fingers ached. She could not let him affect her like this. She'd learned her lesson with Hunt. And yet, she'd desperately prayed it might be different with someone else. With the major. That just once, she would know . . .

That thought scared her to death. The violent needs and desires roiling within her frightened her to her very core. She was plagued by an almost insatiable hunger she was convinced she'd killed seven years ago. But her desires weren't dead. The longing was still there. The yearnings. The lust. All of it, every emotion she'd locked away surged to the forefront, sucking the air from her lungs.

With a shuddering sigh, she spun around and nearly raced for the door. She needed to stop torturing herself with stupid, impossible thoughts. Some women were not meant to be the perfect partner to a man, and she was obviously one of those women. No matter how desperately she yearned to be, or how much it hurt to know she never could be, she had to face the facts she'd lived with her entire marriage.

The desires and passion that came to the forefront when she was with the major would lead to nothing but heartache.

She closed the door ever so softly and walked down the stairs. Sleep was the furthest thing from her mind. Ignoring her traitorous emotions could only be achieved if she kept busy. Finding the necklace was foremost in importance.

She swiped away an errant tear that rolled down her cheek as if it had a right to escape. It was too late for tears. Seven years and a lifetime too late.

Chapter 20

The mantel clock chimed one in the morning, and Claire sat on the floor with the last book in her lap. She was finished. She'd searched through every book in Hunt's study. Every book on shelves that took up two entire walls of the room from floor to ceiling.

"You didn't find it."

It was more a statement than a question, but his voice startled her just the same.

She looked to the door. "What are you doing out of bed? Dr. Bronnely said you weren't to get up until tomorrow."

She scrambled to her feet and rushed to where he leaned against the door frame. It had been three days since he'd been injured and he'd healed remarkably fast, but he still wasn't completely recovered. He shouldn't be out of bed, nor should he have come down the stairs. He could have fallen. He could have injured himself even more than before.

He wore nothing but a pair of dark pants and a full-sleeved, white lawn shirt he hadn't bothered to tuck in. His feet were bare, and Claire couldn't ignore how drawn she was to his casual attire. Hunt wouldn't have dreamed of leaving his room without being fully dressed. The major didn't seem to notice. Or care.

His hair was disheveled, and several strands hung down over his forehead, giving him a dangerous look. His high cheekbones seemed more pronounced, the sharp angle to his jaw more defined, and Claire's breath caught in her throat.

She went to his right side to help him stay steady on his feet. She avoided touching his wound and wrapped her hand around his waist. He put his arm across her shoulder and walked with her into the room.

"Sit here," she said when they reached the oversized maroon sofa sitting at an angle in front of the fireplace. The fire had gone out long ago, but the room wasn't chilled yet. In fact, it seemed noticeably warmer than it had been only moments earlier.

He cautiously sat, then leaned back as if testing his shoulder. With a sigh, he relaxed against the cushions, but he didn't let go of her hand.

"Sit here beside me."

She shook her head, but he refused to release her. When he pulled her toward him, she had no choice but to sit next to him.

"You look tired," he said, touching his finger across her cheek where dark circles probably rimmed her eyes. She could never hide the telltale sign that she'd been out too late or gotten too little sleep. Her eyes always gave her away.

"I'm fine." She looked at the wall of countless books. "It isn't here."

She heard him take a big breath, heard the air fill his lungs, saw the lift of his chest. His arm wrapped around her shoulder, and he brought her close to him.

"Then we'll keep looking. We'll take his desk apart drawer by drawer. Maybe there's a hidden compartment somewhere."

Claire made a move to get up, but he wouldn't let her. "You're not doing any more tonight. You've been up long enough. You're dead on your feet."

"But if there's a chance it's here—"

"Then we'll find it tomorrow."

Claire leaned back against him. Every instinct told her to separate herself from him, but it was as if she didn't possess the will to do it.

She couldn't explain the strange sensation of sitting beside him, of having his arm around her, his body pressed against her. She'd never felt this with Hunt, not even in the beginning. And that scared her. A shiver ran down her spine.

"Are you cold?"

She felt her cheeks warm. "No. I'm fine."

He reached for a cover that was draped over the back of the sofa and placed it over her lap. Then he wrapped his arm around her shoulder again and pressed her head against his chest. She went willingly.

She nestled her head in the hollow just below his chin and breathed a heavy sigh. She molded perfectly into the dips and valleys of muscles that banded across his chest and down his torso. And she ached to be even closer to him.

She curled into him and reached her arm around his middle. With her cheek pressed against him so securely that she could hear every solid beat of his heart, she closed her eyes and gave in to the riotous emotions she'd refused to let herself feel for the last seven years. She belonged here. Some buried part of her knew she did. And yet . . .

Barnaby's words came back to haunt her. The major *was* a threat to her. Bigger than even Hunt had been. Her relationship to Hunt had been nothing short of disastrous. How could she think it would be any different with the major? How could she take such a risk again? The fear she felt was too real.

"It's time I went to bed," she whispered, her breath ragged and forced. "I'm very tired."

He didn't apply pressure to keep her from escaping, nor did he lift his arm to let her go. And yet, she couldn't find the strength to leave him.

"What's wrong, Claire?"

"We shouldn't be sitting here like this."

"What are you afraid of?"

"I'm not afraid. I'm just wiser than I was before and—"

Claire clamped her lips together and held her tongue. If only she weren't so desperate to have him hold her. If only she didn't want to stay in his arms forever.

"I'm not ready for this," she said as if she owed him an explanation.

"For what? To sit here like this? For us to hold each other? Comfort each other?" He sat forward on the sofa and turned until she had no choice but to look at him. "Hunt's dead, Claire. He's been dead for months."

She shook her head. How could she explain that Hunt had been dead to her for seven years? It wasn't Hunt or his memory she was afraid of. It was Major Samuel Bennett. It was every warning Barnaby had issued. It was her.

She knew it wasn't possible to give him just a small piece of her heart and keep back the rest so it would be safe. He would demand it all. She knew he would. He was that type of man. Even though she wasn't sure he would give her his heart in return. Just as Hunt hadn't been able to give her his. And in the end she would be left with nothing but an empty existence that robbed her of any chance for happiness, and the renewed vow to never trust a man again.

She shook her head, her whole body trembling in a mass of regret and confusion. And he calmed her with a touch.

He placed his finger beneath her chin and tilted her head upward. With the side of her face cradled in the strong, steady palm of his hand, he stroked her cheek.

His eyes didn't leave hers, their gazes locked until she could do nothing but match her breaths with his. And at that moment, she forgot every warning Barnaby had given her. She wanted the major more than she'd ever wanted anyone before. Enough that she could fool herself into believing that the look in his eyes said he wanted her equally as much.

He was going to kiss her. She knew it as surely as she knew the sun would rise in the sky at dawn. As surely as she knew the moon would be there at night. And she was just as confident that when he kissed her, every star in the sky would explode into a thousand fireballs.

She should run. She should turn her face away from his while there was still time. But she didn't. She could do nothing except watch his head move closer to hers.

Then it was too late.

His mouth covered hers, his lips firm and gentle, warm and devouring. And she was lost to him. She could do nothing but take what he offered and pray it didn't destroy her. Pray she was strong enough to risk this much, without any expectations for the future.

His lips gently moved atop hers, touching briefly before lifting, then touching again. Fiery swirls spiraled through every part of her, the heat of desire converging low in her belly. A wet heaviness seemed to settle there, pulsing, throbbing, until she thought she might go insane. And he deepened his kiss.

His lips moved with greater intensity, as if asking for some favor, seeking some treasure, demanding some great secret. And Claire kissed him back.

It was a natural thing they did, this mating of two people, their hands twined about each other, their lips pressed together. And Claire gave in to the pleasure she received. She drank from him, then threaded her fingers through his hair while holding him close to her. She moaned her delight.

It was a mystery. The emotions raging through her were a myriad of confusion she'd never experienced before. And she was ready to risk it all and take the gift he offered.

Obviously he didn't know what Hunt had discovered so soon after their wedding. She'd evidently satisfied the major's passion enough that he didn't find her as lacking as Hunt had. And when he kissed her again, she prayed he would never discover her secret. Because she didn't want him to stop. She was on fire, and it was impossible to tear herself away from him.

His chest was heavy against her and pressed her back against the cushioned sofa, trapping her in the warmth of his embrace. They were still sitting, but a part of her knew if he pushed against her, she would lie down on the settee and welcome his weight on top of her.

He didn't. Instead, he braced his weight on one forearm on the cushion beside her and kissed her again. And again, until she was certain flames consumed her.

"Open for me," he said, his ragged voice a whisper against her lips. And with gentle urgency, he pressed his thumb downward against her chin, and she opened for him.

The feeling was amazing. He drank from her with greater immediacy—taking, demanding, and giving. Her chest heaved as harshly and erratically as his, and she couldn't think, couldn't breathe. Couldn't have stopped him if she tried.

His tongue delved into her mouth as if searching the unknown, seeking in desperation, and finding. He pressed harder against her and moaned his pleasure. Their tongues touched, battled, then mated in a ritual previously unknown to her.

She didn't understand this new game he was teaching her; a game that left her wild and in a heated frenzy. She was left with no choice but to hold on and let him be her guide.

She wrapped one arm around his neck and pulled him closer. Her rapid breathing meshed with his while the need building inside her grew to a fevered pitch. She'd never experienced such passion, such a giving and taking and sharing of primal desires. She was hot with need, and she reached for him as if by pulling him closer against her she could take him into herself.

She lowered her hand and touched him beneath his shirt, skimming her fingers over his chest, caressing his bare skin; then she moved upward to the part of him covered with bandages. His flesh was hot, his sinewy muscles hard. They rippled beneath her fingers when she touched him, and he ground out an earthy moan before kissing her again.

She needed him like she'd never needed anything before. Wanted him more than she knew it was possible to want anyone. And she wasn't sure what she should do.

His hand held her by the waist, his fingers branding her flesh with his touch. The fire burning inside her was all-consuming, each touch adding fuel to the raging inferno. His fingers moved upward until they touched the underside of her breast. Then he moved further upward until her heavy weight was nestled in the palm of his hand.

An array of fireworks soared through the air, exploding in the darkness, their bright rays bursting into blinding flashes of light before her eyes. She knew where this was leading. Knew what would happen next. He would reach for her, then pull back as if his disappointment was more than he could overcome.

It was how it had always been. She'd look into the major's eyes, expecting to see the same passion as was raging through her, but it wouldn't be there. All she would see was the regret he couldn't mask before he turned away from her.

For seven years she'd battled the same blinding humiliation, and she wouldn't endure it again. Hunt had conditioned her well, and a part of her had died each time she'd been rejected. The pain she'd suffered was a torture she'd never endure again.

A cry came from deep within her, a heartrending sound that released years of anguish and bitterness. She couldn't survive one more humiliation. Not when her body was on fire and in a few short minutes the major would look at her as if his lack of desire was her fault.

She stiffened beneath him and held herself still, refusing to participate in the blazing kiss that a moment ago had set her on fire.

It took a few seconds for him to notice she was no longer kissing him back. When he did, he pulled away from her and moaned as if the separation was painful.

"Claire?"

She turned her head and pushed away from him. She needed to separate herself from him. She couldn't look into his eyes—didn't want to see all the questions he'd expect her to answer. She couldn't shoulder the blame another time.

Guilt for what she'd done raged inside her. She'd known not to kiss him. Known the risk she was taking. But she was like the moth drawn to the proverbial flame. What was there about him that pulled her like it did? Why did she ache to be near him? To hold him? To have him hold her? Hadn't she learned from the past? Hadn't her marriage to Hunt been enough of a lesson?

With the same regal detachment she'd developed throughout her marriage, she braced her shoulders and turned to face him with her chin held high. Her breathing was still more labored than she wished and her cheeks hot to the touch. But the damage was not irreparable. She hadn't let it go that far. She was still safe. As long as she didn't let this ever happen again.

She faced him squarely. "You need to get back to bed. There's always a chance fever will set in if you don't take care of yourself."

He leaned back against the cushion, his breathing heavier than hers, his discomfort more obvious. She could tell his fury hovered just beneath the surface, near enough it was almost plain to see. His words brought it closer.

"I'm fine. The only fever I'm suffering from has nothing to do with my back."

"Don't!"

"There nothing wrong with what is happening between us."

"Nothing is happening between us."

"That sure as hell wasn't the impression I was getting."

"Then you made a mistake."

"How long did it take you to learn to turn off your emotions like that? Like blowing out a candle? Is this a game you played with Hunt? Hot as fire one minute, cold as ice the next. No wonder—"

She braced herself for what he implied, then rose from the settee and walked away from him. "No wonder what, Major? No wonder my husband chose to spend months at a time away from home? Away from me? No wonder a life with me wasn't enough for him to give up his life with the government? No wonder I wasn't important enough for him to stop taking risks that might get him killed?"

Claire turned to bravely face him. "Or, do you now think you have the answer to why I failed to provide Lord Huntingdon with an heir? I'm sure you and the rest of Society are wondering why after seven years there wasn't a child."

She hid her hands in the folds of her skirt and clenched them until her nails bit into her flesh. Then she smiled the smile she'd perfected over the last seven years. "It would be well of you not to dwell too much on any of these questions. Or on me. If you have need of female companionship, Major, I'm sure there are many other women you'll find more to your satisfaction. You are free to leave my house at any time and seek them out. Barnaby is here to protect me, as well as help me look for the necklace. It's not likely I'll have any further need of you. Now, I think I'll go to bed. Do you need assistance up the stairs, or can you manage yourself?"

He rose from the settee, the grimace on his face a sign that he was in pain. "I'm not going to allow you to do this. That isn't what I meant and you know it. You're as tightly strung as an overly wound clock."

She felt her temper rise. "You have no authority to allow or disallow anything I do. If I am tightly strung, it is only because of you. You have made my life miserable from the day you walked into my home, interrogating me like I was a common criminal. Accusing me of crimes against humanity as well as against my country."

He reached out to touch her. Whether to hold her or just as a manner of apology, she didn't know. Nor did she care. She stepped out of his reach and shoved his hand away from her.

"Claire, talk to me."

"There's nothing to say."

"Then explain what just happened here."

"I made a mistake, Major. A terrible mistake. And it won't happen again."

"You can't mean that. I—"

He took a step toward her; she halted him with an angry glare. "Get away from me! I don't want you to touch me ever again." She held out her hand to stop him from coming any nearer. She wasn't sure he would stop and was prepared to do what was necessary to keep him from her. But an angry voice coming from behind them made her efforts unnecessary.

"That's enough, Major!"

Claire and the major both turned to the open doorway. Barnaby stood there with his hands clenched at his sides and a lethal look on his face. "Are you all right, Claire?"

"Yes, fine," Claire stammered, as if she'd been caught kissing the major instead of arguing with him. "I was just on my way to bed. Would you please help the major to his room?"

"Of course."

Claire nodded, then escaped the room without a look at either the major or her brother.

She forced her feet to carry her up the stairs and away from him. Even though there was nothing more she wanted right now than to rush back into his arms and give herself to him the same as she had earlier. To prove to herself that with him, everything would be different.

Chapter 21

Sam leaned his head back against the carriage squabs and absently rubbed his aching shoulder. He hadn't slept, had barely rested since the angry words Claire had spoken last night. He still didn't understand what the hell had happened. One minute she was kissing him with a desperation that stunned him, and the next she was a cold, unfeeling statue beneath him.

He released a frustrated sigh and asked himself for the hundredth time what happened to cause such a change. And for the hundredth time, he was unable to come up with an answer.

The carriage slowed, and he sat forward. Before he reached for the door, he wiped at the fine sheen of perspiration from his forehead that hinted that he hadn't allowed himself to heal enough before going out. The ache in his shoulder confirmed it. But what choice did he have? Time was running out, and he had to do everything he could think of that might answer the many questions nagging at him.

The minute the carriage he'd borrowed from Hunt's stable came to a stop, he disembarked and walked up the short walk to Claire's town house. He was returning from a very frustrating meeting with McCormick. A meeting where too many accusations were tossed out, too many angry words spoken. And where too many explosive tempers flamed an already explosive situation.

McCormick realized the importance of finding the necklace as much as Sam did. It had taken every argument Hunt could come up with to keep the head of the Foreign Office from sending an army over to tear Claire's home apart to search for it. Sam needed to find it. Soon.

If only he knew what Hunt meant when he said, "She has it. My marchioness has it."

They'd searched the house from top to bottom, from the attic to the cellar, even going so far as to pour out some of Hunt's vintage wines. But had found nothing.

Sam raked his fingers through his hair, then gently rubbed his aching shoulder again. Why had Hunt told him to get the necklace from her if she didn't have it? Why had he said to get the papers from Claire if he hadn't given them to her?

Sam clenched his teeth in frustration. Hunt's dying words meant no more to him now than when he'd whispered them all those months ago. It was a riddle Sam was afraid he'd never figure out. And thousands of young British soldiers would pay for his incompetence with their lives.

There were only days left before the peace negotiations began. Days in which to discover the traitor's identity. And Sam hoped they went better than the last twenty-four hours had gone.

Everything had been in turmoil since he'd kissed Claire last night. He remembered the passion in her kiss, the heated desire. Which was totally at odds with the fear he saw in her eyes when she ended the kiss. As if she was suddenly afraid. Terrified that he'd want something she wasn't willing to give. Something she wasn't able to give. But what? Unless there was something she was hiding.

He stopped in midstride on his way up the stairs. Suddenly he realized how much the outcome of her battle to keep her emotions locked away mattered to him. The realization of how much he cared for her hit him with the force of a battering ram that broke through the barrier he'd erected around his heart. The realization of how much he wanted her—needed her—was even more surprising.

Sam stood on the top step of Claire's town house and wanted to laugh. How had this happened? In all his nearly thirty years, he'd never once entertained the notion of caring for someone. He'd never once let down the protective guard that kept a woman from penetrating his heart. All that had ever been important to him was his country and his job with the military.

But each day, Claire became more important to him. And for the first time ever, the thought of settling down on the estate he'd been left by his father was more appealing than his life of intrigue and danger. The thought of having a home and children, and growing old with someone he loved was suddenly very pleasant. He yearned to stay alive long enough to see his children grow, and perhaps even his grandchildren.

He was at a crossroads, and the path his future would take depended on finding the necklace. That was the key to bringing about a quicker end to the war. Then his services wouldn't be needed anymore. There wouldn't be a reason for him to stay with the Foreign Office.

Sam walked through the front door and handed Watkins his hat and gloves. He stopped when he saw Claire standing at the foot of the stairs.

She was dressed in black again, as was expected of a woman in mourning. Her hair was pulled back from her face and wound into a tight chignon at the nape of her neck. Loose tendrils had escaped from their binding and framed her face. Bloody hell, but she was a beauty. And from the frown creasing her forehead, an angry beauty.

"Good evening, Lady Huntingdon."

Sam walked toward her when she didn't close the distance between them. "Is something wrong?"

"No."

The short clip of her single answer indicated otherwise. He looked over to where Watkins stood. "Watkins, would you have tea served in the study?"

"Right away, sir."

"And have Cook make some of those meat sandwiches she served for lunch yesterday. I'm starved."

Watkins smiled. "Of course, sir. It won't be a minute."

"Thank you." Sam turned back to where Claire stood and held out his arm for her to take. She didn't, but brushed past him and walked to Hunt's study.

Claire waited until the door closed before she spun around to face him. "It's only been three days since you were hurt."

"Three and a half."

She glared at him. "Don't make light of this, Major. You shouldn't be out of bed, let alone out of the house."

He smiled. "I'm glad to see you care."

"Did you go to see McCormick?"

"I happened to see him, yes."

The major sat down in one of the maroon cushioned chairs before the fireplace and crossed one leg over the other as if he didn't have a care in the world. The look of pain in his eyes said otherwise. The brief shadow that darkened his expression said the meeting had not gone well.

Claire clenched her hands at her side. She didn't know why she was so angry, but she was. How could he pretend to be so calm? She knew the stress of the last few weeks had pushed her closer to the breaking point. To see him sit there as if he hadn't a care was nearly her undoing. She could think of nothing except finding the necklace. And rescuing Alex. And . . .

And the kiss they'd shared.

Claire couldn't sit; she could barely stand still. "What will you do when you don't have the necklace?"

"You mean *if* we haven't found it yet?" He shrugged as if that were a moot point. "The only thing left to us—we'll bargain without it. We'll promise the Russians we won't tell the world that they were selling off some of their most valued crown jewels in exchange for military secrets. And we'll promise them that as soon as we have the necklace in our possession, we'll return it to them. But Roseneau will not get it, Claire. We'll save your brother without paying that price."

She stalked across the room to where she didn't have to face him. "Why do you think Hunt took it?" she said, staring into the dancing flames in the fireplace. "He didn't need it."

He hesitated as if searching for an answer. "I think he just didn't want Roseneau to have it. I don't think Hunt knew what he had or the repercussions taking it would cause."

Claire clasped her hands around her middle. "Damn him!" she said, squeezing shut her eyes. She stiffened when she realized the major had come up behind her.

"Claire?" His voice was a soft whisper, and Claire knew he was going to reach out to her.

"Don't!"

She spun around and held out her hands to ward him off. She couldn't let him touch her. For more than a day, her life had been in a constant turmoil because of the kiss they'd shared. From the minute he'd held her, she'd yearned for things she could never have. Even though she'd vowed she wouldn't let thoughts of him consume her, they did. He was everywhere. And the more she tried to tell herself she didn't need the passion he'd shown her, the more she knew she did.

She tried to forget what it felt like to have his arms around her or his lips pressed to hers, but every time she saw him it was like living that magical time all over again. And with every second she became more desperate for him to pull her into his arms and hold her. And kiss her. She'd never wanted anything so desperately in her life. Never wanted to take the chance that with the major everything would be different.

For seven years she'd stomped down every emotion the minute it surfaced. She'd replaced the passionate void in her life with new gowns and a rush of activity. She'd taught herself she could exist without being touched or held or loved. Until *he* came. The major. With his bold and daring ways, his blatant masculinity, and his self-assuredness.

Now a day didn't go by that she didn't hunger for what she'd gone a lifetime without. A night didn't go by that she didn't dream of lying in his arms, of him taking her as a man takes a woman.

Every time she told herself she couldn't take the risk, a thousand voices screamed that she would die if she didn't. That she couldn't live the rest of her life without the passion that exploded in her every time he touched her. Her existence had been so empty that just once she wanted to know . . .

Just once.

He stared at her as if waiting for some sign as to what she wanted him to do. Some hint of the direction she wanted to go. But how could she think of anything other than Alex and how he was suffering every day for something that wasn't his fault?

As if the major knew her thoughts, he grasped his fingers around her upper arms and turned her to face him.

She pulled away from him when a servant brought in a tea tray with sandwiches. Claire stared at the familiar china service but didn't make a move to pour from it. As the servant was leaving, Watkins stepped into the room. There was a frown on his face, and Claire felt a jolt of warning.

"Excuse me, Major, but Monsieur Roseneau is here to see you."

Claire felt as if someone had stolen the air from her lungs. She couldn't breathe. There wasn't enough air in the room to take a breath. She darted a look to where the major stood and watched his shoulders lift and his body stiffen to the battle-ready stance he took on whenever he faced danger. The look on his face turned hard as granite and the glint in his gray eyes as cold as steel.

"Watkins, show Lady Huntingdon to her room."

Claire shook her head. She didn't want to face Roseneau, but at the same time, she didn't want to lose even the smallest chance to bargain for Alex's release. The major saw her hesitation.

"Go upstairs, Claire, and stay in your room. Don't come down until I come for you."

"But—"

"Go."

His voice was a harsh whisper. The look in his eyes as cold as ice. Claire debated again whether to follow his orders, then decided it might be for the best. With a curt nod she turned to leave. Roseneau's voice stopped her.

He stood uninvited in the doorway, a look of confidence on his face. A daring glint in his eyes.

"Please, don't leave, Lady Huntingdon. I do so enjoy your company." He took a step into the room. "I see you were about to have tea. How delightful."

A biting assault of panic slammed into her chest. He was here. The man at the center of so much destruction was here demanding to see the major. The man threatening to kill Alex was in her house. She turned her head and met the major's hard look. When he spoke, the unrelenting tone of his voice sent a shiver down her spine.

"What an unpleasant surprise, Monsieur Roseneau. I don't remember Lady Huntingdon mentioning she'd invited you."

"That's not very friendly of you, Major. An obvious lack of good breeding. Your uncle would be sorely disappointed. Fortunately, the lady doesn't share your lack of hospitality."

Claire faced him squarely. "I'm afraid I have no desire to entertain someone who's caused my family so much suffering. Please leave my home."

Claire nodded for Watkins to show Roseneau the door, but he stopped her with a malicious grin and a wave of his hand. "I have come to give you one last chance to save your brother."

Claire's heart skipped a beat. Every nerve in her body screamed. All she wanted to do was run to where he stood and scratch his eyes out. To make him suffer like she knew Alex was suffering. She must have taken a step toward him because the major reached out to stop her.

He stepped in front of her, half shielding her. Half restraining her. When he spoke, his voice contained a blatant threat. "What do you want?"

"The necklace, of course," Roseneau said, his lips curling upward. "And the papers." He turned toward her to issue his threat. "Before it's too late."

Claire lost her battle to the fear racing through her. "I don't—"

The major's hold on her arm stopped her words; the look on his face caught her breath. Roseneau shifted his gaze from her to the major.

"You don't what, Lady Huntingdon?"

Claire looked up at the major. "Nothing."

"Advising the lady to keep the necklace is very foolish, Major Bennett, and will gain you nothing. The Russian authorities already know Lord Huntingdon took it and that your government intends to use it as leverage to end the war. Therefore," he said, walking through the room, "it would be most beneficial to give me the necklace so *I* can return it."

The major took a long breath. "And why would I want to do that?"

"Why, to keep the Marquess of Halverston alive."

"No!"

Claire didn't realize she'd moved toward Roseneau, but she had.

Roseneau held up his hand.

"Don't worry, my lady. As of right now, your brother is still alive." Roseneau walked to Hunt's desk and picked up the round marble paperweight. "How long he remains so depends on you."

The muscles in the major's arms knotted beneath her hand. "You'll excuse me if I have trouble taking you at your word." He leveled Roseneau an intimidating glare. "The Marquess of Huntingdon is dead because of your greed."

"Let me assure you I was not responsible for the marquess's death. Lord Huntingdon and I were, perhaps not close friends, but friendly adversaries nonetheless. I would never have wished him harm."

Claire took a deep breath. "If not you, then—"

Roseneau shook his head. "I can only guess as to the killer's identity. A game I'm afraid would put me in a great deal of unnecessary danger."

Claire felt her nerves bristle. "Release my brother. He doesn't know anything about the necklace."

"I'm afraid I can't do that. In fact I must insist you hand over both the necklace and the papers immediately."

The major stepped forward. "You're too late, Roseneau. The British authorities already have them."

Claire saw Roseneau's face pale and his hands clench around the paperweight.

"Giving them away was very foolish, Major. You had a chance to live before. Now you have none."

The major stepped away from Claire, forcing Roseneau to turn to keep him in view. "Your future is not so very secure either, Roseneau. The Russian government cannot be happy that you stole such a precious treasure from them."

Roseneau shrugged his shoulders. "Failure is the chance one must take in any encounter. As an army officer, you are well acquainted with the risks involved in a battle, Major."

"But I have learned to choose my battles carefully. Why did you get involved in such a scheme?"

"Let's just say I was given little choice. What is the term you English have? Skeletons in the closet? Well, suffice it to say I, too, have a skeleton or two. When a certain person offered me the opportunity to keep these skeletons safely locked away, I could not refuse."

"And this person wanted the Russian jewels?"

"This person wants wealth, Major Bennett. Wealth means power, and some men cannot get enough of either. The whole world knew the Russian government was willing to empty their treasury to gain an advantage in the war. The problem was the Russians were in—how do you put it?—financial straits. They could not come up with the money, so they offered the jewels. There is always someone in the world willing to sell even their soul if the price is right."

"And the necklace everyone is so concerned about?"

"Ah. The Queen's Blood." Roseneau lifted his lips in a noncommittal grin. "Let's just say absconding with the necklace was an impulsive act on my part. One I didn't think would have such negative repercussions."

"And the papers? Why are you so desperate to get the papers back?"

Roseneau shrugged his shoulders. "I'm afraid I don't have the answer to that. I'm not the one who wants them."

The major laughed, and Claire held her breath, watching the look on Roseneau's face turn deadlier.

"Am I correct," the major said, filling the room with the same powerful intimidation she'd sensed in him from the beginning, "that the papers contain a clue as to the traitor's identity?"

"I'm sure I wouldn't know, Major. My part was only to act as courier. I've found it's never wise to be too curious in deals of this kind. Now, about the papers—"

The major spun around and pinned Roseneau with a hostile glare. "It's too late, Roseneau. The government already has them. There's an army of men working to decode them right now."

The fury on Roseneau's face was obvious while the Frenchman held the major's glare. Suddenly it changed. The look in Roseneau's eyes changed to humor, and he smiled as if he was aware of a well-kept secret. "Do you know what I think? I think you are lying, Major. I don't think you have either the necklace or the papers."

Roseneau shifted the marble paperweight from one hand to the other, then carefully placed it back on the desk. "I think the Marquess of Huntingdon hid what he took from my safe and you and the marchioness cannot find it." He laughed. "You are still searching. That is the reason you have not left the marchioness's home. The reason there has been no hint of anyone at the Foreign Office working frantically to decode the messages. The reason no arrests have been made. That possibility was mentioned," he said, stepping to the side of the desk, then turning back, "but of course I discounted it as impossible. Now, I'm not so sure. In fact, I think it more than probable."

Claire's blood roared in her head, and she watched as the two adversaries stared at each other, neither conceding on any point. The major was the first to break the silence.

"I think it's time you left, Roseneau. When you talk to our traitor, tell him his days are numbered. It won't be long before we discover his identity. Then we'll know who was willing to sell out his country, and who murdered the Marquess of Huntingdon."

As if to emphasize his point, the major stepped closer to Roseneau. "I can promise you, he'll swing for his crimes. Because I'll put the noose around his neck myself. And perhaps yours, too. *If* you're still alive, that is. Now leave."

Roseneau's eyes narrowed. A vein bulged in his neck and if anything, he looked more threatening. "You have a day and a half to find the necklace and papers. The Russian emissary is scheduled to arrive on Thursday. If I don't have the necklace in my possession by Wednesday afternoon at three o'clock, the Marquess of Halverston will die. You will find his body floating in the Thames."

Claire couldn't breathe. She took one gasp for air after another, but there didn't seem to be enough air in the whole universe to help her.

The major took another step closer to Roseneau. "Get out," he ordered, and Roseneau's face turned a deeper shade of red.

"You'll regret this, Bennett."

"What I regret is that I didn't realize what Lord Huntingdon had done before he was killed. He'd still be alive and you and the traitor would have already been hanged."

"Time is running out," Roseneau repeated, then stormed from the room.

"Watkins!" the major ordered after the front door closed on Roseneau. "Send someone for Lord Barnaby! I want him here, now!"

Watkins nodded, then rushed to issue an order to one of the footmen. The major walked to a side table against the wall, then over to where Claire had sunk down on the cushion of the nearest chair.

"Here. Drink this," he said, half filling a glass with brandy.

Claire tilted her face and looked up at him. They only had a day and a half left.

He reached out and put the glass in her hand.

"Take a drink."

Claire took the glass but didn't drink any of it. "He's going to kill Alex if we don't hand over the necklace."

Claire couldn't stop trembling. Her hand shook so violently that some of the liquid spilled onto her skirt.

"Just take one swallow, Claire."

"No!" she said, throwing the glass against the wall. "Didn't you hear him?" She bolted to her feet. "He's going to kill Alex unless we find the necklace!"

"No, he won't. We'll find him first."

"How? You don't know where he is!"

Claire knew she'd lost control. Knew fear clouded her mind. Knew she was taking her terror out on the major. She lifted her fist and brought it down against his chest, as if fighting him would somehow get Alex back. Would somehow make the nightmare she was living go away.

She raised her hand again, but he didn't let her strike him. Instead, he wrapped his arms around her, pinning her arms to her sides. He held her close, enfolding her in his strength. And she leaned against him because this was the only place she felt safe.

The clock on the mantel quietly ticked away, counting down the precious minutes they had to find the necklace and papers. But still he held her, not moving, not talking. Only breathing big, deep breaths that lifted his chest. His chin rested atop her head, his hands moved in slow, relaxing circles, and his heart drummed with a pounding beat beneath her ear.

"We have to find him," she said as tears streamed down her face and dampened the front of his shirt.

"I know."

They both heard the commotion from the entry, but he didn't move away from her. Nor did he let her out of his grasp when the door flew open and Barnaby burst into the room.

"What's happened? Watkins said Roseneau just left."

The major didn't drop his arms from around her. He didn't put any space between them. He only lifted his chin from the top of her head to look at Barnaby and said, "Where the hell have you been?"

Chapter 22

Sam waited hours for sleep to consume him. But it didn't. His mind was a whirlwind of jumbled thoughts that ran together in confusion. Everything that had happened today had only added to his frustration. The meeting he'd had with McCormick early in the day played over and over.

But there was something else. Something that caused more questions to arise. It was the frequency with which Barnaby's name came up during their discussion. Not once, but several times. And in regard to totally unrelated incidents. In Sam's mind, there was no reason for his involvement except that he was Claire's brother.

Then, there was the conversation Sam had with Barnaby Linscott after Roseneau left. The man knew details to which he shouldn't have been privy. Just as he had answers for every question Sam asked. Answers an ordinary person shouldn't have known.

Sam brushed his hands over his eyes and tried to empty his mind, but certain questions wouldn't go away. Certain events seemed too coincidental. For example, why had Barnaby Linscott been in Paris the night of Roseneau's ball? He was only a second son, even if his father had been a marquess. Surely that wasn't enough to warrant an invitation to such an exclusive affair. Sam doubted he'd been on the original guest list. So who'd pulled strings to get him invited?

Next, Sam remembered the day Barnaby came back from visiting Hunt's estates, from searching them. It was the first time they'd met, yet Linscott knew who he was before they were introduced. He said he remembered him from Roseneau's ball. But why should he? Sam had been there as Hunt's driver. What nobleman takes note of a driver?

And Sam remembered how elusive Lord Barnaby had been when Claire began introductions. He had the impression that Barnaby Linscott didn't want Sam to realize he was Claire's brother. What possible reason could there be for him to remain anonymous?

Sam sat on the edge of the bed and rested his elbows on his knees. Every question raised another question. The more Sam remembered, the muddier the waters surrounding Barnaby Linscott turned. He wanted to laugh. Claire's brother was nearly as good at elusion and subterfuge as her husband had been.

He remembered the night they'd attempted to free the Marquess of Halverston. How Barnaby Linscott's actions had mirrored his own. As if they'd both been taught the technique by the same master.

Maybe that was the problem. Too many things about Linscott reminded him of Hunt.

Sam swiped his hand across his face in frustration. What did it all mean? He knew he could figure it out if he weren't so damn tired. If he weren't so worried about Claire and what would happen if they couldn't save her brother.

He bolted to his feet and took one step forward, then stopped when he heard a door close downstairs. Sam listened to the muffled footsteps he heard moving somewhere below and reached out to pull the gun from the drawer in the table by his bed. He wrapped his fingers around the cool metal and walked across the room.

He didn't light a candle, but opened the door to his room and stepped out into the hallway.

The house was dark except for a single light in the foyer that cast shadows on the wall. Sam made his way to the stairs and descended slowly so as not to alert whoever was there.

When he reached the bottom, he looked around. Nothing seemed out of the ordinary until his gaze stopped on the floor in front of Hunt's study. There was a light beneath the door.

Sam's first instinct was to surprise whoever was in there, but a tiny voice told him he already knew the intruder. He lowered the gun to his side and slowly opened the door.

Claire sat behind Hunt's desk going through drawers that had already been searched over and over again. She leafed through stacks of papers, rereading them to make sure they weren't the papers Roseneau wanted.

He stood in the doorway until she noticed him.

"Oh!" She clutched her hands to her chest. "I didn't hear you come."

"I'm not surprised."

"It's not here."

"I know."

She slid the drawer shut and dropped her hands to her lap. "I don't know where else to look."

Sam stepped into the room, and she lifted her gaze. A frown appeared across her forehead and with eyes wide and grief-laden, she watched him come near her. Before he reached her, she stood, but kept the desk between them as if she were afraid to step out from behind the protection it offered.

He stopped. Even with Hunt's desk as a barrier between them, he could smell the scented soap with which she'd bathed. The urge to hold her was almost more than he could bear.

As if she realized his thoughts, she took a step away from him, putting a measurable distance between them. Sam let her separate herself from him.

"You're sure this is the only room Hunt came to when you returned from Roseneau's?"

"Yes. He didn't go anywhere else."

He turned to look around the room. Floor-to-ceiling bookshelves spanned two entire walls on either side of the room, the expensive leather-bound books a tribute to Hunt's intelligence and appreciation for literature. The books had all been opened to make sure there wasn't a pocket secretly cut out in the inside to hide the necklace and papers.

The door to the room was on the wall opposite them. Two large paintings flanked the thick oak door on either side, but Sam had already searched each of them, going even so far as to remove the canvases to make sure nothing was hidden inside.

Behind them, wide double French doors leading to the terrace cut the wall in half. There was nothing else in the room except Hunt's desk, two leather chairs, and a sofa. But they'd all been thoroughly searched.

If this was the only room he'd stayed after he returned from France, where the hell could he have hidden them?

Sam closed his eyes and breathed a deep sigh. When he opened them, Claire was standing in front of him. She was so different from the picture she'd presented each time he'd seen her with Hunt. Still as strong and self-reliant, yet fragile somehow. Suddenly he couldn't imagine her with Hunt at all. "Why did you marry him?"

She lifted her chin just enough to focus her eyes on him, and Sam thought he noticed a hint of sadness.

"You mean, why did the Marquess of Huntingdon marry me?"

She turned, and Sam watched her move closer to the terrace doors. Each step exhibited that natural grace he remembered from the times he'd seen her before.

With barely a hint of emotion, she said, "Because neither of us was given a choice. My father considered a match with the revered Bridgemont heir the coup of the year. Hunt would be a duke someday, you know. And I would be a duchess. But that would be after Hunt's father was dead."

"He's still alive, isn't he?"

Claire nodded. "And he still controls everything and everyone with an iron fist. Just as he always did." She paused. "Does that surprise you?"

"A little, I suppose. I can't imagine anyone controlling Hunt."

"His father did. Especially before we were married. From the money he allowed Hunt to spend on his lavish lifestyle and his mistress—yes, I knew about her," she said with a smile, "—to the woman he would marry. His father chose me. Not Hunt. It was all rather flattering at the time. I was barely nineteen years old and selected to wed the rakish heir to the Bridgemont dynasty. Except the esteemed heir didn't want me."

Sam let her open the French doors and stand in the cool night air.

"Hunt was nearly thirty-four years old when we married," Claire continued, "and according to his father, had not done his duty as the only heir. His father decided it was more than past time he married and set up his nursery. The Bridgemont line must be preserved, you know. And I was chosen to accomplish the deed.

"I can still remember the day Hunt was told we were betrothed. It happened in this very room," she said, looking back over her shoulder, as if the events of that day were alive before her. "My father brought me with him to sign the marriage contract he and the duke had drawn up. I was to spend some time with my new betrothed so the two of us could get to know each other. Afterward, I realized Hunt knew nothing about the arrangement. Or about me. He exploded with the fury of a violent thunderstorm.

"They sent me from the room, of course. But I could hear him raging through the walls. I'm surprised all of London didn't hear him. He was adamant in his refusal to marry me. He told both his father and mine he would marry when he was ready to marry, and choose the woman with whom he'd live the rest of his life himself. He had no intention of letting anyone else make that decision for him. And, to quote him, 'It sure as hell wouldn't be some simpering young chit just out of the schoolroom.'"

Sam watched her head tip back as she looked up into the nighttime sky. He wanted to go to her but didn't. "Then what happened?"

"I'm not sure. The Duke of Bridgemont said something I couldn't hear and there was nothing more. When they brought me back into the room, Hunt was gone. All that remained was the marriage contract with his bold signature. Three months later I was Hunt's wife and the two of us lived happily ever after."

Sam watched her take a big breath, as if she had to reach deep inside to ease some painful memories buried far inside her. But Sam couldn't imagine what they could be. He was sure everything had turned out for the best. Hunt may have started his marriage resenting the woman his father had chosen for him, but surely it hadn't ended up that way. How could it have with someone as magnificent as the woman standing in front of him? How could Hunt have lived with her for even a day without coming to love her? It would have been impossible. And it had been. Sam knew that from Hunt's dying words. From his demand for Sam to protect her. From his admission that he'd loved her, his marchioness.

She took a step back into the room and closed the doors that led onto the terrace, then leaned her forehead against the cool glass. As if drawn to her, Sam walked up behind her until his body was pressed against hers. He stood there for several seconds, her back and hips nestled against him, then he reached around her from behind and locked his fingers at her waist.

He tightened his hold ever so slightly and after a brief hesitation, she leaned back against him.

The heat from her flesh set him ablaze. He lowered his head and nestled his face against the crook of her neck. And he kissed her beneath her ear.

She angled her head, exposing more of herself to him, then sighed softly when he rained gentle kisses up and down the graceful column of her neck. He kissed her again, her clean fragrance seeping into every inch of his body.

At first he thought she would stop him, but she didn't. It was the most wondrous torture he'd ever endured. They stood there, their bodies touching for what seemed an eternity, until he knew it would be impossible to let her go.

He turned her in his arms and nestled her close to him. He wanted her to wrap her arms around him and hold him, and he thought she might. But something held her back. He wasn't sure what it was until she tilted her head and looked into his eyes. He nearly staggered from the depth of emotion he saw.

If she understood the danger of their situation, she didn't show it. Instead, she breathed a deep sigh and leaned into him to bury her face against his chest.

He wondered if she could hear his heart pound beneath her ear and knew it was impossible for her not to. Even though they were adversaries of sorts, every inch of him burned with a desire he couldn't fight any longer. He placed his finger beneath her chin and tilted her face upward, and kissed her.

He was on fire, the connecting of their bodies igniting an inferno of desire that had smoldered from the moment he'd first seen her. He wanted her like he'd never wanted anyone before.

He deepened his kisses and opened his mouth atop hers, searching for that perfect mate he knew awaited him.

She hesitated for a moment, an obvious indication of her mixed emotions. He knew there were ghosts tormenting her. He was without a doubt the first man she'd kissed since Hunt had died. Such intimacy had to be difficult for her, and yet, it was more than that. He remembered her first kiss. It had seemed almost . . . virginal.

He deepened his kiss, tasting her, teasing her, devouring her. Her hands skimmed up his chest, then her arms wound around his neck. She held on to him as if she didn't intend to let go. And yet, he was afraid she might.

"Don't ask me to stop," he whispered, kissing her again and again, molding her body to his because he needed to feel her against him.

"No," he heard her whisper against his mouth. "I won't."

And he kissed her again.

She sagged against him as if her legs were too weak to hold her upright, and he moved his hands over her body. She was perfect to his touch; her waist narrow, her hips seductively curved. He cupped her breasts while still kissing her and swallowed her gasp when his thumbs brushed over first one hardened bud, then the other.

"Let me love you, Claire."

He sensed her hesitation before she nodded as if she weren't able to form the word *yes*.

Sam kissed her again, his hands worshipping her lithe body, his tongue delving deep into her honeyed cavern. Oh, how he wanted her. How he needed her. Like he'd never needed anyone before.

He led her across the room and opened the door. "Not here," he said softly. "Upstairs."

He'd not take her here. Not on a narrow sofa or on the hard floor. He'd make love to her in a bed, but it wouldn't be in Hunt's bed, or in hers. They'd make love in the room where he'd been sleeping. Where the memories would be all their own.

He led her up the stairs, stopping once or twice to kiss her thoroughly. When they reached his room, he opened the door and followed her in. He closed it behind them and took her into his arms. She went willingly, although Sam thought he noticed a hint of trepidation. He brought his mouth down on hers to take her fears away. There was a nervousness in her kisses he wanted to ease, a trembling he wanted to calm. He knew how much this night was costing her, how difficult it was after being Hunt's wife.

With a hungry kiss, he vowed she would never regret what they were doing.

Chapter 23

Claire didn't remember climbing the stairs or walking down the hall, but somehow they'd reached Sam's room. She couldn't stop trembling. She was taking the biggest risk of her life. And yet, there was no way she wanted him to stop what they were about to do. She wanted him too much. Trusted him that much. She'd never felt this way before.

Surely this time it would be different. She'd waited seven years and she had to know for sure.

She clung to him and met his fiery kisses with a desperation she was afraid was more than her body could control.

Claire followed his lead, kissing him with an intensity that matched his. His hands moved over her body, touching her, feeling her, setting her flesh on fire. Yes, this was what she'd waited a lifetime to experience. Sam was the man she'd waited a lifetime to find.

She reached up to touch him, cupping his stubbled cheek in her hand. He turned his face to gently kiss her palm. The feel of his mouth on the tender inside of her hand sent a warm heaviness swirling to the pit of her stomach. Then lower. She shivered.

This was how it was supposed to be between a man and a woman. She knew it was. Even though she'd never experienced it before.

She placed her palms against his warm flesh. She couldn't touch enough of him, couldn't hold him close enough. Couldn't kiss him deeply enough. Being in his arms was like being caught up in a violent turmoil she didn't know how to battle.

She was desperate to feel his flesh beneath her fingertips, his rippling muscles beneath her hands. As if he read her mind, he stripped his shirt over his head and threw it to the floor.

"Touch me, Claire. Like I'm going to touch you."

Claire ran her hands over his shoulders and his back. She avoided the bandage across his shoulders and moved her hands to his waist, then up again to his shoulders.

She almost didn't notice his hands at work on the buttons that ran down the back of her dress. One by one they popped loose, freeing her. With his mouth still on hers, he pushed the material from her shoulders and ran his fingers over her exposed flesh. Claire couldn't suppress the shiver that shook her.

Next he worked on the tabs of her petticoats, pulling them until the yards of material puddled at her feet. His mouth moved to her neck while his hands ran along the side of her body. His warm breath sent shivers racing up and down her spine while his tongue traced fiery circles at the side of her neck just below her ear. Her legs weakened beneath her, and she clung to him with greater fervency.

Claire wasn't sure what happened next. His hands moved over her, and she couldn't think. She sighed, and he covered her mouth and kissed her again.

"Please," a voice whispered when their kiss ended, but it didn't sound like hers. It couldn't have been hers. This voice was raw and needy, husky with desire. "Oh, please . . ."

"Please, what, Claire? This?"

She didn't know what he meant, didn't know what she wanted, but he did. He must have. Because he loved her like she'd never been loved before.

"Yes. Please, hold me. Please, love me."

He smiled, then his mouth came down on hers, hot and demanding. He kissed her with greater impatience, taking her with him headlong into the unknown.

Her blood rushed through her veins, pulsing hot and heavy. When she thought she could take no more, his kisses intensified.

"I need you, Sam. Please. Oh, please."

He kissed her hard on the mouth, then moved over her. She welcomed his weight atop her, his strength against her. She wrapped her arms around his neck and brought his mouth down to hers.

He kissed her hard, then entered her with one swift thrust.

His intrusion was painful, stretching her, then tearing her when he penetrated the proof of her virginity.

He stopped.

"What the hell?"

The look on his face was stark with surprise and something more. Perhaps anger. Perhaps resentment. But mostly shock and disbelief. She read his mind as he realized that what he thought he'd done had to be impossible.

His breathing came in hard, jagged gasps, his muscles tensed in agitation, his nostrils flared wide. His smoldering gray eyes held her captive. She prayed he felt enough passion that he wouldn't reject her. But she knew he intended to.

He was going to reject her. Abandon her like she'd been abandoned before.

She couldn't let him. All would be lost if he did.

"No. Please, no. Don't stop. Please."

She was begging. She knew it and hated herself for it. But this was important. He didn't know how important. She needed to be loved just this once. Not that he loved her. She knew he did not. But in that instant, she knew she loved him. And she needed to know what it was like to be loved by the man she loved.

"Please."

She cupped her palm to his cheeks and smoothed the lines of fury that stretched taut across his face. "Please. Just this once," she whispered.

She urged his head downward until his mouth was atop hers and waited, praying he'd want her enough to close the distance on his own.

He stared at her, his chest heaving, the muscles across his shoulders and chest as tight as strings on a bow. A heavy sheen of perspiration covered his forehead. Through clenched teeth he asked, "Are you all right?"

She nodded, then raised her head to kiss him. He kissed her back.

His kiss was at first tentative, hesitant, but then he kissed her deeper, harder, with more passion. His tongue entered her mouth, and she met his invasion with all the expertise he'd taught her. Their tongues touched and battled in a fevered frenzy, then mated with a consuming heat that sent her soaring.

"Are you sure?" he gasped, his arms braced on either side of her, his gaze boring into hers.

"Yes. Oh, yes."

She felt him move inside her and wanted to cry out with joy. She tightened her fingers around his shoulder as they began their journey.

"Relax, Claire. Just relax."

Claire tried, honestly she did, but he was working her to a mindless state. Carrying her with him on a journey even more incredible than she imagined it would be.

She gripped his muscled arms until she knew she must be leaving marks in his flesh, but she couldn't ease her hold. He was her lifeline, and she would drown if she let go of him.

Claire didn't think she could survive soaring this high into the unknown. "Major!"

"Samuel," he gasped. "Say it!"

"Samuel. Yes. Oh, Sam!"

Claire's head thrashed from side to side as she lost herself in the wild abandon of their lovemaking. She writhed beneath him, her mind a useless part of her body that no longer functioned. And still he took her higher into the unknown.

His thrusts left her with no control as she cried out his name again. "Sam!"

"Yes, Claire. Claire!"

At the sound of her name, Claire leaped from a precipice high into the Heavens. She tumbled downward toward earth, through billowing clouds, blinding sunshine, and vivid rainbows. And still she tumbled further. Through darkness and blinding light.

If given the choice, she would choose never to fall back to earth. Never allow this miracle to end. Never allow this wondrous sensation to conclude. But it did. And she lay wondrously sated beneath him.

She opened her eyes as he thrust into her a final time. Then, with eyes closed tightly and teeth clenched, he threw back his head and found his release.

When at last he collapsed atop her, she wrapped her arms around him and held him close, pretending for just a moment that he was hers forever. That she'd never be forced to give him up.

His weight was wonderfully heavy atop her, his skin slick with perspiration from their lovemaking. She ran her hands over his shoulders and down his arms. His muscles rippled beneath her fingertips.

She couldn't stop herself from touching more of him. She memorized the feel of him against her, inside her, atop her. It was a memory she would never forget. A memory she'd cherish her whole life.

His face was nestled against her neck, his breathing harsh and raspy against her throat. His chest heaved while his heart thundered, and she felt every beat against her breast.

The minutes passed in blissful quiet, their bodies replete, their passion sated. And she thought how wonderful it had been.

But that euphoria was quickly replaced by a devastating sadness when his body separated from hers.

He rolled away from her and lay on his back, his eyes open wide as he stared at the ceiling above him. She knew he had a million questions to ask. Just as she knew she owed him an explanation. She just wasn't ready to give it. Not yet.

"Claire?"

His voice came to her as from a distance. As if he was struggling to invent at least one possible reason that she was still a virgin.

"Don't," she answered, curling into him.

He reached out his arm and nestled her to him as if he understood her need for his closeness.

Claire rested her head on his shoulder and wrapped her arm around his waist. And she slept.

A woman.

At last.

Chapter 24

Claire watched the sky turn from a dusty gray to a hazy blue, then brighter yet as streaks of varying shades of pink spiraled through it. She studied the changing colors through half-drawn drapes at the window and knew dawn was not far off.

He slept now. Finally.

He'd been awake when she'd fallen asleep and still awake each time she woke. She'd listened to his labored breathing long after they'd made love and knew it was only a short time ago when it slowed that he'd finally given up his fight to understand. And he slept.

She lifted herself from him and moved to the edge of the bed, then slipped out from beneath the covers he'd thrown over them. She tried to be as quiet as she could, but realized when his breathing changed he was probably awake again. She was glad he let her slip on her gown and leave the room without stopping her.

The night had been wondrous. Even more perfect than she'd imagined it would be. She didn't want him to change its rightness with the questions she knew she'd eventually have to answer. Questions that would color the major's opinion of Hunt. So she left him without a word.

She reached her own room without being observed, but wasn't really concerned. It was too early for even Cook to be up.

How strange that seemed this morning. That life would go on as usual, the same as it did every morning, when it wasn't at all an ordinary morning. When no morning would ever be the same for her again. All because of what had happened to her last night.

Claire filled the basin with water and dared for the first time to look into the mirror. She didn't know what she expected to see, but knew she must look different. Knew it must be plain for everyone to see that she'd changed. That the person she'd been yesterday was gone. Had been transformed into a different person. A woman.

She rinsed a cloth and washed. She was sore, she realized, but it was a wondrous soreness. A completeness she'd never thought to feel.

When she finished, she dressed in a fresh black gown. Oh, how she wanted to wear the green-and-white-striped muslin she'd worn before Hunt's death. Something gay and pretty. Something that would reflect her joy.

She combed her hair, pulling it loosely back from her face and letting it fall down her back. Tilly could fix it in a more severe style later on, but for now, she wanted it loose. Wanted it as free as she felt.

With a smile on her face, she turned from her dressing table and stopped short. Her door stood open and the major filled the entryway.

His feet were planted sternly, his hands locked behind his back, and he wore a severe expression on his face. He'd washed and shaved, his face clean, his thick, dark hair brushed back like she was used to seeing. But this morning his exposed face only emphasized his serious demeanor.

He wore dark pants over his boots and a loose-fitting white cotton shirt tucked into his waist, but open at the collar. She tried not to stare at the wide V at his neck that exposed the bronzed skin and thick hair she'd touched with such abandon last night, but failed to move her gaze from him. She could not keep her eyes from him. Nor could she keep that strange warmth from settling deep inside her.

He stepped into the room and closed the door behind him.

An uncomfortable tension engulfed her, a dark foreboding that entered with him and filled every nook and crevice of the room. She'd studied his formidable presence often, but had never felt its full threatening force more than she did now.

"Good morning," she said, struggling to stand up to him when what she wanted was to lower her gaze to the floor so she wouldn't have to look at him. She knew he was seething with questions about last night. Knew he wanted answers to secrets she'd just as soon not reveal.

"Good morning."

He stepped farther into the room, his gaze riveted on her. An aura of determination surrounded him, and she felt like a prisoner he'd come to interrogate. Like an enemy concealing secret information. She would rather he didn't stand so close. That he didn't tower over her.

She rose, then moved to the window and drew back the drapery. It was not yet dawn, but the openness helped. It gave her a feeling of confidence. She needed all the confidence she could gather.

"You didn't wake me when you left."

"I didn't see the need."

"You didn't."

His two words made up such a simple statement, but the hard tone of his voice suggested any reply she gave him would take her to a place she didn't want to go.

"It's too early to ring for coffee," she said, praying he'd take her hint and go downstairs and wait for her there. "If you'd like—"

"What I'd like," he said, crossing the room in two angry strides, "is for you to tell me what the hell happened last night."

She stepped away from him. Not out of fear, but because she needed the distance to battle the confusion she saw on his face.

"Why didn't you tell me you were a virgin? My God, you were married to Hunt for six—"

"Seven."

". . . seven years."

His expression turned harder, the condemning look in his eyes blatant along with the disbelief.

"Bloody hell, woman. Didn't you once, in all that time, allow him to come to your bed?"

Didn't she *allow* him?

Claire staggered under the weight of his implication. She gripped the edge of the nearest chair angled in front of the window. She had imagined him coming to many conclusions, the most obvious being that her husband had never *wanted* her as his wife. But never had she expected him to think *she* was the one who would not be a wife to her husband. She swallowed hard. "Is that what you think?"

"What else am I to think? You said yourself the purpose for your marriage was to give Hunt an heir. How could you deliberately deny him that right?"

He thought the worst of her. Thought she was callous and deceiving enough to forbid her husband his right to get her with child. That it was by choice she was still a virgin. She nearly doubled over from the pain.

She didn't think it was possible to hurt any more than she'd hurt every day during the seven years Hunt had refused to make her his wife. But she'd been wrong. It hurt far more to realize Sam thought she was capable of such deceit.

She pulled deep within herself as she had for seven years. Far inside until she reached that empty place where no hint of emotion or hurt could touch her. Why had she assumed the major would realize that she couldn't be at fault for the lack of intimacy in her marriage? That it was Hunt's fault she was still a virgin?

Didn't he know her well enough to realize that? Or care enough for her? She'd learned years ago that no one had thought for even a minute that Hunt might be the reason she'd never conceived a child. But she thought Sam would be different.

She was a fool. For seven years she'd faced Society's pitying glances when month after month there was no sign of a child. And for all that time, she'd suffered with her own feelings of inadequacy when her husband refused to come to her. She'd locked away her emotions and convinced herself it did not matter if her husband could not love her.

She'd survived the disgrace of not being a woman her whole married life. What did Major Samuel Bennett's opinion of her matter? Let him believe she'd refused to be a wife to her husband. If he didn't know what kind of woman she really was, then let him believe the worst of her. It would solve the impossibility of a commitment between them. It would be the excuse she needed to pretend last night had never happened.

Claire forced a well-rehearsed smile and turned on him.

"Perhaps," she said, forcing down the lump lodged in her throat, "I wanted Hunt as little as he wanted me. Perhaps our marriage was a one of mutual dissatisfaction."

"So you refused him for all that time?"

"Do you find it hard to believe that I could remain untouched for so long? Oh, Major. That was not difficult. You knew Hunt. He was hardly the type of man to force himself on a woman."

The major's hands clenched at his side. "Do you know what you've done? Because of you, the Huntingdon title will cease to exist."

She wanted to laugh. Oh, how often she'd thrown that same argument up to Hunt in the beginning when she was naïve enough to think she could save her marriage. When she'd tried every tactic and argument she could think of to force him to be a husband to her. Even if it was only to provide him with an heir.

Before Hunt had, in his quiet, forceful way, told her that no child of hers could be his heir. Even though she couldn't understand his reasoning, she knew his meaning. He hadn't been able to fight his father's demand that he take her as his wife, but he refused to have her as the mother of his children.

Even though Claire thought she might be ill when she looked at the disappointment she knew she'd see on the major's face, she braced herself to face him. "I obviously expected him to live longer."

She heard the sound of his fury when he sucked in a harsh breath. "How did you do it, Claire? There was never a hint of scandal involving Hunt. No rumors of a mistress or an affair with a widow or bored and unhappy wife. How did you force someone so undeniably male and accustomed to female companionship to lead the life of a monk?"

"Stop it!"

With long, angry strides he took himself to the other side of the room and turned his back on her.

Claire waited, praying he'd realize how wrong he was. Praying he'd say the words that would take away the bitterness she heard in his accusations. She waited for him to realize she wasn't capable of doing something so horrendous. But he said nothing. He only braced his hands against the fireplace mantel and hung his head between his outstretched arms.

For a long time he stared into the cold, lifeless embers of a fire long gone out. When he spoke, his voice was soft and deadly, his words cutting through the silence like a knife. "Why me?"

Hundreds of painful needle points pierced her heart. A lump formed in her throat, and even though she tried, she couldn't speak.

"Why did you deny your husband for seven years, then not even six months after his death give yourself to me?"

Claire knew what it felt like to have her heart ripped from her breast. She was still alive, yet she knew a part of her had died.

For seven years she'd thought she'd lived her worst nightmare. Thought nothing could be worse than knowing the man who'd vowed before God to love and cherish her didn't want her. But that hadn't been the worst. She knew that now.

Her worst nightmare was watching the man she'd come to care for—no, love—stare at her as if she were the most vile, disgusting creature on earth. It was having the man to whom she'd just given her body accuse her of being such a scheming manipulator that she'd denied her husband his right to an heir. It was having the man to whom she'd given her heart think she could do something so abhorrent. That was the worst.

And a large part of the heart she'd exposed to him crumbled and broke, making it impossible to tell him the truth . . . that her husband had been too repulsed by her to touch her. She could save herself that disgrace, at least.

"Why you?" Claire said, her voice sounding unnatural to her ears. "Who better?"

She took two steps into the center of the room and faced him squarely. "Who better to expose my secret to than Hunt's best friend? Who better to trust with the knowledge that I'd never let my husband bed me than the one person I knew would never divulge my secret?

"Just imagine the scandal my virginity would have caused once it was discovered the Marquess of Huntingdon had not been man enough to force his wife to fulfill her wifely obligations. Imagine the laughing-stock Hunt would have become if I would have let just anyone bed me and my virginity became common knowledge."

She paced the room, clasping and unclasping her hands. Her breathing was rapid and shallow. She had to keep moving or she would fall apart. "I consider choosing you as my first lover a magnanimous act in protecting Hunt's memory. Hunt would have been grateful for your participation, Major."

She saw him stiffen as the impact of her words registered. His jaw clenched, and the narrow glare of his eyes contained more bitterness than she believed could be leveled at any one person.

"Think of bedding me as doing Hunt a favor. Of saving your fellow comrade-in-arms from being posthumously disgraced." The room spun around her, and she reached out to steady herself against the corner of her small writing desk. "Can you imagine the laugh Society would have had at his expense, knowing the manly Marquess of Huntingdon could have had any woman in England—except his wife?"

Claire managed a laugh even though the blood thundered in her head with such violence she could barely breathe. A painful weight pressed against her heart. And through his hate-filled glare, she tried to pretend the look of horror and disgust she saw on the major's face wasn't killing her inch by painful inch. But it was. "Now, get out!" she demanded. "And leave me alone!"

Claire turned away from the look of revulsion on his face. She waited to hear him storm from the room. When he didn't, she repeated her demand. "Get out! Now!"

She squeezed her eyes shut to keep the tears from running down her cheeks. When he didn't move, she prayed she'd hear him tell her he knew her words had been lies. That he knew her well enough—cared for her enough—to know she would never have turned Hunt from her bed. That he knew Hunt would never have let her. That there must be another reason.

But if he did, he didn't get a chance to utter those thoughts. Her door flew open and Barnaby stepped into the room.

"What the hell is going on, Claire? I heard the yelling from my room."

Claire gave the major a final look, then turned her gaze to the confused look on Barnaby's face. From the furious look on the major's.

Barnaby was right. The major wasn't capable of giving her what she so desperately needed. She'd been a fool to think he could.

"Claire?" When she didn't answer him, Barnaby turned to Sam. "Bennett?"

Claire knew her brother expected the major to explain what his sister obviously wouldn't. She knew he wouldn't. Knew her secret was safe now for eternity.

Just as she knew the most wonderful night of her life, the night she'd anticipated for more than seven years, was now a night she wanted to forget had ever happened. All her beautiful memories had been destroyed.

"Linscott," she heard the major issue to her brother, "get everyone up. I want them in Hunt's study in fifteen minutes."

"What?"

"You heard me. I want that room stripped from floor to ceiling. I want every picture off the walls and every book off the shelves. Now!"

The major didn't give Barnaby time to answer. His hard, angry footsteps stormed from the room. She clutched her hands tight around her middle.

"Claire?"

She felt Barn step up behind her, but she couldn't turn around to look him in the eyes.

"What was that all about?"

"Nothing. It was nothing."

Claire felt Barn's hands grip her shoulders, then turn her gently until she faced him. She forced herself not to shrink from his discerning gaze, but kept her back rigid and her chin high.

Barn dropped his hands from her shoulders and stepped back to look at her. Claire knew the moment he realized how desperately she was hurting.

"Ah, Claire. I warned you."

"Yes, you did."

Claire smiled a bittersweet smile, then turned away from her brother and walked to the window. The sun was up now. It was a beautiful day.

"Have Watkins get everyone up and send them to Hunt's study. We don't have much time left."

"Are you all right?"

"Yes. I'm fine. I'll be down in a minute to help. We have to be there in case he finds the necklace. It's the only way to save Alex."

Claire held her breath while Barnaby hesitated. She breathed a sigh of relief when the door closed behind him and she was alone.

She stood as long as her legs would hold her, then sank to the floor beneath the window and buried her face in her hands. She didn't want anyone to witness the silent, complete demise of a heart in agony. It was not something she wished to share with anyone.

Chapter 25

Claire worked alongside the servants, removing armload after armload of heavy books from the shelves and placing them on the floor. The astronomical number of volumes Hunt had accumulated was amazing. But even though some of them were rare editions, priceless in monetary worth, they were worthless when valued against Alex's life. Which was why Claire watched every move the major made. If the necklace was here, she had to make sure she found it.

She glanced across the room to where he was busy stripping everything from the walls. He was without a jacket or waistcoat, and the sleeves of his white lawn shirt were rolled midway up his muscled forearms. He was the most powerfully masculine male she'd ever seen. As well as the most dangerously angry.

He'd said very little to anyone since she'd entered the room, and had been careful not to cast even one glance in her direction. He was quite successful at keeping his attention centered on the monumental task before him. She was glad. She wasn't sure she could stand up under his condemning scrutiny any longer.

Barnaby worked with him, taking everything the major handed him and helping lift the objects that were too heavy for one person. Even the draperies from the windows lay in heaps on the floor. The major's energy seemed boundless, but she knew it was raw fury that drove him.

In the scant hour since Sam had come downstairs, he'd accomplished as much as half a dozen men. He worked as if the hounds of hell were biting at his heels. As if he could burn off the frustration and anger that ate at him.

Claire knew such an effort was impossible. Hard work wouldn't make anything go away. It wouldn't take back the cruel words they'd both said. It wouldn't make what they'd shared good again.

Each pass she made with another armload of books forced her to walk closer to him. She tried not to let her gaze linger too long where he stood on the ladder, but found it impossible. Her eyes were naturally drawn to his powerful physique. To his dominating presence. And each time she caught a glimpse of the fury on his face, she died a little more inside.

More than once she had to swallow past the painful lump in her throat, then berate herself because she'd allowed herself to reach for a future she should have known was impossible.

"Watkins. Remove the books from this wall next," the major ordered in curt, precise terms. He pointed to the shelves closest to where he stood. Two servants rushed to move a second ladder to the spot he indicated, then Timothy, one of the footmen, quickly climbed the rungs.

She walked to the ladder where Timothy stood at the highest shelves and was forced to look up. From just beyond Timothy's shoulder, the major's gaze locked with hers. Her heart slammed against her ribs when she recognized the unyielding hardness in his eyes. He was still struggling to come to terms with what he thought she'd done. She could see it. He was still fighting emotions he was unable to control. Every shred of anger and bitterness she saw on his face was directed toward her.

Oh, she'd expected the questions. Expected to have to explain how she could still be a virgin after seven years of marriage. But she hadn't expected the accusations. Hadn't expected him to believe she was at fault for her failed marriage. That was the harshest blow of all. His words still left her heart aching.

Didn't you once, in all that time, allow him to come to your bed?

She tore her gaze away from him and took the books from the footman's outstretched hands. It was too late to wish for things that could never be. Nor did she have the luxury of changing the events of her life so things would be different. She would concentrate on something else. On finding the necklace and saving Alex.

The major evidently thought the necklace and papers were hidden here somewhere or he wouldn't be going to such lengths to empty this room. And if they were, both she and Barnaby were here to make sure they got the necklace to exchange for Alex's freedom.

Claire set her armload of books on the floor and went back for more. Then more. Then more. Until one wall was done and the other nearly finished.

"Claire, why don't you sit down for a while?"

Claire turned to see Barnaby behind her. His features were strained, and there was a genuine look of concern in his eyes.

"I'm fine."

"No, you're not. Even the major—"

Barnaby cut off the rest of his sentence when she flashed him a hostile look.

"You need to rest. Why don't you go to your room for a while?"

"We need to be here in case he finds the necklace. We can't let him have it, Barn. He won't give it to Roseneau. He'll let Alex die."

Barn wrapped his arms around her and pulled her to him. There was nothing unusual in such a show of affection from Barn. Of her two brothers, he was the most like her. The closest to her. The one who understood her best. He was also the one from whom she'd had to work hardest to keep the problems in her marriage secret.

"We have a few hours yet, Claire. We're not out of time, and we have a small army watching Roseneau. The minute he makes a move, we'll know it."

Claire leaned against Barnaby and welcomed his embrace. It made her feel safe for at least a little while. But she knew it was a false sense of security that wouldn't last. "Do you think it's here?" she said, her cheek against his chest. "Do you think there's a chance Hunt has a safe concealed somewhere in the walls?"

"If there is, Bennett will find it. Even if he has to bring the room down around him."

Barnaby pushed back a strand of hair that had come loose, then held her at arm's length. "Get some rest, Claire. You need it."

"I'll be fine once we have Alex home."

Barnaby looked uncomfortable. "That may not be possible, Claire. You know that."

Claire's heart skipped a beat. "No, Barn. Not you, too." She pushed herself away from him and looked into his face for an answer to the alarming fear growing inside her. "Surely you wouldn't let the major keep it? It's our only chance to save Alex."

Claire knew her voice was louder than it should be, and when she looked around, several servants were staring at her. So was the major.

Barnaby led her farther away from everyone, then turned her toward him. "There are a lot of lives at stake, Claire. Alex's is only one."

"No!"

Claire pulled out of Barnaby's arms. She looked at him and for the first time saw a man no different than the major. How had she missed it all this time?

"You don't care what happens to him, do you?" she said, not caring that her words would hurt him. "You don't care that he may die."

"You know that's not true, Claire."

"Yes, it is, or you'd know we don't have any choice but to give the necklace to Roseneau."

"Claire, I—"

"Linscott! I need your help."

The major's voice cut through the tension in the room like a saber on the battlefield. Everyone in the room turned their gazes to him. Including Claire.

She stared at him, struggling to find any softness, any compassion. Any hint of the man she'd lain with last night. A man who would choose Alex's life over the lives of strangers. She found none. He was as far removed from her as he'd ever been. As if he'd shut her out and locked the door. She clenched her fists and held his gaze, making him look away first.

"It'll be all right," Barnaby whispered. "I won't let anything happen to Alex."

"Linscott! Now!"

Barnaby gave her hand a squeeze, then went back to where the major stood. The shelves were empty, and after talking to the major, Barnaby ordered everyone to leave. When the room was cleared of the servants, the major walked to the center of the room and studied each empty wall. Claire stood frozen in place. When his penetrating gaze stopped on her, she struggled not to show any weakness but failed when the floor felt as if shifted beneath her.

"Linscott, get your sister to a chair before we have to pick her up from the floor."

Barnaby rushed to help Claire to the nearest seat, a green-and-burgundy floral sofa someone had moved away from the wall. The major jerked his gaze away from her as if the sight of her was more than he could bear.

He positioned the ladder on the far side of the room, then grabbed a wooden mallet from the floor and climbed the ladder set up before the empty shelves. When he reached the top, he drew back his arm and let it gently fall back against the wall with a thud.

Claire sat on the edge of the settee, her nerves stretched to the breaking point as she watched the major tap the mallet against the wall.

The sound was solid, hard, the dull thud the sound of a hammer hitting a barrel filled with dirt.

For many long, agonizing minutes, the pounding continued. Claire stared as if riveted to the major's arm reaching out and striking the wall. His muscles bulged beneath his shirt, and the further he stretched, the more the material strained over his shoulders.

She remembered the feel of his flesh beneath her hands last night. How his muscles rippled at her touch. How his skin gleamed with perspiration from their frantic lovemaking. She shook her head as the pounding continued. But the visions of him lying on top of her, of his weight pressed against her, of his heat thrust inside her refused to go away.

It seemed to last forever, the pounding. But finally he finished one wall. Barnaby moved the ladder to the other side of the room, and the major climbed the rungs. A strand of hair fell across his brow, and her fingers ached to reach out like she'd done last night to brush it back. The inside of her palms itched to touch his face and feel the biting stubble against her tender flesh. Her lips ached to be kissed like she'd been last night. To feel his mouth against hers, his lips open atop hers, his tongue delving inside to mate with hers.

With each thud of the mallet, her heart thundered harder inside her breast. The steady pounding related every detail about him she couldn't live without . . . his strength, his gentleness, his unflagging honor, his loyalty.

Each time the thuds stopped so he could move the ladder, her heart jolted as if it couldn't beat without his urging. And when he continued, her mind ticked off in rhythm all the memories she cherished . . . the night he'd saved her from Roseneau's henchman, afterward when he'd cradled her in his lap and called her back when he thought she was dying, when he'd held her hand, and carried her to her bed when she was too weak to walk, and forced her to eat when food was the last thing she thought her body could handle.

She remembered the hours they'd talked, the night they'd walked in the garden, the days spent in each other's company, and . . .

Claire understood why the major's rejection hurt more than Hunt's rejection had. She'd taken Hunt as her husband, but she'd never truly loved him. As Hunt had never truly loved her. But she loved Sam.

If only she didn't. If only she could have been satisfied with kissing him that first time, then never again. If only she could have been content with the way he held her and not ached for something more. But she hadn't been.

That was why his rejection hurt so much. She more than cared for him.

She loved him.

Her heart stopped with the same suddenness as the thudding of the mallet on the wall. Everything in the room was alive, and Claire wondered if she'd uttered her most secret thoughts aloud. But it wasn't that. She knew it when she looked at Barnaby and his eyes were riveted on the spot the major had just hit.

He hit it again.

The sound this time wasn't like a hammer hitting a barrel filled with dirt, but a hammer hitting an empty keg. It was hollow—the sound ringing, then echoing as if there were nothing inside to stop it. The major dropped the mallet to the floor and ran his hands over the spot he'd just hit.

Barnaby stepped closer. "What is it, Major?"

The expression on Barnaby's face was so intense Claire wondered that he didn't climb up the other side of the ladder to help investigate.

The major didn't answer, but deftly moved his fingers over a square area. Claire stepped closer, her heart thudding in her chest. If they found it, she couldn't let him have it. Alex's life depended on it.

She looked around the room, searching for something to use to take it away from him. But there was nothing.

She turned her attention back to where he still worked. He ran his fingers over a large spot, then lifted a flap in the wallpaper about two inches in diameter. He looked closer at the circle, then glanced down at Barnaby.

Claire's heart thundered faster.

"Linscott, there's a key in the left top drawer of Hunt's desk. Get it."

Barnaby ran to the desk and opened the drawer. With the key in his hand, he ran back to the major and handed it up.

Claire watched in silence as the major inserted the key in the opening and turned. With a slight pull, the secret square opened, revealing a safe in the wall that had been impossible to see by just looking.

The major reached inside and removed the contents item by item: a small box, a larger envelope, a thin ledger, and some loose papers. Last to come out was a book. A Bible.

The major climbed down the ladder and took the contents of Hunt's safe to the desk, where he laid them out.

Claire didn't think she could stand the suspense. Couldn't stand knowing the necklace was there. Couldn't stand to think she might not be able to get it.

The major sat down in Hunt's chair, and Barnaby stood behind him. Claire took another step closer, her knees trembling, her eyes riveted on the contents.

The major picked up the small box first and opened it. It was the right size for the necklace Hunt had stolen. When he opened it, Claire expected to see the necklace that was responsible for Hunt's death and Alex being in danger.

The major emptied the jewels on the top of the desk and looked at the contents of the box. The jewels were beautiful and without a doubt worth a fortune, but looked more like Huntingdon heirlooms: two rings, a diamond necklace, and a string of pearls. There were two or three brooches and a beautiful diamond pendant. But she could tell from the look on the major's face that the Queen's Blood wasn't there.

Claire's heart lurched in her chest. The necklace wasn't there. Their only means of freeing Alex *wasn't there*.

Chapter 26

Claire sank down on the nearest chair and watched while the major went through the other items. He opened the ledger next, although Claire hardly cared what Hunt had written down in the book. How could she? Nothing else scattered on the desk would save Alex. Even giving Roseneau every Huntingdon heirloom they could get their hands on wouldn't save him. Only the Queen's Blood would.

Claire watched with a growing sense of despair while the major gave the ledger a quick glance, then set it aside to search the large envelope.

Claire could tell it didn't contain a necklace, but only papers. He pulled them out and laid them on the desk in front of him. From where she sat, they all looked like legal documents, probably deeds to properties Hunt's family owned. He scanned each document, then laid it to the side when he was finished.

All but one.

She saw his reaction, the quick intake of breath that lifted his shoulders. A frown darkened his face as he read the paper. When he reached the bottom of the page, he shoved his chair back from the desk and stood. Barnaby stepped to the side to get out of his way.

The look on Barnaby's face said that he was as confused by the wild glare in the major's eyes as she was.

There was a look of utter disbelief on the major's face. He walked to the window with the paper in his hand, and for several long seconds he didn't move. Only read the document again and again.

Claire kept her gaze riveted on his tense body, waiting for some clue as to what he'd found.

He closed his eyes, as if he needed to block out the words he'd just read, then he slowly held out the paper.

Barnaby took it and read the words. His face turned white and his hands trembled.

"Bloody hell! What does this mean?"

The major shook his head, then moved his gaze to where Claire sat in the chair watching them.

Barnaby waved the paper in the air. "This can't be right! Tell me it can't!"

But the major didn't tell him it couldn't. Instead, he crossed back to the desk and opened the large book . . . the Bible.

Claire frowned as he lifted the cover and scanned the first page, then the next. He found what he was looking for on the third page, on the right hand side, in the lower third of the page. Claire could tell because that was where his gaze remained. That was where Barnaby's gaze stopped. Then they both lifted their gazes from the page and stared at her.

The expression on Barnaby's face was the same as it had been the night he'd come to tell her Hunt was dead. The major's was different. Just as stark and threatening, but now filled with confusion and questions.

"Claire?"

Barnaby walked toward her, his movements slow and hesitant, almost as reluctant as someone on his way to the gallows. The news, whatever it was, was not good. She could see it on his face.

But she couldn't focus on Barnaby. She could only stare at the man to whom she'd given herself last night. The man she'd trusted with her secret. Now he stood in the sunlight before the window, his features frozen as if chiseled from granite. His high cheekbones and angled jaw rigid and firm. His dark, thick brows framing eyes so deep a gray they almost seemed black. As they had last night. At the peak of his passion.

It was on him she focused. On him she drew the strength she knew she'd need to face whatever Barnaby intended to confront her with. On the man with the ruggedly handsome features and bronzed skin. With the broad chest and muscled arms. The man she knew she loved. The man she wanted to run to now and have wrap his arms around her and hold her. She knew she could face it then, whatever Barnaby was going to tell her. But he didn't come to her. And she couldn't go to him.

"Claire?"

She nodded her head and moved her gaze to where Barnaby stood. His features were strained, his complexion drained of all color. She clenched her hands in her lap and waited.

"Did you find the necklace?"

She asked the question even though she knew they hadn't. She'd seen what they'd found. But asking somehow drew the attention away from the paper Barnaby held in his hand.

"We found . . . this."

He held it out to her, and for a long moment, she simply stared at it.

She looked past her brother to the major. His gaze didn't waver but locked onto hers while she reached for the paper. She finally took it from Barnaby and held it in her hand. Then slowly lowered her gaze.

She didn't know what she'd expected. Her eyes read the letters, but her mind refused to decipher their meaning.

CERTIFICATE OF MARRIAGE

There was no elegant scrolling or ornately painted designs like on the marriage certificate she and Hunt had signed in the lengthy ceremony after their marriage. The paper seemed rustic and plain in its simplicity.

MARCH 16, 1838

Claire stared at the date. It meant nothing to her. She'd been barely ten years old then. And nothing remarkable had happened then except her mother had died and left her alone. Her gaze moved to the bottom of the page. To the bold script of her late husband's.

BRANDON DURRANT, 10TH MARQUESS OF HUNTINGDON

It was Hunt's title. Hunt's name. But how could his name be here?

Claire scanned further down the page. To the last line. Where a small word denoted the role of the signer. Such a small word with such an enormous meaning.

MARY ELIZABETH SMITHSON

Bride

Claire stared at the words. She read them over and over, thinking perhaps they'd change. They didn't. The magnitude of their meaning loomed larger before her, enveloping her in a vast pit of darkness.

She fought to escape, but it was as if a blanket of cold spread over her, freezing her, preserving the ice that ran through her veins.

She was sure she should do something. Was certain something was expected of her, a specific reaction that was appropriate to this situation. But for the life of her, she couldn't imagine what it might be.

How did one react when they found out the man they'd been married to wasn't one's husband after all?

She rose to her feet and separated herself from Barnaby and the major. She walked across the room and looked out the window. Everything seemed normal outside. How could that be?

"Claire?"

The major's voice broke through the haze of confusion and roiling turmoil racing through her mind. He was close, she could hear he was, but he didn't touch her.

She wanted to laugh. Perhaps he knew she didn't want to be touched. That she'd shatter if he did. That she'd crumble into a million pieces with even the smallest gesture.

Except she knew she wouldn't. There was too much anger in her to fall apart, too much rage and hurt. She could thank Hunt for that. For conditioning her to be such an expert at pretending her life was perfect when it was far from it.

"Claire? Do you know what the paper means?"

She jerked her head upward and leveled both him and Barnaby with the most livid glare she could muster. "Yes, Major. I'm well aware of what the paper means. It means it's quite probable I'm not—"

"Excuse me, my lady," Watkins said from the doorway. "But you have a visitor."

"Tell whoever it is your mistress isn't receiving," Barnaby said in a gruff voice.

"Begging your pardon, sir, but I think this is important. The lady says she's . . . the Marchioness of Huntingdon."

⁓

Sam saw Claire stagger slightly and reached for her, but she held out her hand to stop him. She stepped away and anchored her hand against the wall as if she needed its support to steady herself.

None of them moved for several long seconds. Then, as if she'd regained control of her shattered emotions, she squared her shoulders and turned around. She looked first to her brother, then to him.

Sam fought the knot that formed deep in his gut and twisted painfully. There was a haunted and faraway look in her eyes. Her face was void of color. But when she brought her hands around in front of her, she looked unnaturally relaxed and composed.

"Watkins, show the . . ."

She swallowed hard and sucked in a shaky breath, the first visible sign of how difficult this was for her.

". . . marchioness to the morning room and have tea served. Tell her I'll be with her momentarily. See that she is made comfortable."

"Yes, my lady."

"You don't have to go," Linscott said when Watkins left the room. "I can take care of this."

Her eyebrows shot up in dainty arches, then she smiled a placid smile. "She's not some dust that can be swept under the carpet, Barn. She's Hunt's widow. She's the Marchioness of Huntingdon."

"And what the hell are you?"

A gaping silence filled the room. Barnaby had asked the question even Sam hadn't wanted to consider. And for the first time in all the years he'd known Hunt, he hated him for what he'd done to her.

"Major," she said, walking to the center of the room.

Her voice was strong, her words clipped. Sam was glad. He would much rather she strike out in anger than revert inward in quiet solitude.

"Have you gone through all the papers?"

"Yes."

"What else is there for me to know?"

"Are you sure—"

She spun on him. "I've had enough surprises for one day. I would like to meet Huntingdon's widow on at least somewhat equal footing."

"Very well. Why don't you sit down," he said, pointing to the nearest chair. He expected her to argue, but she didn't. She sat with her back rigidly straight and her hands clasped in her lap.

"The marriage papers seem in order. Hunt's name along with a . . . Mary Elizabeth Smithson's are also entered in the family Bible we found in the safe."

"Were there children?"

Sam wanted to hold some of this back from her, but there was no way he could. "Yes."

"How many?"

"Four. Two sons and two daughters."

She sucked in a shaky breath, and Sam was reminded again of how difficult this was for her.

"His heir?"

"Jonathan Alexander Durrant, now the eleventh Marquess of Huntingdon. He should be nearing seventeen."

"And the youngest?"

Sam knew what she was asking. "Claire, don't."

"How old is the youngest?"

"Five."

He heard the strangled gasp and fought the urge to go to her.

"That is why . . . ?"

She didn't finish her sentence, but Sam knew what she meant. That was why Hunt had never lain with her. That was why after seven years of marriage, she was still a virgin. Damn Hunt.

Damn him!

A pain hit Sam in the gut as if he'd been slammed by a fist. He'd been so wrong. Been so unfair to her. He'd thought it was her fault that she was still a virgin. Sam couldn't believe that Hunt hadn't wanted Claire in every way a man wants a woman. He couldn't believe that Hunt's life in private was so opposite the life he portrayed in public. And, Sam needed someone to blame. Someone other than his best friend. So he'd let himself believe that she was the one who'd barred him from her bed. But she wasn't. It had been Hunt.

"It wasn't your fault, Claire."

Her angry gaze locked with his. "No, it wasn't. But you were ready enough to blame me, Major. Weren't you?"

She didn't wait for his reaction, but bolted from the chair and walked to the door.

Chapter 27

Claire walked down the narrow hall that led to the morning room with angry, determined steps. For seven years, the woman behind that door had robbed her of every dream she'd ever had. For seven years, someone else had been given all the Marquess of Huntingdon's love and affection, while Claire was left to live an empty shell of an existence.

Claire braced herself, ready to confront the thief who'd stolen everything from her. A fury unlike anything she'd ever battled raged full force.

"Claire."

The major's voice called out from behind her, but she didn't stop. She marched forward and let him and Barnaby follow her.

When she neared the morning room, a liveried footman scrambled to open the door.

Claire clenched her teeth and stepped inside.

The woman Hunt had loved stood across the room. She had her back to Claire and wore a black gown, a stark reminder that she, even more than Claire, had the right to mourn Hunt. Claire was prepared to dislike her, was prepared to make her pay for every hurt Hunt had ever caused.

Then the woman turned, and Claire looked into eyes drowning in unfathomable sadness. Claire knew it would be impossible to hate her.

Although older than Claire, Hunt's wife was one of the most beautiful women Claire had ever seen. She'd pulled her golden hair back from her face into a tight chignon, but delicate tendrils had fallen loose from beneath her black velvet bonnet to frame her face.

Her complexion was creamy white, her lips full, her eyes a magnificent shade of green. She had a face painters gave everything they owned for the honor of putting down on canvas.

For several long seconds they looked at each other in silence. Claire saw a depth of loneliness in Hunt's widow's eyes that reached deep into her soul. A loss Claire had never felt for the man who'd been her husband. Claire tried to speak but suddenly found herself unable to find the words. The woman across the room smiled tentatively.

"I wondered under what circumstances we would eventually meet," the real Marchioness of Huntingdon said, her voice containing a hint of reserved nervousness. "But I never imagined it would be like this."

Claire swayed at the woman's soft, gentle voice and felt a hand press against the small of her back to steady her. She didn't need to look to know the major stood next to her.

"You'll have to forgive me," Claire said, taking comfort in the major's strength. "I'm at a disadvantage. Hunt failed to mention your existence to me."

"I know. I'm sure there's much Brandon did not mention."

Claire glimpsed an honest regret in the woman's eyes she wasn't prepared to see.

"You must be Major Bennett," the woman said, lifting her gaze to where the major stood. "Brandon spoke of you often. You're exactly as he described you. He was very fond of you."

Sam nodded. The woman turned to Barnaby. "And you must be Lord Barnaby. The marquess told me he'd chosen wisely and repeatedly commented how much he admired you."

Barnaby nodded curtly, but showed no sign of softening.

"Allow me to introduce myself. My name is—"

She stopped. She smiled slightly, then breathed a heavy sigh when she looked at Claire. "This is not easy. I so wish Brandon would have prepared you."

"I'm not sure how he could have prepared me to meet his wife. Mary, isn't it?"

There was a look of surprise on Mary's face before she said, "I see you found Brand's secret hiding place. The safe hidden in the wall."

"Yes. We found it. You can imagine my shock when I discovered your marriage certificate there."

"Yes. I can imagine. I apologize for that. Brand never intended to deceive you as long as he did."

"Then why did he? Why did he have to deceive me at all?"

"For our son."

Claire reeled at the admission. She knew Hunt had a son—the major had already told her—but hearing it said so bluntly stole her breath.

She stepped away from the center of the room. Away from where the major stood ready to reach out to her. Away from where Barnaby stood, ready to comfort her however he could. She didn't need them. She needed to face this on her own.

She walked to where the tea service had been set up and leaned against the table until she'd composed herself, then turned to face her adversary.

"Please, sit down, Lady . . . Lady Huntingdon," Claire said. The words caused a lump in her throat.

Lady Huntingdon took the chair Claire indicated, then turned her attention to Sam. "You were with Brandon when he died, weren't you, Major?"

"Yes."

Hunt's widow lowered her tear-filled gaze to her lap. "Did he suffer at the end?" Her soft voice broke. She dabbed at her eyes, then raised her gaze to meet Sam directly.

"No."

"I'm glad."

Lady Huntingdon cleared her throat as if composing herself, then turned to where Claire sat on the sofa opposite her.

"I'm sorry it took me so long before I came to see you, but I didn't know until a few weeks ago that Brandon was . . . gone."

"How did you find out?" the major asked, moving closer to Claire. He sat on the sofa next to her, his thigh touching her as if he wanted her to know he was there for her. Barnaby sat on her other side.

"When Brand left us that last time, he said he'd be gone at least a month, if not two." She smiled. "It wasn't unusual for him to be detained longer once he came to London. But when three months went by and he still didn't return, I became worried. I sent Parker, Brandon's servant, to London. He's the only one who knew Brand's real identity. As you have probably realized, our relationship was a secret Brand guarded closely."

Barnaby sat forward in his chair and spoke for the first time. "No one suspected who you really were?"

Lady Huntingdon smiled. "Everyone *knew* who we were. Lord and Lady Granville. My husband was rumored to have some position with the government, or perhaps it was a position with a solicitor, or perhaps a connection to a large shipping firm, or"—she smiled—"whatever fantasy Brandon invented that kept him away from home for long periods of time. We lived such ordinary lives, no one paid much attention to our comings and goings."

"You have to excuse my bluntness, Lady . . . Lady . . ." Claire tried to finish, but couldn't.

"Please, call me Mary. And I will call you Claire if you don't object. Because that is how Brandon always referred to you."

Claire squeezed her eyes shut tight, trying to accustom herself to this nightmare. "Very well, Mary. You'll have to excuse my bluntness, but I . . . I . . ."

Mary smiled. "You deserve an explanation."

The Marchioness of Huntingdon—the *real* Marchioness of Huntingdon—rose from her chair and separated herself from where

Claire and the major and Barnaby sat. With a soft, gentle voice, she began.

"I met Brand when I was nineteen. My parents were actors and we were playing in London. One night Brand and a group of his friends came to one of the performances. He came backstage after the performance and asked me to join him for dinner. I found out later he did it on a dare. Not a very romantic beginning," she said, glancing at Claire, "but I think we fell in love that night. I know I did.

"It wasn't long before Brand was talking marriage. I knew from the start a future together was impossible. He was a marquess, heir to a dukedom. I was an actress. I knew his father wouldn't allow his only son to marry me. But Brand was so optimistic. He wouldn't listen to anything I said. Then I discovered I was pregnant."

Mary ran a small gloved hand over the edge of the marble mantel on the fireplace. "I would have been content to be Brand's mistress, as long as we could be together. You see," she said with a faraway look in her eyes, "we both realized how impossible it would be to live without each other. For weeks, every time Brand brought up marriage, I refused. I told him I wasn't interested in his title. That all that mattered was that we were together.

"But Brand wouldn't consider any arrangement other than marriage. He was so confident that when his father found out I was carrying the next Bridgemont heir, he'd agree to our marriage. But of course those were just the idealistic dreams of youth. When His Grace found out, he became livid. He refused to even consider allowing his son to marry an actress.

"Brandon put up every argument imaginable. He even arranged a surprise meeting between us, sure that when his father met me, he couldn't help but welcome me as a daughter-in-law. The meeting was a disaster.

"The Duke of Bridgemont publicly rejected me and announced to all in attendance that he would never despoil the Bridgemont name by allowing his son marry a fortune-seeking harlot. That he'd disown Brand first and let the title be passed down to a distant cousin. So Brand and

I did the only thing left to assure our son wasn't born a bastard. We married secretly."

Mary paced the room. "We were so young then. So naïve. Brand was only twenty-five and I was just nineteen. Brand was convinced that in time his father would change his mind about me. If not, he was content to wait until his father died and he became the next Duke of Bridgemont.

"So, we moved to an estate Brand bought under our new assumed name, and for nearly seventeen years, we've kept our marriage a secret."

Claire clutched her hands in her lap until they ached. "Why did he marry me? What possible reason could he have had, knowing he was committing bigamy?"

"The Bridgemont title. The estates. Everything that went with the name. His father was tired of waiting for Brand to provide him with an heir and threatened to disown him if he didn't marry you."

Claire reached out. The major's hand was suddenly there. Claire held on to him as if he were the lifeline she needed to survive this.

"Somehow, his father found out about us. Not that we were married. He assumed Brand was keeping me as his mistress. Of course, his father didn't have any qualms about that as long as he married you to provide him with a legal heir.

"I begged him not to go through with it. I told him I didn't care about the wealth or the estates. That I would be happy with whatever he provided. And I truly believe until the last second, he didn't intend to go through with his marriage to you. He'd resigned himself to giving it all up. But one thing stopped him. His one weakness. His Achilles heel."

"Of course," Claire said, feeling a bitterness she couldn't fight. "His title was too important to him."

"No. His *son* was too important to him. Jonathan Alexander, Brandon's heir. He couldn't throw his son's inheritance away just to spite his father."

"So, he offered me up as a sacrifice," Claire choked out. "He married the woman his father demanded he marry . . . a woman he didn't want, a woman he wasn't legally free to have, so he could protect his son's inheritance. Why didn't he just tell his father he already had an heir?"

"Because he knew the duke wouldn't allow an actress's son to inherit the Bridgemont title. It may still turn out that way. The Duke of Bridgemont may still decide to disown Brandon's son once he finds out about him."

Mary stood in front of them, her back straight, her head high. "I regret it's turned out this way. I even considered never revealing my marriage to Brand. But I never really had a choice. I had to do what was best for my son.

"Jonathan is the Marquess of Huntingdon, the Duke of Bridgemont's legal heir. Every choice Brand made was to ensure his son would one day inherit that title. He would have expected me to follow through in his place."

Claire rose to her feet and moved to the opposite side of the room. She needed to think. She needed to separate herself from Hunt's wife. She stood stock-still with her back to the room and her eyes staring out the window, seeing nothing.

As if the major knew how difficult this was for her, he stepped up beside her. "Are you all right?" he whispered, placing his hands on her shoulders.

Claire nodded, then forced herself to stand steady when he released her.

The major turned to where Mary stood. "Did Hunt give you anything when he returned from France? Did he leave anything with you for safekeeping?"

The major's question fired through Claire with the force of a gunshot. She turned, waiting for Mary's answer.

"He always brought things with him when he came, gifts for the children, papers to work on while he was visiting."

"Did he bring any papers with him when he came that last time?"

"Yes. I have them out in the carriage. I packed everything in my trunks in case there was something of importance."

"Watkins," Claire said, rushing to the door. "Have Lady Huntingdon's trunks brought inside and have them taken to the blue guest room. Then, send Tilly down to show Lady Huntingdon upstairs."

The major's face turned hard. Claire knew as well as he that there was a good chance the papers Hunt had taken were in one of Mary's trunks. And the necklace. The necklace that would save Alex's life.

"You will, of course, stay here," Claire said to Lady Huntingdon.

"That's not necessary."

"Yes, it is."

"Thank you."

"Tilly," she said when the servant entered, "show Lady Huntingdon to the blue guest room and unpack her trunks." She turned back to Mary. "I'll be up momentarily to see you settled."

Claire watched Mary follow Tilly from the room, then turned to see what course the major intended to take.

"Linscott," the major ordered, "take a message to McCormick. Tell him to stand ready. Tell him not to let Roseneau out of his sight."

Barnaby was already near the door when he stopped. "Do you think she has them?"

"Yes. That's what he meant with his last words. 'My marchioness has them.'"

Barnaby paused. "The Russian emissary is scheduled to arrive tomorrow evening. It doesn't give us much time to discover the traitor's identity."

There was a grim expression on the major's face. "Tell McCormick I'll send word the minute I know anything."

Barnaby nodded then left the room, leaving Claire to battle the major by herself.

Chapter 28

Claire's head ached. She reached up to rub her throbbing temples. She'd known it would come down to this, to the major and her on opposite sides. She only prayed he was more concerned with the papers for the moment. That she would have at least one chance to get the necklace without him stopping her.

Although she knew when she took, it he'd never be able to forgive her.

"Claire?"

Claire wrapped her arms around her middle and hugged tight, praying she could protect herself from the pain that was to come.

"Are you all right?"

She nodded her head, but inside a voice was screaming, *No! I'm not all right.* She'd probably never be all right again. Because when this whole nightmare was over, she'd be forced to face the fact that her entire life had been a lie. Be forced to announce to the world that she wasn't the Marchioness of Huntingdon. She wasn't anyone.

And worse than that, she'd be forced to live with the major's anger and fury when he realized she'd exchanged the Queen's Blood for Alex. When he realized her brother's life had been worth more to her than her own, because he was the only innocent one in all of this. And she could not live with herself if she let him die.

Then, she'd have the rest of her life to live with the memories of Sam's kisses and the one single night he'd made love to her. Time to come to terms with the fact that the only man she would ever love hated her.

"Claire?"

He'd come up behind her and put his hands on her shoulders. His touch was like a brand searing through her. She wanted him like she'd never wanted anyone in her life. Needed him more than she thought it possible to need anyone. Just once more before he left her. Once more before she was left with a heart so shattered she'd never be able to survive. But loving him again would only make it worse. And she wasn't sure she could survive it.

"I'd like to be left alone," she said, stepping out of his arms.

"He can't hurt you any longer, Claire."

Her breath caught. "No, he can't. No one will ever again."

"Claire?"

"Please, don't call me that."

"What, Claire?"

"Yes."

"That's your name."

"But I haven't given you permission to use it."

The look on his face turned dark. As if she'd struck him. "Why are you doing this?

"Doing what?"

"Closing yourself off from me."

With a stiffening of her spine, she turned her back to him and moved as far away from him as possible.

"Don't you realize it's too late to walk away from me? We've shared too much, Claire. We've held each other and kissed each other, and given our bodies to each other."

"Stop!"

Claire brought her fist to her mouth. How could he remind her of that? How could he throw her mistake in her face like that?

"I'm doing everything in my power to forget that last night happened. It was a mistake. I should never have let things go that far but I—"

She stopped before she revealed more than she intended.

"But you what?"

"Nothing."

"What reasons aren't you able to admit, Claire? That you couldn't stop yourself any more than I could? That you knew from the start there was something between us that even Hunt couldn't destroy?"

"How dare you!"

"Would you like me to tell you what I think?"

"No."

"I think you made love to me because you wanted me. And because you were desperate to disprove all your insecurities. I think Hunt's refusal to physically make you his wife made you doubt your ability to be a woman. That for just one night you wanted to be loved."

Claire stifled a cry.

"What Hunt did to you was unconscionable. He had no right to take you as his bride when he already had a wife. There is no excuse for that, other than he loved his son so much he would do anything—even commit bigamy—to ensure his son's rightful place in Society. But that doesn't excuse what he did. Nor does it excuse what you did to me."

Claire spun her gaze to the hard look on his face. She wanted to demand he explain what he meant, but he didn't give her a chance. He explained without her prompting.

"You used me to prove to yourself you were capable of loving someone, capable of being a woman. You used me the same as Hunt used you."

"No!"

"Why, Claire? Why did you choose me to give yourself to? Why me, when you could have had anyone?"

"That's not why I—"

"Then why, Claire?"

"Because I—"

She clamped her hand over her mouth. She'd almost blurted out the words she could never take back. Almost told him she loved him. But she'd stopped herself just in time. Just before she'd made a fool of herself and was forced to watch the look of shock on his face. Before she had to hear his words of denial.

She lifted her chin and glared at him. "You already know why."

"No, I don't. Tell me."

He took a step toward her, and Claire sucked in a painful breath. How could she tell him she loved him?

"Tell me, Claire," he said, taking another step. "Tell me why you gave yourself to me." He took another step, then another, until he stood so close she could feel the heat from his body. "Tell me," he said, clasping his hands over her shoulders and pulling her close.

"You know!" she cried out, knowing he intended to kiss her. Certain she'd die if he did. Even more certain she'd die if he didn't.

But when he wrapped his arms around her and pressed his lips to hers, she didn't care about anything except having his body pressed close to her and his lips against hers.

She wrapped her arms around Sam's neck and held him close. His lips moved over hers until she ached with a yearning only he could assuage. She didn't think of the rightness of kissing him. Or the pain she would feel when he realized that she'd used the necklace to bargain for Alex's life. When he looked at her with disgust instead of adoration. She only knew that this would be the last time she'd have him near her once he realized what she'd done. This would be the last time she'd know what love truly felt like. She took what he offered with greater urgency.

He deepened his kisses—taking from her, demanding from her, then opening his mouth to begin his assault. His tongue skimmed her warm flesh in search of a treasure. She rushed forward to meet him, to take from him all he could give.

Their mating was magic. Wave after wave of molten heat soared through her chest and down her belly, igniting the beginning of something greater than she'd ever felt before. There was a desperation in his touch, and his tongue battled hers with a vibrancy that stole her strength.

Claire clung to him, rubbing her hands across his shoulders and touching as much of him as she could.

Then she forced herself to stop. Stop before it was too late and there was no turning back.

She turned away from him and stepped out of his arms. She was unable to stand on her own and braced herself against the corner of a table that sat by the door.

"What, Claire?"

Claire gasped for air, praying when the day was over he would understand that she'd had no choice.

"Why did you stop?"

She shook her head. "I only wanted—"

"Wanted what?"

Claire swallowed hard and forced herself to hold his gaze. If he believed nothing else they'd ever shared, she wanted him to believe this. "I just wanted it to be like before. Just once more."

With a heart she was certain was breaking, she took another step away from him. "Tilly should have Lady Huntingdon's trunks unpacked. I'm going to see if she has the papers with her. If she does, I'll send them down. Perhaps it isn't too late to salvage at least that much from this disaster."

Claire walked out of the room and closed the door behind her. She suddenly felt very alone and frightened and closed off from the rest of the world. As if she'd been set adrift in a small, fragile boat upon an ocean fraught with danger and hostile threats.

And she knew the last thing on earth she wanted was to be left alone . . . separated from the one man who possessed her heart and made her feel safe and whole.

~)

Sam leaned his shoulder against the window in Hunt's study and waited for Claire to come down with the necklace and papers. His mind roiled in a whirlwind of confusion. How could Hunt have married her, knowing full well he already had a wife? How could he have used her so cruelly, taking her as his wife, yet never making her his wife?

Everything he was learning about the man he'd admired tarnished his perfection. Disobeying the orders they'd been given was a dishonest move. Pitting himself against a man as dangerous as Roseneau was a stupid thing to do. But the worst was what he'd done to Claire. Marrying her when he wasn't free to do so was a sin Sam wasn't sure he could forgive. And Hunt tumbled from the pedestal where Sam had mentally placed him.

Sam pushed away from the window and took another long swallow of the brandy he'd poured himself. His initial assumption was that it was her fault that she was still a virgin. That she had never allowed Hunt to make her his wife.

Bloody hell, if Hunt were here now, he'd beat him within an inch of his life. He'd make him pay for every day he'd made Claire feel inadequate. For every day she'd believed she was a woman no man could love. Because she wasn't. And he knew it because he—

His breath caught in his throat, and a weight heavier than the world itself was suddenly lifted from his chest. A weight that contained a lifetime of hopelessness and yearning and unfulfilled desires. A weight filled with the dark aloneness that had always made up his life. And in its place he was given the air he needed to breathe and the sun he needed to survive, including every emotion he'd denied he was capable of feeling. Most especially, love.

He dropped his head back on his shoulders and grinned a heartwarming smile. Yes, love. The love a man feels for a woman. The protective giving and sharing that makes a person whole. The love he knew he felt for Claire. A love that assured him that nothing was more important than that she be at his side and in his arms for the rest of his life. When this whole mess was over, he'd tell her.

Then, he'd help her when she was forced to come face to face with the wife and family Hunt had left behind. And together they'd weather whatever was in store for them and forge a future filled with everything they'd both gone a lifetime without.

As soon as he knew the identity of the traitor.

Sam paced the room, checking the clock on the mantel, waiting for her to come down with the necklace and the papers the Marchioness of Huntingdon had brought with her.

It would be over soon. The British representatives would have the necklace, and Sam would have the papers Hunt had taken and could begin deciphering them to figure out the identity of the traitor.

But first he had to free the Marquess of Halverston. The plan was in motion. He'd sent Linscott with instructions to have agents surround the Ambassadors Hotel where Roseneau was staying. Once he knew the necklace was in McCormick's hands, Sam would handle Roseneau on his own. He couldn't promise Claire her brother's life wouldn't be sacrificed to save the lives of thousands, but he'd do everything in his power to get him away from Roseneau.

Then, Sam would take Claire away from this madness and show her how special love between a man and woman could be. He'd give her all the things she'd been denied because Hunt couldn't love her. He'd tell her how much he loved her, and spend every day for the rest of his life showering her with affection.

He remembered how she'd looked the night of Roseneau's ball. How beautiful. How lucky he thought Hunt was and how envious he'd been of his friend. And he remembered how terrified he'd been when he'd rescued her that night Roseneau's henchman almost killed her. How afraid he'd been that he hadn't gotten to her in time. That the bastard had hurt her. That was when he knew he wanted to spend the rest of his life protecting her, taking care of her. Only he hadn't recognized the feelings for what they were.

It wasn't until he saw her in the garden with her brother that he knew how much he loved her. That he realized how much it hurt to think she loved someone else. How much he wanted her for himself. That he wouldn't let anyone else have her.

And Sam knew she felt the same.

She couldn't have kissed him with such desperation if she didn't. Wouldn't have made love to him with such passion. And yet, something about the way she'd pulled out of his arms just now bothered him. Something he couldn't explain. Something he couldn't put his finger on.

Maybe it was fear. Fear because of all Hunt had put her through. Fear for her brother's safety. Fear because of what she'd barely survived. But the words she'd spoken just before she'd left him wouldn't go away.

I just wanted it to be like before. Just once more.

Just once more.

Sam didn't know why those words should bother him, but there was something ominous about them. A warning he didn't understand. Then he remembered the desperation in her kisses. The urgency. As if she were taking as much from him as she could one last time.

Just once more.

Bloody hell!

Sam glanced at the mantel clock, then raced across the room. She should have returned with the necklace and papers long ago. Tilly had had enough time to unpack Lady Huntingdon's trunks ten times over. Why the hell had he given her so long?

Sam took the stairs two at a time, then raced down the long hallway until he reached the blue guest room. He pounded twice, then threw open the door and scanned the room.

"Where is she?"

Lady Huntingdon looked up from where she sat sipping a cup of tea. Her gaze darted to him, her eyes opening wide when the door slammed against the wall.

"Where is she?"

Hunt's wife let out a startled gasp and set down her teacup with trembling hands, then reached for a packet of papers on the table. "She's gone, but she told me to wait here for you, that you'd come to get these." She held out the papers.

Sam felt his heart drop to the pit of his stomach as he took the papers. "Where'd she go?"

"I'm not sure. She just asked me to wait here until you came."

Sam's blood pounded in his head. "Did she take anything with her when she left you?"

"Why, yes. A necklace. Brand gave it to me the last time I saw him. She said it was imperative it got into the right hands immediately."

Sam felt the floor drop out from beneath him. He tucked the papers into his jacket and raced from the room, her words echoing in his head.

Just once more.

Chapter 29

Claire walked down the long hallway that would take her to Roseneau's suite at the Ambassadors Hotel. She clutched her reticule close to her, knowing that hidden inside the red velvet pouch was the necklace that would save Alex's life. And the object that would destroy any chance that Sam could love her. But what choice did she have? How could she live with herself, knowing she'd had the power to save Alex but hadn't used it?

"Are you sure you don't want to send for Major Bennett?" Watkins said, as if her thoughts of Sam were evident for everyone to see.

Claire shook her head, knowing Sam would never let her take the chance she was taking today. That he would hate her when he realized what she'd done.

"No, Watkins. Major Bennett can't help me with this."

She heard Watkins's heavy sigh and turned her head to glance over her shoulder. Watkins stood close. She was thankful he'd refused to stay with the carriage, had insisted on coming with her.

"Be careful, my lady."

Claire smiled a tremulous smile and rapped on the door.

A tall, heavyset servant opened the door and looked down his long, thick nose to where she stood. Claire fought the uncomfortable shiver that raced down her spine.

"Please tell Monsieur Roseneau Lady Hunt—"

Claire stopped short when Roseneau appeared behind the intimidating servant.

"Ah, Lady Huntingdon," he said, clasping his hands behind his back and rocking on his heels. "What a pleasure to see you."

Claire let her gaze rest on her nemesis. Every fear she had slammed into her. Every possible conclusion as to how this might end flashed before her. What if she failed? She tried not to let the terror that raged through her show.

"Please, come in," Roseneau said, welcoming her with effusive enthusiasm.

"Thank you, Monsieur Roseneau. My servant will, of course, accompany me."

The corners of Roseneau's mouth lifted in a sneering grin. "Of course. By all means. Can I get you a glass of wine?" he said when he'd seated her in a delicate plush blue velvet chair angled before a matching settee.

"No. Thank you."

"I hope you don't mind if I have a glass. In celebration, of course."

Claire didn't answer. She watched him pour a deep red burgundy wine into a glass and set the crystal decanter back on the table. She forced herself not to move away from him when he sat opposite her.

With a grin that caused Claire to shudder, he raised his hand in a mock toast, then lifted the glass to his lips and took a swallow.

When he finished, he leaned back against the cushion and casually rested the ankle of one leg over the opposite knee. "I assume your presence means I have reason to celebrate. That you have the necklace and have brought it to me . . . so near to the three o'clock deadline that will save your brother."

Claire glanced at the clock on the mantel and silently whispered a prayer. It was ten minutes before the hour. Ten minutes before the deadline Roseneau had set.

"Where is he? I want to see him."

Roseneau laughed. "Surely you don't think I have him here."

"Yes, I do. Where else would you have him? Especially since you probably realized I wouldn't give you the necklace without proof he was still alive and well."

Roseneau smiled, then took another sip of the wine in his glass. "Louis," he said to the intimidating man standing at the side of the room, "please show the marquess in."

The servant exited the room by a side door.

Roseneau leaned back against the cushion and let his iron-hard gaze burn through her. "This had better not be a trick, my lady. There is far too much resting on whether or not you have the necklace. I'll not allow you to play games with me."

"Believe me, Monsieur Roseneau. I am hardly interested in playing games. Not while you hold my brother."

"Very wise."

He lifted the glass to his lips again, then stopped when the door opened.

"Ah, there you are, Halverston. We've been waiting for you."

Alex staggered into the room, his hands tied behind his back, his haunted eyes sunk deep above his cheekbones, his face dark with a multitude of bruises. He stayed on his feet only with Louis's help.

A painful weight plummeted to the pit of her stomach when she saw what they'd done to him. "How dare you!"

She bolted to her feet and took a step toward Alex. Roseneau was on his feet in an instant and stopped her with a raise of his hand.

"I wouldn't if I were you," he said, his voice a low growl. "The necklace, if you don't mind."

"Untie him first. I'll not barter with my brother bound like a common criminal. He's a peer of the realm and should be treated as such."

Roseneau challenged her with a glare, but Claire didn't back down. She couldn't stand to see Alex mistreated one more second.

"Untie him!"

Roseneau cast a glance over his shoulder. "Untie him, Louis."

The look on Alex's face when the burly brute loosened his bonds was worth the effort it had taken to stand up to Roseneau. But the villain's next words affected her like ice flowing through her veins.

"The necklace, Marchioness."

"Don't give it to him, Claire," Alex said, his voice raspy and weak. "Not for me."

Claire stared at her brother's sallow complexion and lifted the corners of her mouth to form what she prayed came across as a confident smile.

"Claire, no," Alex repeated.

She tore her gaze away from her brother. "Please, sit down, monsieur," she said to Roseneau, indicating the settee where he'd sat before. She sat down in the chair. Her back was to Watkins, but she made sure Alex remained in view. With slow, deliberate movements, she reached into her reticule and brought out a small red velvet bag. She carefully placed it on her lap, keeping the opening toward her.

"No, Claire!" Alex ordered again. He tried to take a step closer, but Roseneau's man stopped him.

"It's all right, Alex. We don't have a choice."

"How right you are, my lady. Now . . ." Roseneau paused, yet didn't lift his gaze from the reticule in her lap. "The necklace, if you don't mind."

"Claire! You can't!"

Claire saw Alex struggle to free himself, but Roseneau's man was too strong and Alex too weak.

With trembling hands, she pulled the gold cord to open the bag, then reached inside. She clasped her fingers around the cool metal and stopped. For one small second, she was consumed by doubts. For one small second she wasn't sure she was brave enough to give the major up, because that would be the result if her plan failed. Because to the major, honor was everything. Sacrifice for the good of country; for the good of all that was important. It was the code by which he lived. Even if what had to be done meant sacrificing an innocent life. But Claire didn't live by those rules.

To her, she had to do everything in her power to save Alex.

Alex hadn't asked to be involved in this. He didn't have anything to do with Roseneau or the necklace or the papers or the traitor. He was the innocent one in all this. The one being asked to sacrifice his life for what Hunt had done.

A violent tremor consumed her. Hunt and the major were the risk-takers. They lived by a code she couldn't understand. While she was the one left to put things to right. The one with the jewels to pay as a ransom. How could she live with herself if she didn't do everything in her power to save her brother?

And how could she survive losing the major if she failed?

The clock on the mantel chimed three and her heart thundered in her breast with each strike. Every second that took her nearer to freeing Alex was another second closer to risking Sam's love.

"The necklace, Lady Huntingdon."

A heavy weight pressed painfully against her chest as she slowly pulled the necklace toward her. With her left hand, she reverently slid the necklace against the black material of her bombazine skirt, laying it out so that the diamonds and rubies shone in all their brilliance.

Roseneau gasped in appreciation as loudly as Claire had the moment Mary had pulled it from the bag to show her what Hunt had given into her care.

Roseneau reached for the necklace, but Claire quickly snatched it out of his reach.

"Not until my brother is free," she said, holding her hand over the necklace so he couldn't get it.

"I'm afraid you're hardly in a position to make demands, my lady. Not as long as Louis is standing so close to your brother."

"Then I suggest you tell Louis to move," Claire said, pulling a pistol from her reticule and pointing it at the middle of Roseneau's chest. The loud click of the hammer being cocked gave her his full attention.

Shock was evident on his face. So was the helpless terror she saw in Alex's eyes.

"That was not wise, my lady," Roseneau said.

"Perhaps not," she said, lifting the pistol slightly. If fired, it would hit him between the eyes. "But be assured I will not hesitate to use it."

"And if the lady misses, be assured I won't."

Sam watched every pair of eyes flash to where he stood in the open doorway. Both Roseneau and Claire bolted to their feet and turned toward him. The amazing relief he felt the second he saw Claire unharmed turned to unbridled fury. What the hell did she think she was doing? How on earth did she think she could stand up to Roseneau on her own?

How can she give away a necklace that could save thousands of lives?

The relieved look on her face made him even more furious. He could barely contain his anger as he watched her slide the necklace back into the velvet bag and with her left hand, slip it into the pocket of her skirt.

Roseneau's face turned purple, his expression livid, and every conceivable outcome flashed before Sam. Every way this might turn out. Even the possibility that he could fail and Claire might die.

That thought sent a wave of terror down his spine.

"I suggest," he said, stepping into the room, "you give the order to release the marquess right now."

Roseneau recovered quickly and moved his hand toward his pocket.

"I wouldn't if I were you," Sam said, inwardly hoping Roseneau would reach for the gun Sam knew he had hidden. "You have no idea the pleasure I would take in relieving the world of your presence."

Roseneau slowly pulled his hand back and lifted it to show he was unarmed.

"Claire, step over here. Now."

Claire quickly stepped around Roseneau and came to stand beside Sam.

He didn't look at her. He couldn't risk seeing the hope in her huge, dark eyes. It took all the willpower he possessed not to pull her up against him, not to take her in his arms and kiss her until neither of them could breathe. "Watkins. Keep your mistress with you."

"Yes, Major."

Sam focused his attention on Roseneau. "Release the marquess. Now."

"Of course, Major. The marquess was only my guest until I got the necklace." Roseneau slowly turned to the side where Louis had Alex pinned in a painful grip. "Louis," Roseneau said, "help the marquess across the room."

Louis gave Roseneau a knowing look, then shoved Halverston forward. Claire's brother was too weak to stand unassisted, and he stumbled as he tried to catch his footing.

Before Sam could react, Roseneau grabbed Halverston by the arm and pulled him in front of him to act as a shield. Then he pulled the pistol from his pocket and pressed it against Halverston's temple while Louis quickly rushed forward and clamped his hands around Halverston's arms.

Sam heard Claire's startled cry and lifted his gun, but realized how helpless he was. Roseneau would kill the marquess before he got off a shot.

"I suggest you drop your gun, Major," Roseneau said, jabbing the pistol hard against Halverston's temple. "I'd hate for my gun to accidentally go off and kill the marquess."

Sam hesitated a fraction of a second, then dropped his gun to the floor.

Roseneau smiled tightly. His grin indicated he considered himself in control. And he was. Sam tried to come up with a way to escape, but the two men who entered the room from Sam's right only lessened their chances.

"Now, Lady Huntingdon. The necklace. Give it to me."

"Claire, no," Sam ground out through clenched teeth.

"Enough, Major! Or you're dead."

One of the men stepped up behind Sam and shoved the barrel of a gun into his ribs

"Pierre," Roseneau said to one of the men holding a gun on Sam, "tell Jacques to bring the carriage round to the back. It is time we left."

The man raced from the room and a few minutes later rushed back. "The carriage is ready. We must go quickly, monsieur. There are several men watching the streets. If we do not leave now, it might be too late."

"How regretful. Lady Huntingdon, I think you have something in your possession you wish to trade for your brother's life?"

There was a gleam of desperation in Roseneau's eyes, and Sam knew if he was going to prevent Claire from giving away the necklace, he had to do something now. His gun lay on the floor to his left, and in a swift move, he dove to get it. Before he could reach it, the man to his right brought the gun in his hand down against Sam's temple.

A searing pain shot through his head and took him to his knees. He struggled to keep from giving in to the blackness that wanted to overpower him. Only Claire's pained cry reached through the hazy fog surrounding his brain and kept him from succumbing to the darkness.

Chapter 30

"No!"

Claire saw Sam fall to the floor, saw the bright red blood stream from a cut above his eye and fought the welling panic rising inside her.

"Enough!" Roseneau shouted, pulling Claire's attention from where the major was slumped on the floor.

"The necklace, Lady Huntingdon. Now! Or I'll shoot both the major and your brother and leave you to bury them."

Claire nodded as Sam anchored his hand against the arm of a chair and staggered to his feet. The blood still ran from the cut on his head and his face was unnaturally pale. She should have turned away from him before he rose, but she didn't.

Her gaze locked with his, studying every feature on his face. From the sharp angles she remembered tracing with the pads of her fingers. To the hard form of his lips that had kissed her with such abandon. To the steel gray of his eyes that had turned almost black in the height of passion. Eyes that now looked at her in anger and rejection. And she was forced to face—as she'd always known she'd have to—a look that would haunt her for the rest of her life. A look that had the power to destroy her.

"The necklace," Roseneau said, his hand outstretched, the glare in his eyes lethal.

"*No, Claire,*" she heard Sam whisper again from behind her.

With a trembling hand, she slowly reached her right hand into her pocket and pulled out the red velvet bag.

"*Don't,* Claire."

She clutched the bag in her hand one last second, then held it out to Roseneau.

"Keep our friends detained, Louis," Roseneau said, tucking the velvet bag into the inside of his jacket. He walked across the room and turned when he reached the door. "Good day, Lady Huntingdon. Major." Roseneau paused. "A special farewell to you, Lord Halverston. I've so enjoyed our time together." Then he left the room.

Claire fought to stand up under the painful weight pressing down on her. Every part of her felt numb. A cold empty void gaped open inside her as the minutes ticked by until this was over. Louis and the second gunman kept their pistols aimed at them. No one moved. Claire, because she couldn't. Alex, because he was too weak. Sam, because moving would have brought him closer to her, and she could tell from the clenched fists at his side and the hostile glare in his eyes, he feared what his reaction might be. He thought she'd betrayed her country.

When enough time had passed that Louis was assured Roseneau had escaped, he and the other gunman made their way to the door. With a mocking salute, they exited the room, locking the door behind them.

Claire breathed a shuddering sigh, then rushed to where Alex sat. "Watkins, help me. We have to get out of here. Alex, can you stand?"

She heard Sam work to open the door while she leaned down where Alex was crumpled against the side of the settee. "Hurry, Alex. Before they come back."

She reached out her hands to assist Watkins, then pulled back when Alex made no effort to try to rise.

"Why would they come back, Claire? You've given them everything they want."

His spiteful words were like a slap in the face. The look of disappointment in his eyes contained the sting of a painful blow.

Claire stepped back and watched as her brother struggled to his feet without her help. He took several labored breaths, then turned to face her. "Pray to God you didn't do this for me, Claire. How do you expect either of us to live with ourselves knowing the necklace you gave to Roseneau guarantees the deaths of innocent British soldiers?"

Claire fought to breathe. She staggered backward and would have fallen if Sam's hands hadn't clamped around her shoulders to steady her. She spun away from him as if his touch burned her and looked upward. Upward into Sam's hard, unreadable glare.

The air caught in her throat, and she stepped away from both of them. "You would rather I let you die?" she said, staring at the desolation in her brother's eyes.

"What do you think?"

The floor fell out from beneath Claire's feet. Her plan had worked. The risk she'd taken had been successful. And yet she felt as if she'd failed. On legs that trembled beneath her, she walked to the open door.

"Claire, wait," Sam said, grasping her arm as she walked down the long hallway to the stairs.

"Don't. Touch. Me."

She shook his hand off her and walked down the stairs, then out into the late afternoon sunshine. Her carriage waited across the street where she and Watkins had left it a lifetime ago. But she couldn't expect to ride home in it. Alex would need it, and she wasn't strong enough to survive hearing him refuse to ride in the same vehicle with a traitor. Instead, she turned the corner and began the long walk home.

"Claire, don't."

"I'd like to be left alone, Major. Go back where you're needed."

"I'm needed *here*."

Claire spun around and fired every hurtful word festering inside her. "No. You'll never be needed here. Go back where men exist who live by the same set of rules as you. Where what Hunt did was, if not admirable, at least acceptable, regardless of the one life that was destroyed. After all, what is just one life? Isn't that how you feel? Isn't that how my brother feels? It was obviously how Hunt felt. Just one life was not that significant. Regardless of whose life it is. It is only *one* life! And Heaven help the fool who goes against such a philosophy. Where the attempt to save just one other person is considered the greatest of travesties."

Claire couldn't hold back her anger and gave vent to the fury raging inside her. "Well, Major. The one life that was destroyed was important to me. Very important. Because it was *mine*!"

She faced him squarely and pointed back in the direction they'd come. "Now, go back and console my brother because I didn't allow him to die for a noble cause. Go back and commiserate with him because he's still alive and Roseneau has escaped. Go—" She glared at him so there would be no mistaking how serious she was. "Go to hell, Major. And leave me alone."

Claire stared at the hard expression on his face, then spun away and continued down the street. Only Barnaby's voice sliced through the blood rushing inside her head.

"Claire, stop."

Barnaby's voice came at her from somewhere, but she refused to stop. If Alex's reaction had been so vehement, Barn's would be twice as severe. He was, after all, an agent of the government everyone believed she'd betrayed.

"Claire! What's wrong?"

Claire walked a little faster to escape a confrontation with her brother, but it wasn't necessary. The major must have halted him before he reached her. His words sifted through her anger even though he stayed far enough away from her not to intrude.

"Linscott. Help Watkins get your brother to the carriage and take him home. Then send another carriage round for your sister."

Claire listened to Barnaby's heavy boots knock on the cement walk as he ran to follow the major's orders. She kept walking. With each step, she prayed everyone would leave her alone so she wouldn't be forced to look at the condemnation in their eyes.

Claire walked on. Her heart sat in her chest like a heavy boulder.

The traffic was heavier as she walked through London's busy streets. She forced her feet to take one step after another and not stop. Oh, how easy it would be to curl up beneath one of the huge linden trees lining the walk and close her eyes and never wake up. How easy it would be to wend her way through the throngs of people rushing about at the end of a busy day and get lost in all the confusion. That was how she felt. Lost. Even though there were crowds of people around her.

She reached the end of the walk and stepped onto the street. The major's hand clamped around her arm and pulled her back as a team of horses raced by.

"Bloody hell, Claire! Watch where you're going."

His voice sounded angry, his hold on her tighter than she was sure he intended. She understood his animosity was in response to what he thought she'd done. Yet, what choice had she had? To hand the necklace over to the major, knowing he would let Alex die rather than give it up?

No. Using it to free Alex was a risk she'd had to take. A risk she'd take again if she had to.

Claire pulled out of his grasp and continued on her way, not sure where she was going or why. Only knowing she needed to be far away from where she'd been. From where she was. She walked faster.

He was close behind her, his presence like a looming thundercloud. His closeness as enveloping as a thick fog from which there seemed to be no escaping. She raced onward, hoping he'd leave her be. Knowing he wouldn't.

Claire ignored the slowing of a carriage on the road beside her and walked faster.

"Claire, one of your servants is here with a carriage. Get in and he'll take us home."

She was suddenly consumed by an unquenchable desire to run as far away as she could. Suddenly desperate to put as much space between herself and Sam as she could. Loving him hurt too much. Losing him hurt even more.

Before she reached the next corner, he turned her around, picked her up, and carried her to where the carriage waited for them.

"Get us home. Now!" he ordered, then lifted her into the carriage and jumped in after her.

"What the bloody hell are you trying to do?" he bellowed the minute the carriage lurched forward. "Get yourself killed?"

Claire grabbed handfuls of her skirt and wadded the material in her fists. Her head throbbed as if someone had fired a cannon inside it. "Of course not, Major. I wouldn't dream of doing anything so accommodating. I plan on living a long eventful life to make up for the years of loneliness Hunt forced me to endure while he raced to the country every spare minute he had to spend time with his loving wife and family. I plan to wake up every day with the renewed vow to think of no one but myself, to make no sacrifices that aren't beneficial to me alone. But most important, I plan to put immediate effort into forgetting these past weeks ever happened.

"Then, if I'm very, very lucky, I might be able to forgive the Marquess of Huntingdon for everything he did to me. And forget how much I love—"

Claire's heart slammed against her ribs. She'd almost said it. Almost revealed her innermost secret. A secret that would not only give him greater power over her, but would expose a heart already broken and bleeding.

"How much you love who, Claire?"

She forced herself to look at him, to meet his gaze and hold it, while inside her heart was aching with a pain that, at times, stole her breath.

"I want you out of my house before nightfall, Major Bennett. The servants will be at your disposal to help you pack and transport your belongings wherever you wish. But, I want you gone."

The carriage turned a corner, then stopped in front of her town house. Before the major could open the door, Claire reached for the handle and pushed.

The door opened, and Claire jumped down without help. She raced past the startled servant and through the open door a footman held for her. She ran across the entry hall toward the stairs, then stopped with her foot on the second step. She lifted her hand from the oak railing of the winding staircase and touched the hard lump nestled in the pocket of her skirt.

She turned as the major came through the door. She hadn't intended to look at him, didn't want the hardened steel gray of his eyes to be the last memory she had of him, but it was too late. Their gazes locked, all the confusion and hurt laid bare for them both to see.

Without flinching, she walked to the center of the hallway and placed a small red velvet bag on the ornately carved receiving table.

Sam's startled expression was plain to see, his gaze moving from the bag on the table back to her.

She turned and walked away.

"Bloody hell, Claire." Sam's hard, quiet voice stopped her on her way up the stairs. "Do you know the chance you took?"

"No, Major. I only know that I lost."

Chapter 31

Sam hadn't been able to tear his gaze away from her as she retreated up the stairs. He held the red velvet bag she'd risked her life to protect, and listened to her muffled footsteps as she walked down the long hallway. When she reached her room, she softly closed the door behind her, shutting herself off from him and everyone else. If he lived another hundred years, he'd never forget the haunted emptiness in her expression. The hurt. The . . . loneliness.

She carried herself away from him with the same regal grace he'd witnessed the night she'd accompanied Hunt to Roseneau's ball. It was a defense posture. He knew that now. The cloak of armor she wrapped around herself to keep all the hurt from showing. To keep from exposing her loneliness to the world. For seven years she'd played as magnificent a part as any actress on stage. She'd convinced the world that her marriage to Hunt was perfect. That there was not a hint of unhappiness. And all the time, she'd been dying inside. Because all she wanted was to be loved.

And she never was.

Sam wanted to go to her, but he couldn't. Not until he took care of the more urgent problems. He swiped the back of his hand across his cheek and wiped the blood that still trickled down the side of his face, then looked up as Barnaby hurried down from his brother's room. Sam motioned for him to follow, then went into Hunt's study and closed the door behind them.

Barnaby walked to the small table that held decanters of Hunt's fine liquors and poured them each a glass. He handed one to Sam and took a swallow from his own. "Where's Claire?"

"She went up to her rooms."

"Is she all right?"

"This hasn't been easy on her. It's going to take time. How about your brother?"

"I got Alex settled and sent for Bronnely."

"How badly is he hurt?"

"I think he may have a broken rib or two, and it doesn't look like he was fed too regularly. He'll be fine once we get some nourishment down him. How about you?"

Sam took the clean handkerchief Barnaby held out to him and pressed it against the gash above his eye. "I'm fine, but we don't have much time. I need you to find McCormick."

"Why? Roseneau's got the—"

Sam reached in his pocket and held out the red velvet bag. Barnaby looked down at Sam's outstretched hand, then up to his face. His eyes opened wide. "What the—"

"Your sister switched bags."

"She what! Do you know what could have happened to her if he would have discovered what she'd done?"

Sam nodded. "Only too well. We've got to get this to McCormick. Take every available man with you. We only have hours before the Russian emissary arrives. Negotiations begin tomorrow. Offering to return the Queen's Blood will perhaps prove we're negotiating in good faith." He held out the necklace, and Barnaby took it.

"What about you? What if Roseneau comes back?"

"He won't. Once he realizes he doesn't have the necklace, if he's smart he'll take himself where he can never be found."

"Do you want me to take the papers to McCormick, too?"

Sam shook his head. "I'll keep the papers. Hunt thought they might hold a key to our traitor's identity. I want to study them first before I hand them over. Maybe I'll see something Hunt missed. Besides, McCormick doesn't know they exist."

Barnaby nodded his assent, then looked down at the velvet bag in his hands. "Would you like to see what cost Hunt his life and caused such a nightmare for so many other people?"

Barnaby didn't wait for Sam to answer but opened the bag and pulled the diamond-and-ruby necklace from its hiding place. He laid it out on top of Hunt's oak desk and stepped back. The sight of it stole Sam's breath.

"Bloody hell," Barnaby said in a reverent whisper. "Those are the most beautiful jewels I've ever seen. They've got to be worth a bloody fortune."

"Yes," Sam answered. "A . . . *bloody* . . . fortune."

Barnaby didn't say any more. He carefully put the necklace back in the bag and tucked it into his pocket. "I'll return as soon as I can. You can't take any chances, Bennett, so lock up after me. Even if Roseneau doesn't come back himself, we can't be sure he won't send someone."

Sam nodded and walked out with Barnaby.

"Watkins!" Sam ordered when the front door closed behind Barnaby.

"Yes, Major?" Watkins said, rushing down the stairs.

"Has Doctor Bronnely arrived?"

"Yes, Major. He's with Lord Halverston now."

Even though Claire wasn't aware that Alex was there, Sam knew when she calmed she'd be thankful. Sam knew it would be easier to protect Claire and her brother if they were both in the same place. The last thing they needed was to underestimate Roseneau. There was an outside chance he would retaliate when he realized Claire had deceived him.

"I want every door and window in the house locked and barred. Even the windows in the attic."

"Yes, Major."

"Have someone stand guard at every entrance—the footmen, gardeners, servants, all of them. Tell the stable hands to lock the carriage house and watch the back of the house. Is that understood?"

"Yes, Major."

"Lord Barnaby will be back shortly and he'll bring more men with him. Until then, don't let anyone in."

Watkins nodded, then rushed to issue orders to the staff. Sam walked to the stairs, taking note of every pounding thud of his heart. He wanted to laugh, or shout, or rail at the Heavens. Each one of those emotions raged through him when he relived what he'd just gone through. What she'd put him through. What she'd—

He stopped.

With one foot still on the floor and one resting on the first step, he froze where he was. He'd never felt like this before, even in the midst of the most dangerous mission or after. And never when there had been a life in danger. He'd never lost control like he was doing now.

He'd been a master at evaluating every situation. A master at handling anything thrown at him. He always followed his gut instinct to adapt to the unknown. But today he'd almost lost control of the situation, and he shouldn't have. This was no different than any other mission he'd been assigned. Except Claire had been involved and . . . he could have lost her.

I could have lost her.

Every ounce of energy rushed from him, stealing with it the air he needed to breathe.

I could have lost her.

He reached out a trembling hand and clenched his fingers around the stair railing. For an agonizing second, he thought he was suffocating.

Bloody hell. He could have lost her. And if he had, he wasn't sure he could have gone on. He wasn't sure he'd want to. Because . . .

Sam dropped his head back on his shoulders and squeezed his eyes shut. Blood roared inside his head as he came to grips with what he'd known for weeks now. He loved her. He loved Claire more than life itself.

He needed to go to her. Needed to make sure she was all right. Needed to set things right before he sat down with the papers in his pocket. The papers that might identify the traitor.

Sam reached the top of the stairs and walked down the hall. Did she have any idea the risk she'd taken? The danger she'd been in? Every time he thought of her facing Roseneau on her own, he broke out in a cold sweat. She couldn't possibly have been sure that he wouldn't look inside the bag. Or kill her when he realized she'd switched necklaces.

And I would have lost her.

By the time he reached her room, he was nearly as angry with her as he'd been when he thought she'd given Roseneau the necklace. He knocked, then waited, but she didn't bid him enter. He knocked harder. When his second knock went unanswered, he sucked in a deep breath and opened the door.

It took him a second to find her. She wasn't sitting in front of the fire Tilly had started for her, or resting in bed. But standing by the window with her back to him.

She didn't turn when he entered her room, only looked over her shoulder to where he stood, then looked back out the window as if ignoring him could make him go away.

"Please leave. I don't want you here."

"I know you don't."

Sam stepped into the room and closed the door behind him. At the soft click, she spun around.

"I asked you to leave. If you don't, I'll call Watkins to have you removed."

"Watkins doesn't have time. He's busy watching the house in case Roseneau comes back."

Her face showed the slightest hint of concern. "He won't come back."

She seemed confident, but Sam noticed the question in her voice. "Most likely not. He'd be a fool if he did. He knows it's too late to get the necklace, and without it he has no choice but to run. England's no longer a safe place for him."

She paused as if thinking over his words, then asked, "What did you do with the necklace?"

"Your brother has it. He's on his way to give it to McCormick."

He stepped farther into the room, not stopping until he was so close to her he could touch her. "Are you all right?"

He waited, but she didn't answer him, so he said, "Your brother thought it best to bring Lord Halverston here to recuperate. He's in a room down the hall. Bronnely's with him now."

She nodded, then turned away from him. "Have you discovered the traitor's identity?"

"Not yet." Sam placed his hand over the papers in his pocket. "I'll look at the papers when we're finished here."

"Then don't let me keep you, Major. I consider everything between us finished."

"Well, I don't."

Sam saw her shoulders sag. "Please don't make this difficult."

Sam couldn't stop the laughter. "Nothing about what we've shared has been anything *but* difficult, Claire."

"And impossible."

"Is it?" He stepped closer until her back was pressed against his chest. "Who do you want to forget you love?"

"No one." She took in a shaky breath that emphasized the hopelessness in her voice.

"Do you know how afraid I was when I walked into Roseneau's room and saw you with that pistol in your hand? Do you know how afraid I was at that moment that something might happen to you? That I might lose you?"

She tried to step away from him, but he stopped her by anchoring an arm against the window. Then he turned her to look at him. The confusion on her face was almost comical.

"Do you know how afraid I was when I thought you'd given Roseneau the necklace?"

"What I saw on your face wasn't fear, Major. It was far worse."

"Yes. Because unlike you, I knew what your brother's reaction would be. I didn't know you'd switched bags but I knew, even though you thought saving Alex was your only choice, it was a choice no one would be able to live with. Especially you."

"I could have lived with it."

"No, you couldn't have," he said, leaning in so close he could smell the fragrant soap she'd used to wash her hair. "Every time the papers published a casualty list from the Crimea, you'd hold yourself to blame for every name. You'd think each one of those men would be alive if only you'd given the necklace to me instead of Roseneau. What you'd done would have haunted you for the rest of your life, and you'd never have a peaceful night's sleep until the day you died."

She lowered her gaze to a point in the center of his chest. The worry lines on her face deepened. Sam brushed the back of his fingers across her forehead and down her cheek.

"Who do you want to forget you love, Claire?"

She shook her head.

Sam placed his finger beneath her chin and tilted her head until she had no choice but to look at him. "Who, Claire?"

"Don't "

"Ah, Claire," he said, lowering his head until his cheek touched hers. Then he whispered in her ear, "It's too late to fight it."

He wanted to kiss her. Needed to kiss her. He wrapped his arms around her and gathered her to him, then lowered his mouth to hers and took her.

He could count the seconds she fought him. Could tell how long she tried to keep from giving herself to him.

He knew the exact instant she yielded.

With a small cry, she wrapped her arms around his neck and met his kisses with full surrender.

Claire fought him as long as she could. She struggled not to give in, not to reveal by her kisses what she dare not speak in words. But the second his warm, inviting lips touched hers, she lost all control. She wanted his hands on her. Wanted his body pressed to hers. Wanted the feel of his touch burning every part of her. And she met his kisses with a greater urgency.

How could she reject the love she'd discovered? How could she not take what she was desperate to have? What Sam offered?

With a soft cry, she clung to him and kissed him with all the emotion she'd denied was a part of her. He held her close, his chest heaving like he'd run a long race, his breathing coming in ragged gasps.

"Oh, Claire," he whispered. "Who can't you forget you love?"

"Don't ask. Just want me. Just . . ."

She reached up to kiss him again, and he took what she offered. He pressed his mouth to hers while his fingers worked at her clothes.

"Tell me, Claire," he said, bringing his mouth back to hers, kissing her with a desperation that matched her own.

"Want me, Sam. Please, want me."

His only answer was an earthy growl that echoed in the shadows and settled deep in her belly. He threw off his clothes with alarming speed then carried her to the bed. She opened her arms and held him to her.

This time was more wondrous than before. He took her with a desperation that carried her far away from the dangers connected with this world. To a place that made her forget all the reasons she'd vowed she would never give in to him again. The reasons she had for never trusting him with her heart.

"Who, Claire?" he asked, his voice strained with passion.

"Sam. Oh . . ."

"Who?"

"You. Oh, Sam."

With his name on her lips, Claire spiraled through the stars. Her release, when it came, was alarming. She shuddered in its wake for what seemed an eternity before she spun back to earth. Sam thrust inside her once more; then, on a loud moan, he found his release and collapsed against her.

Claire lay silent and still for several long minutes, loathe to move. She'd almost admitted that she loved him. Almost said the words she'd vowed never to say. But she hadn't. She sighed with relief because saying them would have exposed her heart and left her too vulnerable.

Claire squeezed shut her eyes and listened while the quiet house echoed her thoughts. She'd already lived in a fairy-tale world where she'd imagined it would be possible for a man to love her. She'd had seven years of disappointment as her lesson that it couldn't happen. How could she take such a risk again?

"Would saying the words have been so difficult, Claire?" he asked, rolling to the side.

"Yes," she whispered, and suddenly realized it truly would. "The cost is too great."

"What are you afraid of?"

Claire couldn't give him an answer. How could she when she didn't understand the answer herself? "It doesn't matter, Major. Please, leave now so I can dress."

The mattress sagged and she knew he sat on the edge of the bed. But he didn't leave her.

"What do you mean, the cost is too great? What cost, Claire?"

Claire jerked her gaze to where he sat. He wasn't going to give up until he'd totally humiliated her. Wasn't going to give her any peace until he'd forced her to admit every fear that kept her from giving her heart away. But she wouldn't give him that satisfaction.

"What would you like me to admit, Major? That I care for you? That I'm foolish enough to make the same mistakes I made with Hunt? Would you like me to give myself over to you so you can remember my surrender as your crowning achievement? So you can have a hearty laugh when my name comes up and you recall what a fool I was? You'll have to excuse me, Major, but I'm not as young and naïve as I was when I married Hunt."

"Are you comparing me to Hunt?"

"I'm comparing you to no one. What I'm comparing is my experience with love. I was married seven years to a man who made a mockery of the emotion."

The mattress sagged when he moved closer to her.

"Claire, look at me."

She didn't. She couldn't.

"I haven't had a lot of experience with love. With lust, yes. But never with love. Perhaps that's why it took me so long to recognize the emotion. But you have to believe me when I say—"

"Don't. I don't need kind words. I don't need lies."

"These are no lies. I love you, Claire. I've loved you from the night I cradled you in my arms and prayed I could keep you safe from harm. Loved you even though I thought you had the necklace and intended to give it to Roseneau because you were lovers. Loved you even more when I found out you didn't have it. Your bravery is unmatched by anyone I've ever known."

He placed his finger to the side of her face and turned her head to look at him. "For whatever his reasons, Hunt put you through an unimaginable hell. I know you carry the scars from what he did. But know this, too—I love you, Claire. And someday I pray you can trust me with your heart, just as I'm trusting you with mine."

Claire stared at him for a long, agonizing moment. How could she risk giving away her heart again? Where was the guarantee that loving him would be any different than loving Hunt?

The emptiness she felt when the major rose from the edge of the bed was like taking away the warmth of the sunshine on a summer day. Claire wrapped a quilt around herself and sat in the middle of the bed. She tucked her legs to her chest and fought to find enough air to fill her lungs. Sam loved her. The man to whom she'd given her heart wanted it. He loved her.

Claire watched him pull on his trousers and boots, then slip on his shirt and shrug into his waistcoat and jacket. When he was dressed, he walked back to the side of the bed.

"I'm not going to take my words back, Claire. I'm not going to change my mind. When this is over, I'm going to say them again and again and again. Until you're so used to hearing me tell you I love you it won't frighten you any longer. Until you're so accustomed to hearing the words you'll be able to tell me you love me without being afraid I'll trample your heart in the process."

Claire stared at him with a longing that grew stronger with each passing second. He loved her.

"Get some rest now. I'll be below if you need anything."

He walked to the door and stopped with his hand on the knob. "I love you, Claire. More than my life. More than words can express. It's a wondrous feeling, Claire. When you're brave enough to look for it, you'll know what I mean."

She didn't need to give him an answer, and he didn't wait for one. It was as if he knew she needed more time. As if he knew it would take her a little longer to realize what he already knew—that only love could make her whole again.

She watched as he opened the door and left her alone with her thoughts. Every word he spoke assured her that he wasn't going to let her give up on the love they had.

Claire stared at the closed door long after he left and swiped at the tears that dared to spill from her eyes.

The pain and loneliness she'd lived with the last seven years bubbled to the surface, then slowly evaporated. Sam was giving her another chance to know love. Now, all she had to do was find the courage to open her heart and accept what he was offering.

Except, she wasn't sure she could.

Chapter 32

The light from the lantern on the corner of the desk flickered with erratic inconsistency as Sam stared at the papers laid out in front of him. It was nearly ten o'clock, hours since they'd returned with the papers and necklace. Hours since Sam had left Claire and opened the message to study the numerical code in front of him.

Hours since he'd realized his world had changed forever.

He fought the jarring disbelief as he stared at the coded message, praying the configurations on the page would change. But they didn't. Recognition sucked the air from his body. Ice flowed through his veins, paralyzing him so he couldn't move. He looked at the formula for the hundredth time only to realize he hadn't made a mistake. He knew the code, understood the formula. He should. He'd created it.

Sam swiped his hand down his face. There was no doubt as to the identity of the traitor.

On unsteady legs, he walked to the study door and opened it. Watkins stood at the front, watching the street from a window. An eerie silence converged on Hunt's town house. It had seeped into every corner and crevice the minute Barnaby had returned and set up guards around the perimeter of Claire's land. The laying of a trap, the waylaying of the traitor. Even though he could not hear or see them, Sam knew the guards were there. Claire would be protected.

"Watkins, inform Lord Barnaby and Lieutenant Honeywell that I am expecting a guest. Be sure they let him pass when he comes. Then show him to the study."

"Yes, Major."

Sam turned around and went back into the room. He sank down in the chair that had been Hunt's and waited.

The clock struck eleven, then twelve. Before the last chime of the midnight hour, Sam heard muffled voices from the hallway and sat with his eyes focused on the door.

"The Earl of Cardmall to see you, Major."

Sam rose to his feet. "Show him in, Watkins."

Watkins stepped back and Sam's cousin entered. His cheeks were flushed, his hair plastered to his head, no doubt from riding bareheaded in the drizzling mist that had been falling since late evening. His clothes were askew on his body, as if he'd come in from a night of wild revelry as Ross was known to enjoy, never expecting to have to leave the house again. But it was the frantic look in his eyes that gave Sam the first warning. The wild desperation Sam saw on his cousin's face that sent a shiver down Sam's spine. "Come in, Ross. You look like you could use a drink."

The Earl of Cardmall walked unsteadily across the room, then stopped while Sam poured them both a drink. Cardmall watched him as if in a daze, then took the glass Sam held out to him with trembling hands. Sam pointed to the nearest chair. "Would you like to sit?"

Ross tipped the glass back and downed the whole of it in one swallow. "You know why I'm here," he said, bracing his hand against the back of the wing chair facing the desk. "You've been waiting for me, haven't you?"

Sam shook his head. "I prayed I was wrong, Ross. But I'm not, am I?"

Ross swiped the perspiration from his forehead. His face held a deathly pallor Sam associated with fear. A fear that would prompt a sane man to act with irrational behavior. A fear that would push a desperate man past the boundaries of sanity. Sam stepped behind the desk and slowly opened the top drawer where he'd placed the gun.

"Just give me the papers, Sam, and we'll forget this whole thing."

Sam shook his head. "You know I can't do that."

"Sam! We're family!"

"In all but this, Ross. I'm a loyal British citizen first. I'm an officer in Her Majesty's Army next. And I'm family last. Don't ask me to betray everything I stand for. Don't ask me to step aside and let you betray principles you'll never survive if you abandon."

"I have to. I don't have a choice. I just overheard Father and Roseneau." Ross staggered, then focused his gaze on Sam. His look contained even more desperation than before. "Hell, Sam. Do you know what they've done? I'm begging you—" He took an unsteady step forward, as if looking for a place to run and not finding one.

A jarring terror slammed through Sam's chest as he watched his cousin's frantic pacing. "Who, Ross? What *who's* done?"

"Father! What he's done! We'll never survive this. *He'll* never survive this."

Sam struggled to make sense of what Ross was saying. How could it be his uncle? How could it be the Marquess of Rainforth?

"What are you saying, Ross?"

"You've got to help me, Sam. We have to get Father out of England. We have to—"

"Ross! Tell me what you heard."

"We're ruined, Sam. Ruined! Do you know what he's done? Oh, God, Sam. Do you know the lives he's destroyed? He'll hang!"

The door burst open, and the Marquess of Rainforth stepped into the room. "Enough, Ross!"

Sam's gaze spun to where his uncle stood. The expression on his face was hard, the look in his eyes lethal. But more terrifying was that in one hand he had a gun cocked and ready to fire. In his other, he held Claire hostage, his fingers clamped tightly around her arm.

"Look who I found coming down the stairs." He pushed her forward without releasing her. "Now, Major. Tell the men who followed me to leave." He shoved the gun against the side of Claire's head. "Or I'll kill her."

Sam looked to where Barnaby stood in the open doorway. "Close the door, Barnaby."

Barnaby hesitated, the look on his face filled with uncertainty.

"Leave!" Rainforth bellowed, jerking Claire toward him. "Or I'll kill her!"

"Father! No!"

A small cry escaped from Claire, and Sam's heart skipped a beat. His blood thundered inside his head. He didn't look at her. He didn't dare. One look at the fear in her eyes and he'd go mad.

Barnaby looked at him again, searching for any sign that would indicate what Sam wanted him to do. If Sam were the one Rainforth had the gun aimed at, he'd want them to take the risk. But not Claire. He couldn't chance anything happening to her.

Sam gave Barnaby a dismissive nod, and he backed out of the room and closed the door.

They were alone. Sam felt a fear unlike anything he'd ever known. He couldn't let anything happen to her. He couldn't survive if it did. "Let her go, Rainforth. Don't make this any worse than it already is."

"You are hardly in a position to bargain, Samuel. Now, step back from the desk."

Sam's gaze slowly moved to Claire's, and he fought the urge to leap over the desk and take her in his arms.

"Now!"

Rainforth lifted the gun and pointed it at Sam's chest.

"Father! No!"

"Now, Major!"

Sam stepped back, enough to placate his uncle, yet not so much he couldn't reach for the pistol in the desk drawer.

Rainforth nodded as if satisfied. "Go home, Ross. Or better yet, go to your club and await news of Major Bennett's unfortunate accident."

"No! No one has to be hurt."

The Marquess of Rainforth smiled. "Oh, Ross. You poor fool. You don't understand any of this." He placed the pistol beneath Claire's chin and pushed her head back. "You understand why it has to be like this, though, don't you, Major?"

Sam felt the air leave his chest. He'd assumed the traitor was his cousin. Not his uncle. Assumed because of Ross's flagrant spending and extravagant lifestyle, he'd done the unthinkable so he could continue living as he was accustomed. He hadn't thought for a moment it was the man who'd taken him in when he'd been orphaned; who'd raised him when he had no one else. Not the man who'd been a father to him—who'd instilled in him a love of country and been the example of integrity and unfailing loyalty. Every part of Sam screamed it wasn't possible for his uncle to be the one. But it was true. There was no doubting that the man Sam had looked up to his whole life had sold his soul as well as his country for a few pieces of silver.

Sam inched forward and placed his hand on the top of the desk. "I understand that unless you give yourself over to me, one of us will not survive the night."

"How astute, Samuel. You are right, though. One of us will not survive this night regardless of what happens. I prefer to be the one left to see the sun rise."

"Then let the lady go and there's a possibility you will be."

"Oh, no, Samuel. I would be a fool to think there is more than one way out of this, and I have not reached my advanced years by being a fool. Now, keep your hands where I can see them and step away from the desk."

Rainforth leveled the gun at Sam's chest and squeezed his finger slightly against the trigger.

Sam stepped back from the desk and lifted his hands in the air. He tried again. "The papers are here. Take them. Just let Lady Huntingdon go."

Rainforth shook his head. "You know I can't do that. She's my safe passage out of this."

Fear grew inside Sam, and he lowered his hands, praying he could reach the gun in the drawer. "Why, Rainforth? Why did you do it?"

"Why do you think, Samuel? For the money. For my son."

Ross reacted to his father's admission with abhorrent shock. "Me! You sold government secrets—for me! God help us! No!"

"How else could I support the life you led, Ross? How else could I amass enough to secure the Rainforth holdings after I was gone? The bills I covered to pay for your lavish lifestyle every month were more than all of the Rainforth profits. How was I to leave enough so you'd never have to go without after I was gone? So you wouldn't lose everything that would someday be yours?"

"Why didn't you tell me? Why didn't you ask me to curb my spending? Why didn't you just once talk to me?"

"You're my son. My only son. It's my responsibility to provide everything you needed."

"I *had* everything I needed. *More* than I needed. I would have done with less."

Rainforth shook his head then looked back at Sam. "If only you would have given the papers to Roseneau, Samuel. Then the lady wouldn't be in danger, and you wouldn't have to die."

"But you know I have them," Sam said, lowering his hand inside the desk drawer.

Rainforth laughed. "Yes. Roseneau convinced me you had. But I knew you wouldn't think of me first. I knew you'd think Ross was the traitor."

"Me?"

Rainforth's gaze turned to his son, the look in his eyes one of unadulterated love. "Do you remember the code you and Samuel devised when you were young?"

"That was a game, Father! A code Sam made up so we could pass notes Master Graham, our tutor, couldn't read."

"The code was brilliant. If you hadn't deciphered it for me, Ross, I wouldn't have been able to figure it out, either. No one could. That's what made it so safe. But when Huntingdon stole the papers from Roseneau's safe, I knew it was only a matter of time until he showed them to Samuel."

Ross reached out a hand and braced himself against a chair. "And you knew once Sam saw the coded messages, he'd think I was the traitor."

Rainforth smiled. "And that's what you thought, wasn't it, Samuel?"

Rainforth turned his glazed look in Sam's direction, and Sam saw the demented ruthlessness in his eyes.

"Yes. That's what I thought."

Sam waited, then let his gaze move to Claire's. What he saw tore at his heart. Her face was pale and her lips were pinched tight, but her eyes darted from him to Rainforth, then to the door Barnaby was behind, as if she was planning the best way to save him.

Sam's heart raced in his chest. He already knew the risks she was willing to take. Facing Roseneau on her own had taken more courage than most men he knew could gather.

He clamped his hand over the gun and positioned his finger around the trigger. "Where is Roseneau?" Sam asked, praying to distract his uncle just enough to gain an advantage. Praying Claire would wait a second longer before she made a move.

Rainforth laughed. "He fled England the minute he discovered the lady had somehow switched the real necklace with a fake. Quite like the proverbial rat on a sinking ship. He was squeamish about killing from the start."

"But you weren't?"

"Perhaps I was the first time. One accustoms oneself to it. Self-preservation puts killing on a different level. Don't you find that to be true, Samuel? You've taken more than your share of lives, haven't you?"

"Yes. More than my share. But I never thought I'd be forced to kill the man who raised me."

"How sentimental, Samuel. But we've wasted enough time. Ross, leave."

"No, Father. You can't—"

"Leave!"

The Marquess of Rainforth turned his gaze to his son for a fraction of a second, but it gave Sam the time he needed to raise his gun. Rainforth had his pistol focused on Sam, and Sam knew he wouldn't get a shot off before Rainforth fired. He only prayed it would give Claire the chance to escape before his uncle turned the gun on her.

Rainforth caught Sam's movement and fired. Sam felt a burning sting in his side as his gun flew from his hand and slid across the floor. The force of the bullet being fired from such a short distance pulled him off balance. He heard Claire's scream as he spun to the side. He struggled to stay on his feet so he could get to Claire, but couldn't.

Everything after that moved in slow motion. He watched Claire shove Rainforth away from her. Rainforth stumbled and reached out to right himself. Then lifted his hand and pointed the gun at Claire.

"No!"

Sam yelled and pushed himself toward Rainforth. If he could only step between them he could . . .

A loud explosion rent the air and Sam watched Claire dive to the floor. Rainforth's eyes opened wide, and he stood unmoving for a moment before the front of his pristine white shirt turned a dark red. He staggered, then sank to his knees before crumpling to the floor.

Sam jerked his gaze to the side where the bullet had been fired from and sucked in a harsh breath. Ross stood with his arm still outstretched while smoke spiraled from a pistol clutched in his hand. His face was deathly pale, his gasps of air coming in short, jagged gulps. There was an expression of horror in his eyes.

"Ross," Sam said through the pain. "It's over now. Put the gun down."

Ross's hand jerked, and the gun fell to the floor with a loud thud. His eyes stayed riveted to the spot where his father lay.

Sam fought the urge to go to his cousin, but he had to get to Claire first. He tried to move but stopped when a burning stab of pain grabbed hold of him. He waited until the pain subsided, then crawled another step. She was so far away it seemed to take forever to get to her. The stitch in his side stole his breath, and he clutched his hand to the burning wound and crawled closer.

"Major!"

Sam recognized Barnaby's voice and heard his heavy steps as he rushed into the room.

"Linscott. See to your sister."

Sam checked the spot where Claire was rising from the floor, then looked back to his cousin and realized he hadn't moved. His stillness frightened Sam almost as much as his need to make sure Claire was all right. When he looked at her, he found her rushing toward him.

"Claire."

"Sam!"

Her hands held him down, his back pressed to the floor, and she nestled his head in her lap. "You're hurt. Just lie still."

"Are you . . . all right?"

"I'm fine. Fine. Watkins!" Claire turned when the butler rushed through the doorway. "Send for Doctor Bronnely. Now!"

Sam relaxed until the next wave of pain gripped him. When it receded, he tried to ease the worry on her face with humor. "If we don't change our ways . . . Bronnely will demand we set up . . . a room for him here." Sam tried to smile but gasped as another wave of pain seared through him. Linscott knelt beside him and pulled back Sam's jacket and his shirt.

"I've seen worse," Linscott said, pressing a cloth to Sam's side to staunch the bleeding. "But you're going to be damn sore for a while."

Sam turned his head to where his uncle lay sprawled, a pool of blood darkening beneath him. Lieutenant Honeywell and another officer were kneeling over him. "Is he dead?"

Barnaby shook his head. "Not yet."

Sam locked his gaze with Barnaby's. "I need a favor." Sam knew he was crossing a line he never thought he'd come near. "Take my uncle home. It won't do anyone any good to know he died here. Then send for McCormick."

Barnaby nodded. "I'll take your uncle home. Perhaps it would be best if Society believes Rainforth had an accident while cleaning his gun. It's not so implausible, and his son is not in any condition to dispute anything right now."

Sam moved his gaze to where Ross now knelt, clutching his father's hand. Sam knew his cousin's sanity hung by a fragile thread. "Thank you," he said to Barnaby, fighting another stabbing shard of pain.

Barnaby nodded, then issued orders for Honeywell to bring a carriage round back. "I'll make sure everything's taken care of before I bring McCormick back here."

Sam breathed a painful sigh, then said, "You're him, aren't you?"

It was impossible to mistake the slow hiss of Barnaby's breath or the lift of his shoulders.

"You're the man Hunt was training to take over for him, aren't you?"

Claire's brother arched his brows. "Lord Huntingdon thought I might be of some use to my country, yes."

"He chose well," Sam said, then closed his eyes and sucked in as deep a breath as his body would allow. "He would be glad we found the necklace and uncovered the traitor."

"Yes. He would."

Sam listened to Barnaby's retreating footsteps. When he opened his eyes, several men were carrying the Marquess of Rainforth from the room. His son walked at his side, clutching his hand. Ross's face was already gaunt and pale, as if he realized his father's death hovered just hours away.

"Doctor Bronnely is on his way," Watkins said, rushing into the room when Rainforth was gone.

"Bring him right in when he arrives," Claire said. "And send in some men to carry Major Bennett to his room."

Watkins rushed from the room. When Sam looked up, his gaze locked with Claire's tear-filled eyes. "Don't cry, Claire. It's over now."

"You could have died. I could have lost you."

"You aren't going to lose me. I'm right here. Nothing's going to happen to either of us ever again."

Sam looked at Claire's pale face and wanted to reach his finger to still her trembling lips. Instead, he took her hands and held them in his. Her gaze was fixed on his, and tears ran steadily down her cheeks.

"It's all right, Claire."

She nodded as she struggled to speak. Finally her lips parted, and she whispered a very shaky question. "Do you really love me, Sam?"

"Ah, Claire. You know I do. With all my heart."

She nodded as if confirming a fact she already knew. Through the tears brimming in her eyes, she cupped her palm to Sam's cheek. "I love you, too."

Sam's breath caught in his chest. "As soon as this is all over, we'll marry."

"There's bound to be a scandal when Society finds out I was never the real Marchioness of Huntingdon. When they discover I lived with

Hunt for seven years without the bonds of matrimony. They'll think the worst, of course."

"After what we've survived, we'll hardly notice a scandal." Sam's heart swelled when she smiled. He locked his fingers with hers and held her gaze. "I can't offer you a title, Claire."

"Is that what you think I want?"

Sam smiled through the pain. "It's what you deserve."

She shook her head. "I deserve to be loved. It's all I've ever wanted. For seven years I woke up each day thinking this would be the day Hunt could love me. But it wasn't. Even though now I know why, it didn't make the years I lived without my husband's love any easier."

Sam reached up to wipe a tear that dared to run down her cheek.

"I didn't think I'd ever know love, Sam. Then I met you. For the first time in my life I know what it is to love and be loved. I can't give you up now that I've found you."

She lowered her head to kiss him. When she lifted her lips from his, she placed her cheek against his and whispered in his ear. "I would be proud to be your wife."

She kissed him again and only broke away from him when Bronnely walked into the room.

"You'll never regret it, Claire," Sam said before Bronnely reached them.

"I know I won't. I'll make you so happy neither of us will have a chance to regret it."

Sam gave her hand a gentle squeeze and held on because he never intended to let go. He'd finally found what he'd been searching for his whole life. A jewel worth more than a king's ransom.

Epilogue

April, 1857

Claire lifted her gaze to the mirror on her dressing table and saw Sam relaxing inside the doorway. He stood with his shoulder against the door frame and his arms crossed over his chest. She recognized the look in his eyes and fought the blush that warmed her cheeks.

"You can go now, Tilly."

Claire's maid smiled, then closed the door behind her as she left the room.

"Ah, Claire," he sighed. "You're beautiful." He crossed the room and took her in his arms.

"It's the dress." Claire lifted her lips to his and returned his kiss with the same passion she'd felt for more than two years now.

"It's not the dress. It's you."

"If we don't stop," she said, kissing him again, "we're going to be late for the ball. It's not every day the young Marquess of Huntingdon gets introduced to Society. And you haven't even begun to dress."

"It won't take me long. Come sit with me for a minute."

Sam took her hand and led Claire over to the wing chair. He sat with her on his lap, then placed his hand on her stomach. "Are you feeling all right?"

She smiled. "Yes. I'm fine. I only seem to get ill in the mornings. It was the same when I was increasing with Matthew. Maybe I'll present you with another son, Samuel. Would that be all right?"

"Whatever pleases you, my dear. As long as you and the babe are healthy I don't have a preference either way."

"Did you just return?"

Sam nodded and pulled her to him. He would hold her close every time he came back from visiting his cousin, Ross. It was as if he needed her nearness. Her understanding. She knew it would be more so today. "How is Lord Rainforth?"

"I couldn't talk him out of it, Claire. He was determined to go through with it."

"You've done everything you can for him, Sam."

"I know, but nothing has helped."

She felt the agonizing breath Sam released.

"He's determined to give it all away, Claire. I swear he'd give away his title if he could."

Claire snuggled closer to her husband. She wished she could take away some of the guilt he carried. "He hasn't wanted any of the wealth his father left him since the night his father died. I think a part of him can't come to terms with the lengths his father had gone to provide for him."

"But you should have seen him, Claire. In one stroke of a pen he signed his inheritance away without even as much as a blink."

"He didn't sign it away. He signed it over to you. Because he knew you'd taken care of it after he refused to have anything to do with it. Because you proved how capable you were at running the Rainforth holdings."

"But I don't want them, Claire. I never have. I'm satisfied with the estate my father left me. I don't want more."

"I know," Claire said. She wrapped her arms around his neck and kissed his cheek. "You have never envied Ross his wealth. That's one of the things I love most about you. Yet you've devoted every day for the last two years to taking care of the Rainforth holdings."

Claire saw the sad look on Sam's face and knew his thoughts before he said them. "I only wish Ross wanted to claim it."

"I know," she whispered, knowing Sam's cousin never would. She took a deep breath and changed the subject. "Barnaby came to visit this afternoon."

"Where's he off to?"

"He wouldn't say. But then, he never does. I worry about him, Sam."

"I know, but he's not in quite so much danger now that the war is over."

"Is that supposed to make me feel better?"

"No. It's supposed to make you worry less."

"How did you do it, Sam?"

"It was easier then. I didn't have you to come home to. Now I'd be of no use to the government at all. I can barely tear myself away from you for an afternoon, let alone think of leaving you for days."

Claire smiled as she snuggled closer to him. "You should get ready. We can't be late. No one will want to miss a minute of the ball to introduce the Marquess of Huntingdon."

Claire pushed herself away from Sam. "Did you talk to the Duke of Bridgemont like you said you were going to?"

"Yes. I stopped on my way home. Hunt's son was there when I arrived. As resistant as His Grace was to accept Hunt's son as his heir when he first met him, he's that determined to have Society accept Jonathan as the Marquess of Huntingdon, and future Duke of Bridgemont. Hunt would be so proud if he could see the bond that's grown between his father and his son."

"I'm the one who's proud," Claire said, kissing Sam again. "Of you. You're the one who convinced the Duke of Bridgemont it would serve no purpose for him to disown Hunt's heir."

"It wasn't that difficult once he saw the boy. Jonathan's the picture of his father. He has all Hunt's noble characteristics, and the same intelligence and integrity as his father. He's so mature, and has the confidence and the wealth to back him up."

"I know," Claire said on a heavy sigh. "He's also too handsome for his own good."

"Are you worried about him? Or all the eligible young women you invited tonight?"

"Lord Huntingdon, of course. Females can be ruthless, you know. And nothing stops us once we set our minds on someone."

"I know. Look what happened to me."

Claire gave him a playful swat on the shoulder, then leaned up to kiss him again. "You were hardly a challenge, Major. I was the one who was afraid to take another chance."

Sam held her close and pressed his lips to her temple. "Yes, you were. I don't even want to imagine what my life would be like if you would not have given in." Sam kissed her cheek. "Now, I think I'd better get ready before I'm tempted to do something much more entertaining right here."

Claire slid off Sam's lap and pulled him to his feet. "Definitely not. Or we'll be late for sure."

He moaned in frustration. "I am only giving you a reprieve, wife. The minute the last dance has finished, I intend to prove how much I love you."

Claire lifted her hand to Sam's cheek. "Your love is all I ever wanted," she whispered, then wrapped her arm around his neck and pulled his mouth down to hers.

She intended to stop after the first kiss but kissed him again. She felt him work at the buttons down her back and smiled.

It wouldn't take Tilly long to help ready her again. And it would be well worth the time.

Acknowledgments

To my special friend and editor extraordinaire—Mary Schwaner. I write because you are there to help me when I get overwhelmed. I wouldn't be where I am without you.

About the Author

Laura Landon taught high school for ten years before leaving the classroom to open her own ice-cream parlor. As much as she loved serving up sundaes and malts from behind the counter, she closed up shop after penning her first novel. Now she spends nearly every waking minute writing, guiding her heroes and heroines to their happily-ever-after. She has written more than two dozen Victorian historical novels, thirteen of which have been published by Prairie Muse Publishing and seven of which have been published by Montlake Romance, all selling worldwide. She lives with her family in the rural Midwest, where she devotes what free time she has to volunteering in her community.